PRAISE [illegible]
DANE MA[illegible]

"With the thoroughly enjoyable way Mr. Wood has mixed speculative history with our modern day pursuit of truth, he has created a story that thrills and makes one think beyond the boundaries of mere fiction and enter the world of 'why not'?" --**David Lynn Golemon, Author of *Legacy***

"Ancient cave paintings? Cities of gold? Secret scrolls? Sign me up! A twisty tale of adventure and intrigue that never lets up and never lets go!" --**Robert Masello, author of *The Medusa Amulet***

"A page-turning yarn blending high action, Biblical speculation, ancient secrets, and nasty creatures. Indiana Jones better watch his back!" **Jeremy Robinson, author of *Instinct***

"Let there be no confusion: David Wood is the next Clive Cussler. Wood's latest book, *Quest*, is a tremendous classic adventure. Once you start reading, you won't be able to stop until the last mystery plays out in the final line." **Edward G. Talbot, author of *2010: The Fifth World***

"Packed solid with action and witty dialogue, this rousing adventure takes a fresh look at one of the most enduring mysteries of the 20th century, David Wood delivers again with *Quest*." **Sean Ellis, author of *Into the Black***

"An all-out blitzkrieg of a globe-trotting mystery-adventure that breaks from the action just long enough for a couple of laughs." **Rick Chesler, author of *kiDNApped* and *Wired Kingdom***

"David Wood just might become the new master of the Biblical action-thriller." **Megalith Book Reviews**

Books by David Wood

The Dane Maddock Adventures

Dourado
Cibola
Quest
Dark Entry (Short story)

Stand-alone Novels

Into the Woods
The zombie-Driven Life

David Wood writing as David Debord

The Silver Serpent
Keeper of the Mists

DAVID WOOD

Gryphonwood Press

Published by Gryphonwood Press.
www.gryphonwoodpress.com

Cover design by Jeremy Robinson

ISBN 13: 978-0-9837655-0-9

DEDICATED TO GREG LESTER,
IN THANKS FOR THE EMAIL THAT
CHANGED MY LIFE.

Prologue

149 B.C.

"Why have you summoned me? I should be at my place on the walls." Hasdrubal's eyes were afire and his hand trembled as he gripped the hilt of his sword. His anger was understandable, considering who he was and to whom he was related. But, he had come right away when summoned, and that was to his credit.

"You are needed for something greater than waiting to die." Aderba'al laid a hand on the man's shoulder, but he shrugged it off. It was an affront which, under different circumstances, would merit severe chastisement, but this was not the time for such things. Time was of the essence. "Hear my words before you so impetuously assume that you know what is best."

"Very well, but do not delay me unnecessarily." He looked around as if, at any moment, enemies would be storming the temple.

"It is you who is delaying me," Aderba'al snapped. "What I do is the last hope for the survival of our people. You have been chosen for a sacred task."

Now Hasdrubal was curious. "Tell me." Suspicion hung heavy in his words, but at least Aderba'al had his attention.

"That is what I have been trying to do. Follow me, listen, and do not interrupt."

They passed through the temple, now dark because they could no longer spare the oil required to light the lamps. Everything, it seemed, was needed in defense of the city.

Behind the altar, he knelt, running his fingers across the carved surface, the smooth stone cool to the touch. He stopped on an image of a flooded field. "Aretsaya," he whispered as he pressed down.

With a click, a door swung open, revealing a dark passage in the base of the altar.

"What…" Hasdrubal must have remembered Aderba'al's warning against interruption, because he clamped his mouth shut and followed without protest as Aderba'al led them down into the tunnel.

He required no light, so familiar was he with this passage. They walked along in silence as complete as the absence of light. Their footsteps echoed in the empty corridor and it was almost possible to forget the enemy at the gates. Not once, in all the time he followed Aderba'al into the unknowable blackness, did Hasdrubal speak, though he surely was wondering where they were going and why.

When he tasted the salty tang of sea air, Aderba'al knew they had almost arrived at their destination. They emerged in a grotto overlooking a sheltered cove. This place was a temple secret, but it was far from the most important one he would reveal today. Down below, sailing ships were being loaded and made ready to sail.

Hasdrubal looked scandalized at the sight and he rounded angrily on Aderba'al, his face red and his eyes flashing. "You want me to flee like a coward? I shall not do it. You know my bloodline and the obligation it carries with it. How can you ask me to run?"

"What I ask you to do requires more courage than anything you have ever done before." This gained Hasdrubal's attention and he lapsed into an uneasy silence.

Aderba'al drew from his robes an oilcloth pouch and handed it to him. "As you are well aware, our ancestors were the greatest sailors in history. They passed down to us knowledge of a land, wild and unconquered by civilized man. It lies far across the great water beyond the white stones. These maps will show you the way."

"Beyond the white stones? *Across* the water?"

Aderba'al nodded gravely. "There is no other choice. You must go beyond the reach of our enemy."

Hasdrubal held the bundle in his hands, looking sadly at it. "Surely there are other sailors who can take this command. Other men…"

"But there is only one man with your blood. One man who can sail, fight, and command their unwavering allegiance. It must be you."

"So I am to find this faraway land and found a new colony?" Regret filled his voice and it was obvious the man would rather fight to the death on the walls than abandon his home.

"That is a part of it, but there is something much more important that you must do. It is a sacred duty that reaches back beyond the history of our people. Few know of it, and should our city fall, as I fear it will, you will perhaps be the only living man with that knowledge."

Aderba'al remembered the day the secret had been passed down to him. He had not believed it at first, but when he had seen the proof with his own eyes, it had been a wondrous revelation. He wondered how Hasdrubal would react to what he was about to be told. Taking a deep breath, he began his tale.

"The ship on which you will travel carries…"

148 B.C.E.

Hasdrubal stepped off the ship onto sand as white as snow and as hot as a forge. The deep green of the forest was a pleasant change from the months of unrelenting blue sea under blue sky. They had sighted land a few times in recent days, and the others had pleaded with him to take the ships ashore, but he had refused. The maps indicated that these were small islands and wholly unsuitable to their purpose. They needed to disappear in this strange new world. He would lead them into its dark depths until the gods told him they had found their new home. When they reached that place, they would plant the seeds of their new civilization… literally.

A man stepped out from the darkness of the forest. Short of stature, with dark skin and glossy, black hair, the man looked at him, not with enmity, but curiosity. He carried a primitive spear, but no other weapon. Hasdrubal's hand itched to reach for his sword, but he remained calm. Step by hesitant step, the man came closer, until he stood only a few feet from Hasdrubal, certainly close enough to use that spear if he chose to do so.

A tense silence hung in the air as everyone waited to see what would happen next. The roar of waves crashing on the shore filled Hasdrubal's ears and the cool breeze ruffled his hair. This would not be the worst place to die, but he somehow sensed this was not his day. His mission was not yet complete.

The dark man looked up at him in wide-eyed wonder. The moment stretched into an excruciating span of three heartbeats. Then, without preamble, he let his spear drop, and fell face-down alongside it.

Hasdrubal thought, for a moment, that the man had died, but then, more figures melted out of the jungle. Like the first man, they too laid down their weapons and fell prostrate in the sand.

"It is as if they think we are gods," Shafat whispered. A fine sailor, his was one of only four ships that had survived the journey.

"It is well that they do," Hasdrubal replied. "Perhaps they shall be of some use as we search for our new home."

"And where will that be?" There was no disrespect in Shafat's voice, only curiosity.

"I will know it when I find it."

1922

"Colonel! You must come quickly!" Adam poked his head

into the tent, his excited eyes shining, in contrast to his dirty face. "Someone has come to the camp!"

Percy Fawcett looked up from his book and frowned. "Tell me, would you open the door to someone's house and shout to them, Adam? Or would you knock first?" Adam hung his head. "And wash your face. You embarrass me." Apologizing profusely, the man backed out of the tent.

Fuming, Fawcett pulled on his boots. Weak men who could scarcely maintain their humanity in the jungle were an affront to his sensibilities. Why was it so difficult to find men with pride, dignity, and a bit of backbone? Disappointments, every one of them.

He pushed aside the flap of his tent, wondering what absurdity had prompted them to bring him out so late. Despite the lateness of the hour, it was still hot and muggy out. The others had kept their cookfire burning and were huddled around it, seeming to find comfort. Weaklings! Doubtless they had called him out here for something preposterous. Perhaps a large insect or something of the sort. When he saw the young man lying beneath a blanket by the fire, however, he revised his opinion at once.

Fawcett knelt down beside the young man and pushed back his hair to get a better look. He did not resemble the natives of this region. In fact, he had a distinctly Mediterranean look about him.

"Who is he? Where did he come from?"

"We don't know," Adam replied. "He came staggering into camp and collapsed. He hasn't stopped babbling. Alberto understands some of what he says, but he can't make out the half of it."

Fawcett listened closely. The language was an odd one. Some of the words were recognizable as a dialect similar to that of the natives of this region. The rest was…

Fawcett gaped, the pipe falling from his mouth. He found that he could understand much of what this young man was saying, but the language was…

It couldn't be!

"Adam, be a good fellow and fetch my book and my

pen." Heart pounding, he stared down in excitement and disbelief at the strange young man who had so fortuitously stumbled into his encampment. And if Fawcett understood his words correctly, this youth just might be the key to what Fawcett had been searching for all these years.

CHAPTER 1

Thomas had never felt so hot in his entire life. The heat was sweltering, unrelenting, and scarcely a breeze stirred beneath the canopy of green. Creeping, clutching foliage dogged his every step. And the insects! They were an unrelenting cloud, biting and stinging him, and invading his every orifice. Civilization's finest insect repellent had waged a losing battle against the onslaught.

"It's getting late." Denesh, his neck twitching in that annoying nervous tic of his, glanced up at the tattered bits of sky visible through the canopy of trees. "You know how quickly night can come on in this jungle. I don't want to be stuck out here when it does."

"I know." Thomas took another look at his notebook. He had found all the landmarks up to this point, but this next one continued to elude him. Perhaps just a bit farther. Of course, he'd been telling himself that for the better part of the last hour, with no success. With a sigh, he tucked the notebook back into his pocket. They were close. He just knew it. His research had proved to be accurate up to this point, with all the landmarks exactly as they should be, so there was no reason to assume it would not continue to be so. They were on the verge of a discovery that would rock the world.

"Did you hear that?" Denesh shifted his weight from one foot to the other, looking all around. He looked like a nervous bird, his head jerking to and fro as his eyes probed the jungle.

"I didn't hear anything." The truth was, Thomas was so focused on his thoughts that a truck could have driven over him and he probably would not have noticed until it was too late. "Let's head back. Tomorrow we'll get an earlier start and see how far we can get. We might even break camp and haul the gear along with us. That way we can range even farther."

Denesh's coffee complexion paled at the suggestion, but he nodded. A brilliant graduate student, he was finding the expedition difficult, to say the least, but he had braved it all without complaint. The young man had potential, assuming Thomas could ever get him back out into the field after this experience. He now stood stock-still, his knuckles white as he clutched the hilt of his machete. "I'm not crazy, Professor Thornton, I swear I heard something. It was the strangest sound. Like a giant sheet of sandpaper being dragged across the ground."

"That's probably what it was, then. Congratulations. You've solved the mystery." He elbowed Denesh in the ribs, coaxing a weak smile. "All right, it's time to test your woods craft. Do you think you can guide us back to camp without getting us hopelessly lost?"

Denesh took up the challenge, and only managed to lead them off course twice, but both times he found the trail again without any help from Thomas. By the time camp was in sight, he had a bit of bounce in his step. The promise of food, no matter how poor, and a camp bed beneath a screen of mosquito netting, seemed like high living in this part of the world.

Thomas sensed something was wrong the moment he entered camp. A quick inspection revealed nothing obvious that might be amiss, but still, things were not right. There was a tension in the air, as if the world were as taut as piano wire.

Derek and Emily appeared from the shadows on the far side of the encampment and hurried to meet him. They both appeared agitated.

"Doctor Thornton, I did not sign up for this trip only to

be stranded in the middle of nowhere." Emily's freckled face was bright red, but whether from sunburn or anger he could not tell.

"Wait, what are you talking about? We're not stranded." The psychological toll this place took on travelers sometimes caused a person to crack. He hoped this was not the case with Emily, who, despite having a face and body that screamed 'delicate flower,' had been a trooper up to this point.

"Victor is gone." Her voice trembled as she spoke and she looked like she was on the verge of tears. "He said he was going to hike back to the lagoon, take one of the boats, and go home."

The news struck Thomas like a punch to the gut. If their guide was gone, that left him alone to get three students back to civilization. He supposed he could do it, but this meant the expedition was over. Damn. Another day or two might have done it. With serious effort, he regained his composure. Under the circumstances, it would not do to appear rattled in front of the others.

"But we still have the other boat, so we aren't stranded." He stared through the trees in the direction of the lagoon, as if his eyes could penetrate the miles of tangled greenery and see their remaining boat, their only path back to civilization, waiting there beside its dark waters. "But why did Victor just up and leave? Did he say anything?"

Emily gave Derek a look that said, *"I told you so,"* and Derek nodded.

"I think it's been coming on for a few days, Professor," Denesh said. "He didn't like it here, and kept telling us it was a bad place and that we should not stay. He knew it would do no good to say anything to you, though. You were so focused on whatever it is you're still doing out here." He held his hands out to his sides in a gesture of confusion. "I do think Victor was on to something, though. There's a wrongness about this place, and it's got us all spooked."

"Superstitious nonsense." Thomas was embarrassed that he had been so focused on his search that he had failed to notice that one of his team was on the verge of abandoning the group. "He got into your heads, that's all. He fed you tales about spooky stuff, and it took root in your psyche. Don't let it control you."

"It's not just that, Professor," Derek said. "I had to kill an opossum today."

"Chestnut-striped," Emily chimed in, proving she had been paying attention to her field guide.

"An opossum," Thomas repeated, unable to keep the disbelief from his voice. He could not begin to fathom where Derek was headed with this.

"I know how it sounds," Derek protested. "You had to be there, I suppose, but it's not just that I killed it. I *had* to kill it. It came marching into camp in the middle of the day, which is strange enough in itself, and it went straight for our food. It ignored me when I tried to shoo it away. Then I kicked it and it…" He swallowed hard. "It attacked me. Turned on me, made this crazy noise, and sprang up like a mountain lion or something. It tore up my pants leg, but I got hold of it by the tail before it could bite me. Even then, it kept snarling at me."

"An opossum snarled at you." Thomas didn't get it. Perhaps this was all just an elaborate ruse to get him to pack up and leave. Or maybe it was a joke.

"It was a snarl," Emily added. "It sounded like a ferocious predator."

"I flung it across the camp and it smashed into that tree over there." Derek nodded at a kapok tree with a trunk nearly ten feet in diameter. "It should have crawled away, but it got up and came right at me again. I kicked it away and it still kept on coming at me. Finally, I had to stomp it to death." Derek's eyes fell, clearly upset by the memory.

"So you had an encounter with a rabid opossum and now you believe Victor's stories about the bogeyman. I'm disappointed in you."

"It was not rabid." Frustration was now clear in Derek's every word. "You don't understand. It didn't appear crazed at all. Its actions were purposeful, and, I don't know, it was almost as if it thought it was a giant predator and I was the small animal in its way. It never seemed the least bit frightened, or even wary, just determined. It was like there was no question of it doing what it wanted to do, and I could pose no threat to it in any way."

"I work at a vet's office every summer," Emily added. "Even in the early stages of rabies, if an animal goes into the aggressive state, it's accompanied by other symptoms, like disorientation, trembling, loss of muscle coordination. I saw none of that. That animal was different. We kept the body if you would like to look at it."

They led him to the spot where the opossum lay. Thomas took his time examining the disfigured remains of the small mammal, though, in truth, he doubted he would recognize even the late-stage signs of rabies. He kept his features calm, letting the silence and his own serenity settle the nerves of his upset students. Finally, he gave a diagnosis of "perhaps" and rose to his feet.

"Our notebooks are complete, Doctor Thornton. They have been for two days. Victor took half the remaining supplies. Let's just go home." Emily sounded as if she were on the verge of tears.

The pleading tone grated on his nerves. They had to leave, he understood that, but that did not mean he had to be happy about it. To have come so close and yet failed. It would be another year, at the soonest, before he could return, and that was assuming his sponsors would fund another trip. He had promised results, and they were not going to be happy when he returned empty-handed. "Fine," he said, rising to his feet. "Pack up as much as you can. We'll leave in the morning."

Derek's and Emily's faces relaxed, and each thanked him profusely, assuring him that this had been the best field ecology trip ever, and that they couldn't wait to get home and tell their families all about it.

Denesh did not appear to share in their joy. He frowned, his eyes fixed on a spot deep in the jungle.

"What's wrong with you?" Emily nudged him. "Lighten

up a little."

"Quiet." The tone of his voice silenced everyone in the group. "Something's coming."

Thomas turned to look in the direction Denesh indicated in time to see three figures stride out of the jungle. They were short and stocky, with glossy black hair cut short in the Yanomami style. Their bodies were painted orange-brown with black smudges all over that put him to mind of a jaguar. Each was armed with a stone-tipped short spear and a stone axe. They moved directly toward the camp, their faces blank, and their strides resolute.

"Who are they?" Derek whispered. "There aren't supposed to be any natives in this area."

Actually, very little was known about this region. The area was so remote that it had remained unexplored in modern times. The satellite photos Thomas had inspected revealed nothing but a blanket of unrelenting green.

"I have no idea. They must be from an undiscovered tribe." Thomas shook his head. These men had the general look and build of the natives of this region, but he noticed subtle differences. Their faces were narrow, and their noses longer. He could not discern eye color from this distance, but they were definitely not the brown one usually found here. Curious, he took a step forward, but Denesh stopped him with a firm grip on his forearm.

"Let me do it. I know a smattering of languages from this area. Perhaps I can get them to understand me. If this actually is a tribe that has avoided outside contact, and we can communicate with them, I could write quite the paper on it."

He walked toward them, his open hands at his sides, and spoke to them in a language Thomas did not recognize. The natives neither acknowledged his words, nor broke their stride. Denesh tried again in three other languages unfamiliar to Thomas, and then in Portuguese. Nothing.

The men continued their silent approach, their faces still devoid of emotion. Their movements were not exactly robotic, but were steady and measured, almost military in their regularity.

"They're like zombies," Emily whispered.

Thomas grew more nervous with each step they took. Maybe he too had been spooked by Victor's suspicions, but something was very wrong. His hand itched to take hold of the machete that hung from his belt, but he dared not make any movement that insinuated violence. The results could be deadly.

Denesh gave up his attempts at verbal communication. He dropped to one knee, slipped off his wristwatch, and held it out as a supplicant would a tribute.

The men stopped in front of him. The one in the center gazed down at the wristwatch and then, as casually as a businessman would brush lint off of his suit, he raised his hatchet and brought it crashing down on Denesh's head. The young man crumpled to the ground, blood pouring from his split scalp.

Emily screamed at the sight of her friend lying dead on the ground, and she turned and fled. Derek drew his .38 revolver and emptied it in a wild spurt of gunfire. At least two bullets hit one of the warriors, punching through his chest and spraying gore on the man who strode directly behind him—yet the wounded man did not stumble, nor did he so much as blink. He kept coming.

Derek stood like a statue for a moment that seemed frozen in eternity. With a sudden gasp, he shot a glance at Thomas, and then back to the bloody warriors who bore down upon him, their implacable gazes locked on the frightened young man. Derek shrieked, threw his pistol at the first warrior, watched it bounce harmlessly off his chest, and then fled after Emily.

Thomas felt for his own pistol and realized he had not even bothered to carry it with him today. He didn't own a gun in his "real life," and still was not in the habit of keeping one at his hip. Now he was quickly altering his opinion on the necessity of firearms.

As the silent warriors turned their attention to him, he slid the machete from his belt and raised it in what he hoped was a threatening pose, but they stalked after him, undeterred. His courage draining faster than his bladder, he turned on his heel and fled blindly into jungle.

CHAPTER 2

Kaylin looked up and down Meeting Street for what must have been the tenth time. Traffic was light in the historic section of Charleston. More importantly, there was no carriage to be seen. Also for the tenth time, she re-read the text message she'd received the night before.

be in front of circ church at 10 get in carriage drop you at powder mag leave your car there its about thomas – andy

Andy was Thomas's closest friend, and in the time she and Thomas had been dating, she and Andy had gotten to know one another fairly well. That was why she knew there were several things wrong about this message. Foremost was the fact that he had texted her rather than calling, which was unusual for him. Second, was the lack of capitalization and punctuation, to which the English Literature professor always paid fastidious attention, even in text messages. Finally, the text had not come from Andy's phone, but from an unfamiliar number.

Thomas was more than two months overdue from the field ecology trip he had taken with his graduate assistant and two other students. He had assured her something like this might happen, and told her not to worry. The Amazon, he said, was not like other places. Plans frequently got fouled up, connections were missed, or wires crossed, resulting in a giant mess. She wanted to believe him, but could not help wondering if Thomas was penning a cover story which would allow him to spend more time with Emily, the cute redhead who called, texted, and emailed Thomas far more often than Kaylin thought appropriate for a professor-student relationship. Now she regretted having entertained such ideas. Andy's message had filled her with a dark sense of foreboding.

Right on time, a carriage appeared in the distance. It belonged to one of the small, private companies that catered primarily to couples looking for a romantic ride around the old parts of the city. As it drew closer, she recognized Andy's shock of short, dark hair, high brow, and fair complexion. The carriage came to a halt and Andy offered his hand to help her inside. His palms were sweaty and his eyes were alive with a manic energy.

"Take this, but don't look at it until you're somewhere safe," he whispered, handing her a small manila envelope as the carriage rolled forward. He leaned up and whispered instructions to the driver, who nodded and began loudly describing the historical significance of the Circular Congregational Church.

"Andy, what's going on? You said it's about Thomas. Have you heard from him?"

"We don't have much time." Andy looked around as if expecting someone to leap into the carriage with them at any moment. "Before he left, Thomas gave me that." He indicated the envelope. "He said that he might be delayed on his trip, but if I had not heard from him by sixty days after his expected return date, to get help from someone I trust, and come for him. He said I should do it without drawing unnecessary attention." Andy paused, his expression tense. "He also told me to watch my back."

"But I've already contacted the authorities. They say they've checked the entire stretch of river where his party was to have traveled, and found nothing. Their best guess is that Thomas and the others probably went into the rainforest and their boat was stolen while they were gone. They tell me they'll keep an eye out, but they figure Thomas will show up at one of the settlements along the river and send for help. What else are we supposed to do?"

"Thomas didn't follow his planned path. This field ecology trip was just a front to get the university to approve an expedition into the Amazon. He's gone after something bigger. Much bigger."

An icy sensation of disbelief crept up Kaylin's spine. What was Andy talking about?

"For several years now, Thomas has been working on a research project that he's kept top secret, except to say it was a very old mystery. He said he couldn't share it, even with the people he trusts. He seems to think knowing nothing might keep us safe, though he didn't say from whom. In fact, he said he didn't have all the pieces, but he thought he had enough to succeed."

"This is nuts! Are you sure he didn't just concoct this crazy story as a cover so he could spend more time with Emily?" She regretted the words the moment they left her mouth.

Andy gave her a soft smile of understanding, took her hand, and gave it a squeeze. "There is nothing between him and Emily. You can take the word of his closest friend on that."

"I'm sorry." She buried her face in her hands. "That was so selfish of me. It's just something that's been bothering me for a long time. God, I feel like such an idiot. Thomas is lost, maybe in danger, and I'm acting like a jealous teenager."

"Don't beat yourself up over it. Thomas needs your help, not your regrets. Now listen carefully. I can't be the one to do this. I'm an English Lit professor, not an explorer, and I don't have any friends who are. Thomas specifically wanted me to tell you if it came to this. He seemed to think you might be able to mount a rescue mission." Andy looked puzzled. "No offense, but you're a Fine Arts teacher, so it seems odd to me. Maybe because of your father's military background?"

Kaylin shrugged, too lost in thought to form a reply.

"So, *do* you know someone, anyone, who could go into the Amazon, find him and the students, and bring them back out alive?" He didn't add, *if they're still alive.*

Actually, Kaylin did know one person who fit that bill. She knew him quite well, in fact, but the mere thought of asking him to risk his life to save her boyfriend made her stomach churn. "I think so." She bit her lip and stared out at the street. "But I don't know if he'd do it."

"Thomas swore that solving this mystery, whatever it is, would rock the world—his words, not mine. He seemed to think he was going to be rich and famous."

"But that doesn't make sense. He's an academic. Even if he solved some sort of mystery in the Amazon, there's no money in that. What would he get out of it? Mostly fame among scholars, maybe a few mentions in the media." Closing her eyes, she took two deep, calming breaths and rubbed her temples. Before getting Andy's message, she had convinced herself that Thomas was not truly in danger. He'd been overdue before and always returned safely. Now, her whole world had been turned upside down. She almost wished for a return to a few hours ago, when her greatest concern had been an irrational fear that her boyfriend was cheating on her. She needed to think about this calmly and logically. "Okay, so we don't know what mystery he was working on. What do we know?"

"Nothing. I've looked at what's in the envelope, and I'm baffled, though he insisted it would be sufficient to set us on his trail without giving anything away were it to fall into the wrong hands. I think you might have more luck with it than me. When you see it, you'll understand why."

"There's so much about this that doesn't make sense. Why didn't he tell me anything? If he thought he might not come back, why didn't he leave us a map or something? He could have written a note saying, *"Look for me here,"* and put it in a safe deposit box. And why did he confide in only you?" She wanted to add *"and not me,"* but she'd already embarrassed herself once today with her jealousy.

"In respect to the first two questions, I can only tell you that he believed someone might be after not only him, but anyone else who might know something about what he was doing. I think he was right. I've been on holiday for the last week, and yesterday I received a call from a colleague who told me that a man has been asking after me around the university. I called a neighbor, who said someone had come to her door asking about me as well. Now I'm afraid to go home." He sighed. "As to the latter question, he knows I keep his secrets."

Before Kaylin could follow up on that last cryptic comment, his head snapped up and he once again looked up and down the street before turning to face her.

"There's no more time for talk. The Powder Magazine is coming up on the right. The carriage is not going to slow down, but he will pull as close to the curb as he can. I want you to slip out right in the middle of the tour group that's waiting at the gate, and then get to your car as quickly as possible. I don't know if you should go home, but you definitely need to get help. In fact, you should probably get out of town, just to be safe. I've gotten you involved now, and I regret it."

"Andy I…"

Ever the professor, he hushed her with a raised index finger, as if she was a student. "I'm sorry to bring you into this, and I hope the situation is not as grave as I fear, but who really knows?" He gave her a small, sad smile. "Here's your stop."

He gave her a gentle shove and she sprang from the carriage. Her last thought before she hit the ground was, *Why did I wear heels?* And then she was stumbling into the midst of a dozen or more tourists waiting to see the colonial-era gunpowder magazine and its museum.

She landed in the arms of a dark-skinned young man in sagging jeans and an Under Armour shirt. He helped regain her balance and looked her over, though his expression was one of concern rather than lewdness. Satisfied she was all right, he looked toward the carriage, which was now rounding the corner onto Church Street. "Did that dude try to push you out?"

"Oh, no." She forced a laugh. "He didn't want me

jumping out of the carriage in heels, and he tried to grab me, but I was too quick. I guess I should have waited for the carriage to stop."

"Why didn't you?" He was still staring at the carriage, as if he didn't want to let it out of his sight until he was satisfied with her story.

"That's my divorce attorney. My estranged husband's kind of crazy, and while we were talking, I saw his car come around the corner. I guess I freaked." Someday she would have to write a note to Mr. Harper, her high school drama teacher, thanking him for all those improv lessons. She looked around, not needing to feign nervousness. "I just want to get to my car and get out of here before he finds me."

"I'll walk you there." The young man offered his hand. "Tariq."

"Kaylin." He had a strong grip, but his hand was surprisingly soft. "I appreciate it, but I wouldn't want you to get into trouble because of me."

"It's all good. Which way's your ride?" He stayed right beside her, shielding her from the view of passing vehicles. As they walked, he told her a little bit about himself. He was a high school senior, and hoped to attend Citadel next year. She told him that she was a Navy brat, which elicited a nod of approval.

As they neared the spot where she'd left her car, she looked down the street and gasped. The carriage was stopped on the side of the road, and someone was pushing Andy into a waiting vehicle. Another man, tall, barrel-chested, with short, ash-blond hair was talking to the carriage driver, who turned and looked back down the street, spotted her, and pointed. The man turned, his blue eyes locked on her, and he started in her direction.

They want to take me too! Her heart pounded and she nearly stumbled.

"That's him, isn't it?" Tariq pushed her behind him and made a beeline toward the man. "Get in your car and go."

"I don't want you to get hurt because of me. Just run."

She couldn't believe this was happening, and she certainly hated that she'd gotten an innocent young man caught up in it.

"Just get in your car, alright? I got this."

Kaylin fished her keys from her purse with trembling fingers and struggled to unlock the driver's side door.

"Hey, lady! I need to talk to you!" The unfamiliar voice must have belonged to the man who was coming after her.

"Yo man, what's up?" Tariq stepped in front of the larger man as Kaylin pulled the door open and slid inside.

"Get out of my way."

"I said, what's up?" Tariq gave the man a hard shove, but he barely budged. Kaylin slammed and locked the door, and promptly dropped the keys. Spewing curses, she retrieved them and started the car. Outside, Tariq was grappling with her would-be abductor. Horns blared as she gunned the engine and backed blindly out into the street. The man broke loose from Tariq, shoved him away, and ran toward her car.

She spun the wheel, did a donut in the middle of the street, and floored it, heading the wrong way back up Church Street. Glancing in the rear-view mirror, she saw the man quickly give up chase, and run back to the vehicle in which they'd put Andy. She wondered why the driver had not given pursuit, but then she saw bodies twisting and jerking inside the car. Andy was trying to fight them so she could get away.

Her inattention almost cost her. She returned her attention to the road in time to see a van blowing through the yellow light, coming right at her. She yanked the wheel hard to the right, going up on the sidewalk as the van shot past her, the stunned driver staring at her as he whizzed past.

Back on the road, she took another look behind her and saw the man who had come after her reach the car, draw a gun, and point it through the window.

She lost sight of the vehicle as she turned back onto Market Street. She gunned the accelerator, flew past the Powder Magazine, and blew the red light as she turned onto

Meeting Street, skidding through the intersection, and barely missing a taxi cab, which swerved and took out a garbage can on the corner. She hoped no one got her tag number, but an appearance in traffic court was small potatoes compared to kidnapping.

By the time she turned onto Broad Street, she dared to hope she was not being followed. She prayed Andy was alive, and that the man had drawn the gun only to get him to stop fighting. Her eyes clouded with tears as she thought of the gentle professor fighting for his life.

She finally breathed a sigh of relief when she pulled into the parking lot of the Charleston Police Department Administrative Building. She knew someone there she could trust, and hopefully he could help her, Andy, and Thomas.

CHAPTER 3

"Let me see if I've got this straight." Captain Ray Gerard tapped his square chin with the envelope Andy had given to Kaylin. A friend of her father, Hartford Maxwell, during their Navy days, he had remained close to Kaylin after her father's passing. "Your boyfriend is overdue returning from the Amazon and you think he's in trouble." Kaylin nodded. "But the only evidence you have is this." He held up the manila envelope.

"I know it sounds crazy, but putting that aside for the moment, Andy was definitely kidnapped. I watched it happen." She winced at the fresh memory and thought of the gun the man had drawn. "He might even be dead."

"Yes, about that." Gerard looked down at his desk, perhaps not wanting to meet her eye. "We can't file a missing persons report just yet. Andy hasn't been gone long enough. What I did do was put out an alert, giving the description of the vehicle and the passengers. Hopefully something will turn up."

Kaylin knew the odds were slim. She had been so surprised by the entire incident that she had not gotten a good look at the car. The best she had been able to tell the police was that it was a silver sedan, as if there weren't thousands of those out on the road. She had been able to give a fair description of one of the men, the one whom Tariq had confronted, but not the driver.

"I don't know what to do now. I don't feel safe going home, but I also wonder if I'm being foolish. This all really has nothing to do with me, except for the fact that I'm dating Thomas. But I don't know anything about his expedition."

"Well, if this thing," Gerard taped the envelope, "is of any significance, and I don't see how it could be, the people who've kidnapped your friend might come after you if they find out if you've got it."

"But I don't have it any more. That was the whole point of turning it over to you."

"Even if they find out you've given it to me, they'll figure you at least looked at it. They might want to make you describe it to them, or to stop you from telling anyone else about it. Either way, you could be in danger. You have anywhere you can go? Any one you can stay with for a couple of days?"

Kaylin sighed. "I'll get a hotel for tonight, and then maybe I can stay with friends. But what about Thomas? Isn't there anything you can do?"

"If your friend Andy is right, and Thomas didn't follow his planned path, I don't see that there's much anyone can do, short of going down to South America and asking around. But even that would probably be a waste of time, especially since we don't even know for certain where he started his expedition."

"But there's got to be some way you can help!" Kaylin realized she was grasping at straws, but the thought of Thomas being in trouble and her doing nothing to help was more than she could bear.

"Kaylin, I want to help you, I really do, but we're just a local police department. We don't have any international connections, and even if we did, what would I tell them? A professor is missing in the Amazon? That happens all the time. What if they were to ask me for his itinerary, and I tell them we don't think he followed it, but we have this here clue..." Once again he held up the envelope and gave Kaylin a meaningful look.

"I understand." She wished she could keep the disappointment from her voice. Gerard was a good man, and she knew he would do what he could. Unfortunately, in this situation, what he could do was not much. "I suppose I'll try the dean of his college, and maybe my congressman's office. I have to do something." She rose from her chair, shook Gerard's hand, and thanked him for his help.

"I really wish I could do more for you, but my hands are tied. I will keep up the search for your friend Andy, though."

She assured him that she understood, and gratefully accepted his offer of a police escort to a nearby hotel. He walked her out to the lobby and they made small talk for a few minutes, and she promised to drop by for dinner with him and his wife sometime soon. A young officer walked her out to her car and followed behind in his squad car. Her mind was abuzz with a swarm of confused thoughts and jumbled questions. What should she do next? Was Andy okay? Where was Thomas? And, perhaps most important, what should be her next move?

Jay Newman watched Gerard leave his office with the blonde and escort her down the hall. The moment they turned the corner, he looked around to make certain no one was watching. Certain he was in the clear, he hurried to Gerard's office and tried the door. He was pleased to find it was unlocked, and he slipped inside and closed the door behind him.

A manila envelope lay on the desk. He had seen the girl carrying it when she entered the captain's office. It must be the one to which the message had referred. Jay opened it and removed the single item it contained. He frowned. What was this and how could it be important? Not his problem. He laid it on his desk, snapped a couple of pictures with his iPhone, and slipped it back into the envelope.

Knowing time could be short, depending on how long Gerard took walking the girl out, he hurried back to the door. Easing it open, he peeked out, and was relieved to find that the hallway remained empty. Closing the door behind him, it occurred to him that he should have just stepped out of the office acting normally, as if he'd simply been looking for the captain and had not found him in his office. All of this cloak and dagger was not for him. If he hadn't needed the money, he would never have agreed to help these guys.

"Detective!" Gerard's voice boomed down the hall. "Are you looking for me?"

Newman was proud of how calmly he turned around to face Gerard who, despite nearing mandatory retirement, still could intimidate him with a mere glance. "Yes, Captain, I was just wondering if there was anything I could do to help you with that young woman's situation."

Gerard fixed him with an appraising look, but then his stony features cracked into a smile. "Don't bother with that one. She's all broken up over her missing boyfriend."

"You mean the guy that was kidnapped?" Newman's heart raced. Perhaps he could glean some useful information from this conversation, which could mean more cash, and hopefully being shut of these guys sooner.

"No, a different fellow. Went on a university field trip and got himself lost." Gerard smirked. "College man. We'd all be better off if everyone had a mandatory tour of duty in the service after high school. It made a world of difference for me."

Newman had heard Gerard's pontifications on mandatory service more times than he cared to remember. He thanked the captain, reiterated his offer of help, which elicited another smirk from Gerard, and returned to his cubicle.

He wasted no time in sending the photos to his contact number, and wasn't surprised when he received a response less than a minute later.

CALL

This was not a conversation he could risk having overheard. He hurried to a small, single-head restroom near the break room and locked the door. Inside, he turned on the water and retreated to the stall before making his call.

"You sent the wrong attachment." Not so much as a hello. *"What the hell is this picture you sent me, anyway?"* The voice belonged to the man who had first contacted him with the business proposition.

"No, really, that's it. That was the only thing in the envelope."

"The next two words out of your mouth had better be 'April Fool' or else my employers are going to be very unhappy with both of us."

"I'm serious." Newman forced himself to remain calm, though his heart was racing. What kind of people had he gotten himself hooked up with? "That is what the girl turned over to my captain."

"And you're certain it was the right envelope?" Suspicion lay beneath every word. *"If you're messing with me, you won't see one penny of the money. And that's only if they take the news well. If they don't..."*

If I don't get that money, certain other people are going to be after me, too. Either way, I'm toast, Newman thought. "I'm one hundred percent sure. I saw the girl take the envelope into the captain's office."

"Fine." The caller gave an exasperated sigh. *"What about the back? You didn't send me a picture of the flip side."*

Newman froze. Had he even looked at the back? Surely he had taken a quick glance to see if anything was there. He must have looked at it, seen nothing, and just taken pictures of the front. In any case, he wasn't going to tell this guy that he might have overlooked something that simple. No way was he going to make this fellow any angrier than he already was.

"The back was blank. What you've got right there is everything." He held his breath, wondering what the reply would be, and what it might bode for his future well-being.

"All right, whatever. I don't get why this thing is such a big deal, but that's not for you and me to decide. We do need to make sure this is the real thing, and the girl didn't pull some sort of switch on us. I'll check her place. You find out if she might have decided to stay somewhere else."

It was a good thing Newman was in the head, because he felt like he was going to throw up. He'd agreed to provide information, not help track down and interrogate innocent women. He hoped the man had nothing in mind more serious than interrogation. He swallowed hard. "I understand. Do you have her name?"

"Yeah, it's Kaylin Maxwell."

Thirty minutes and the walls were already closing in on Kaylin. She sipped a cup of hot tea, which was not bad for a complimentary hotel brand, and tried to relax. It was lunchtime, but she had little appetite.

Her conversation with Thomas's dean had been a waste of time. The man claimed to have no connections in South America, but promised her he would "ask around." The call to her congressman's office was equally fruitless. She'd left a message with a skeptical-sounding aide, who asked that she email him with the details so he could look into it, whatever that meant.

Now that she was calm enough to reflect, she felt like a fool for panicking when the man had come after her, and letting a teenager fight her battle for her. What happened to the tough, self-reliant girl her father raised? She'd been in worse situations before. Since she and Thomas had become serious, she had allowed herself to get soft. Why, she didn't even carry her .380 in her purse any more. It was still in her glove compartment where it had lain for a couple of years now. What would her father think if he could see her right now, cowering in a hotel room, hoping other people would solve her problems for her?

No more of this. It was time to take action. She took out her phone and scrolled down to the D's. There was the name, still there, though the two of them hadn't talked in… she didn't know how long. What if he had changed his number? No, that wouldn't be like him. Never mind. She'd call him later. Telling herself she was putting first things first, and not being chicken, she called her neighbor, Amber.

Perhaps she could safely go home and get her laptop, clothes, and personal items.

Amber picked up on the first ring.

"Hi Amber, it's Kay. Would you mind taking a peek over at my apartment and seeing if things are… all right?"

"Sure. Your key's hanging right here. I'll go check it out. Is everything all right?"

"No! I mean, I think things are okay, but no, you don't have to go inside. Just take a look and see if things look… normal." She was feeling a little foolish. What exactly did she want Amber to look for? Masked men hiding on the balcony? The door kicked in? "You know what? Don't even worry about it."

"It's no problem. I'm already here. Besides, what are next-door neighbors for?"

"No, really. Forget about…"

Amber's scream cut her off in mid-sentence. She heard the clatter of a phone falling to the ground.

"Amber!"

The call ended. She punched up the number again, but no answer. She tried again and, this time, it went straight to voice mail. That sealed it for her. She snatched up her purse, the only item she had with her, and headed for the door, calling 911 as she went. She gave the operator an abridged description of the phone call and the scream, making it sound like she and Amber had been on the phone when Amber screamed and the line went dead. She worried that the incident she described would not seem serious enough to merit police attention, but the operator assured her they would check it out.

The elevator reached the first floor, the doors opened, and she hurried toward the side entrance nearest the spot where she had parked her car. As she passed the front desk, she heard someone say, "Kaylin Maxwell's room, please." She jerked her head around in surprise, and caught a glimpse of a tall, lean man in a navy suit. Distracted, she bumped into an elderly man who was engrossed in a large print novel.

"I'm so sorry," she said, hurrying away.

"Not at all," he called to her. "I wasn't watching where I was going."

She glanced back to discover she had caught the attention of the man at the counter, who was now following after her.

"Ms. Maxwell!" he called. "Hold on a minute! Please!"

She banged through the door and hurried out into the parking lot, once again cursing her high heels and vowing to wear flats for the rest of her life. She was just slamming the car door when she heard the man call out to her.

"Wait! I'm with the police!"

She locked the door and turned to see him approaching, holding up his shield and identification. She let her shoulders sag, and lowered the window an inch.

"I didn't mean to freak you out." He tucked his badge inside his coat pocket. "I'm a detective. Can we talk?"

"First, you can send someone to my apartment. I think my neighbor is in trouble."

"I know. I mean, I came to tell you not to go home." He leaned down, putting his face inches from the window, and lowered his voice. "You're in danger."

Kaylin tensed. "How did you already know about my neighbor? I just called it in maybe two minutes ago."

"I didn't." She was certain he was lying. The way his eyes shifted to the left as he spoke, his demeanor, even the sound of his voice set off alarms. "I just wanted to warn you about going home. If something has happened, then I guess I was right."

"Thank you for your concern. If you'll please follow up on it and make sure help is on its way, I need to go." She put the key in the ignition and started the car.

"Wait! The envelope you brought in to the station. Are you sure you gave us everything? Was there anything else inside?"

"What? No. Captain Gerard has everything. Why would I go to him for help and then withhold the only piece of evidence I have?" Why was he asking about the envelope?

This situation was all wrong.

"That's fine. Just one more question before I go. Was there anything on the back?"

"I don't know. Flip it over and look for yourself." Not waiting for a reply, she put the car in drive and hit the gas, leaving him standing alone, looking dumbfounded as she sped away. She looked back, praying he wouldn't follow her. If the man was truly working on Andy's case, why did he need to ask her a question he could easily answer for himself simply by taking a look at the evidence? It just didn't add up.

Just then, her phone vibrated. The number was local, but unfamiliar. She hesitated for an instant, then remembered her vow to start taking action.

"Hello."

"Kay, it's Amber." Kaylin breathed a deep sigh of relief at the sound of her friend's voice. "I'm sorry about that, but there was somebody in your apartment. He ran for it when I opened the door. He knocked me down and I dropped my phone. I'm talking it went flying. Two stories to the parking lot. Toast."

"I'm so glad you're okay. I'll buy you a new phone."

"Crazy!" Amber laughed. "I've got a replacement plan." Her tone now turned serious. "Kaylin, I'm not stupid. Something's wrong with you. What's going on?"

Kaylin would have liked nothing more right now than to unburden herself to her friend, but she couldn't do it. She needed to stay strong, and crying on Amber's shoulder wasn't the way to do that. "It's one of those proverbial long stories. I'll tell you sometime, but not now."

"The police are here. They want you to take a look and let them know what's missing."

"Oh, okay, I can be there shortly." She was about to hang up, but a thought crossed her mind. "By the way, did you get a look at the guy?"

"I got a look at the huge hand he put in my face when he shoved me out of the way. Other than that, I don't know. The apartment was dark. He was a big white guy with short hair. Sorry."

"No problem. I'm just happy you're safe. I'll be there soon."

She ended the call, and stared blankly ahead as she drove along Murray Boulevard. A few boats, gleaming in the midday sun, plied the waters of Charleston Harbor. Looking at the boats, she sighed. They probably did not constitute a sign from above, or anything like that, but regardless, it was time to make the call.

CHAPTER 4

Daylight was fading, and the murky waters of Altamaha Sound grew dark. This would have to be the final dive of the day. That was all right. It had been a productive one, and the beer and ribs would go down nice and easy while they sat around a pile of Spanish gold. Dane Maddock tapped his wrist and motioned toward the surface. His partner, "Bones" Bonebrake, nodded, and they returned their attention the spot they had almost finished excavating. Bones held the dredge over the spot, sucking away the sand and silt, while Dane scooped up coins and deposited them in a mesh net. A few minutes' work and he was satisfied that this area had been thoroughly culled. He gave Bones the thumbs up and, together, they began their ascent.

He broke the surface on the port side of their boat, the *Sea Foam*. To the northeast, the shadowy form of Wolf Island was already growing dark as the sun settled down for the evening. To the west, the Altamaha River shone blood red in the fading light.

Matt Barnaby, one of his crewmen, offered a hand and hauled him up and over the rail.

"We did it!" Matt clapped him on the back, relieved him of the coins he had collected on this last dive, and held them up for a closer look. "These babies will clean up nicely! Good work, guys. How about we find ourselves a place to anchor and fire up the barbeque?"

"Sound like a plan." Dane grinned and turned to give Bones a hand. They stripped off their dive gear and settled into deck chairs, letting the fatigue from the day's work melt away in the cool air.

"It's Miller time!" a loud voice proclaimed. Willis Sanders, an old Navy buddy and occasional workmate, came up from below deck carrying a cooler, followed by Corey Dean, the last member of the crew. As Matt guided the boat toward shore, Willis passed out the drinks.

"You'd better have something better than a Miller in there." Bones said, languidly stretching and yawning. "I am beat and I deserve a Dos Equis at the least."

"At your service." Willis produced a dark bottle with a black label, popped the top, and handed it to Bones, who rubbed the cool condensation across his forehead before taking a long pull. His eyes suddenly narrowed, focusing on something in the distance. "Hey, Maddock." Bones sat up straight. "You see that blonde on the shore over there? Looks like she's trying to get our attention." He pointed to the south shore of Wolf Island, where a young woman stood waving.

Dane smiled. "I forgot to tell you guys. We're expecting company."

"No way, man. Why didn't you tell me this was a coed trip?" Willis jibed. "I'd have brought me some company."

"I don't think your mom would fit in on this crew." Corey blushed as soon as the words passed his lips.

"Ooh! The computer geek is trying you!" Bones clinked bottles with Corey. "Make it quick, Maddock. It's your night to cook, and I'm hungry."

Matt slowed the boat down and Dane headed to the stern, where they had secured their Sea Doo jet ski craft. He hopped on, fired it up, and headed out across the smooth waters of the sound.

Kaylin Maxwell waited on the shore. A wave of nostalgia passed through him when he saw her smile. The daughter of his former Navy commanding officer, he and Bones had once helped her solve a mystery her late father had been working on, and murdered over, and she had joined them on one of the improbable adventures that seemed to have become the norm for Dane and Bones in the past few years. Dane and Kaylin had dated for a short while afterward, but it had fizzled, mostly due to distance and disparate lifestyles. Dane was now seeing someone off-and-on, but long distance was an even greater impediment to that relationship. In any case, he had been surprised to get Kaylin's call earlier in the day, and was curious why she wanted to see him on such short notice.

He was thirty yards from shore when a shrill scream split the air. He looked to his left to see a young girl on a canvas raft paddling furiously toward shore. Behind her, the long, dark form of an alligator swam toward her, its broad snout cutting a v-shaped wake in the water. Gators preferred fresh water, but it was not unusual to see them in brackish water, especially when they were hunting.

Dane veered the Sea Doo toward the intervening space between the girl and the predator that pursued her. For a brief instant, he considered trying to scoop her up on to his jet ski, but that would require perfect timing and impeccable balance, his craft being too wide for him to simply reach out and grab her. Meanwhile, Kaylin had spotted the girl, and was splashing into the water toward her and the gator. Great! Dane would have to go for the alligator.

The primordial reptile, which looked to be a twelve-footer, closed the gap on the girl, who was still paddling furiously. In the distance, a man and woman were running along the shore in their direction, shouting and frantically waving. Dane was barely aware of them, so focused was he on his target. The alligator opened its jaws wide and Dane sprang off the Sea Doo.

He came down on the gator's back, his momentum pulling it to the side, and causing its jaws to clamp down on empty air. Dane got an arm around its snout, wrapped his legs around its torso, and held on as the beast rolled in the water. Dane went under, had time for a quick breath as he came up, and then was taken under again.

Okay, I've got it. Now what am I going to do with it? he thought. He broke the surface again and took another breath of sweet air. He felt like he was riding the world's wildest bucking bronco as the gator thrashed and twisted in the water. His body shifted forward and, for a moment, he feared he might lose his grip on the deadly jaws. He locked his legs tighter around and punched it in the head once, twice, three times. If the blows had any effect on the beast, they served only to further annoy it. It rolled again, and Dane banged into the seabed, almost losing his hold. He had not realized they had reached the shallows. If he could wrestle the gator to shore, he could get safely away, but, in the water, the gator had the advantage, and he did not dare take the chance of letting go of it.

With one arm around the gator's snout, and another around its head, he unlocked his legs and scrambled for purchase in the sandy bottom. The beast thrashed its tail wildly, sending up a furious salt spray, and Dane felt the snout slipping from his grasp. He gritted his teeth and roared with the effort of holding on, but inch by inch he was losing his grip.

Dark forms burst from the water. Bones and Willis had come to his aid. Willis took hold of the gator's tail and fought to keep it under control. Meanwhile, Bones hastily looped a rope around the snout, and wrapped it around several times. Holding the rope in his right hand, he took control of the head, wrapping his left arm around its head, covering its eyes. Dane moved to take hold of it around the middle, and the three of them hauled the gator, its struggles now subsiding, to shore.

"On the count of three," Dan instructed. "One, two, three!" Everyone let go of the gator at the same time and moved well away as it twisted and shook until Bones' rope, which he had not tied off, came free. Giving an angry hiss, it turned and took to the water, and soon had disappeared back into the sound.

The little girl, frightened but unharmed, had been returned to her parents, who thanked Dane and his friends profusely before departing.

"Not bad, Maddock." Bones grinned. "But gator wrestling's a sport for Indians, not white guys."

"Bones, you're a Cherokee, not a Seminole. How many gators did you wrestle up there in North Carolina, anyway?"

"All I know," Willis interjected, "is I don't want the tail next time. Reminded me too much of a snake." He shuddered and exhaled sharply.

"Dude, how many hard, knobby snakes have you handled?" Bones looked at him with a mix of amusement and scorn.

"I ain't handled no snakes, man, and I ain't ever going to. You feel me?"

"Did you guys plan this show just for me, or is this all in a day's work?" Kaylin walked up and stood between Dane and Bones, who gaped when his eyes fell on her.

"Maxwell! Maddock didn't tell us it was you he was hooking up with!" He pulled her into a crushing bear hug, which she didn't seem to mind, despite his salt water-soaked body. Willis greeted and hugged her as well.

And then she turned to look at Dane. "You told him we were hooking up?" Her flinty stare took him aback, and he found himself at a loss for words. She folded her arms and moved closer until they were almost touching.

"No, I didn't say that. Really."

Her eyes softened and she broke into laughter. "Come on, Maddock." She wrapped her arms around his neck and pulled him close. "I know Bones better than that."

He looked down into her emerald eyes and remembered all too well their time as a couple. Funny how time could erase the bad memories and leave him wondering how he had ever let this picture of perfection get away. "It's good to see you." He wondered if his words sounded as lame to her as they did to him.

Bones cleared his throat, drawing their attention to him. "So Kaylin, what brings you here?"

Blushing, she pulled away from Dane. "Actually, I feel kind of bad coming to you guys like this after not having stayed in touch, but there's no one else who can help me." She shot Dane a pleading glance and continued. "I'm pretty sure I'm in danger, and..." she bit her lip "...I sort of have a mystery I need help solving."

"You're freakin' kidding me." Bones took a step back and raised his hands. "If you tell me we've got to fish the Holy Grail out of a volcano or some crap like that, I'm retiring." He smiled to assure her he was joking.

Kaylin grinned. "No, it's nothing like that, but I do need your help." She looked at Dane again, and he knew that, no matter what it was she needed him for, there was no way he could refuse.

"Well," he began, "why don't you come aboard and tell us all about it?"

CHAPTER 5

They sat on the deck of *Sea Foam*, watching the sun set and enjoying cold drinks after a long day. After a few minutes of awkward starts and stops to the conversation, they settled into an easy give-and-take. He and Bones filled Kaylin in on their exploits since the last time they had seen one another, and she, in turn, told them about her current faculty position at Charleston University, where she taught Fine Arts, and about her boyfriend Thomas, who was also a faculty member at the university.

Not wanting to seem like he was engaging in one-upsmanship, Dane did not mention his girlfriend, archaeologist Jade Ihara, but Bones being Bones, her name came up almost immediately.

"So, Maddock, have you told Jade that you're hanging out with your ex?" Mischief glinted in his dark eyes as he grinned at Dane.

"Jade? Is that your girlfriend?" Kaylin's expression was one of polite interest, though her voice sounded hollow. "Tell me about her."

"She's also a college professor and an archaeologist. I met her on our last little 'adventure.'"

"You do seem to have a knack for that, don't you?" Kaylin's coquettish smile brought back good memories.

"It sure seems that way, doesn't it?" Dane laughed. "I guess I can't really call her my girlfriend. We don't have any sort of commitment, what with her working about six thousand miles away."

"You never change, Maddock. You know that? There's always a reason not to get too close." Seeming to realize she'd revealed something a bit too personal, Kaylin blushed and took a long drink, while an uneasy silence fell over the group.

"That's me," Dane added lamely, trying to ease the sudden tension. "So, are you going to tell us about this thing you need help with?"

Kaylin's face fell. "My boyfriend, Thomas, is missing in the Amazon." She dug into the small backpack she had brought with her, took out a picture, and handed it to Dane. "He left this picture with a friend of ours. It's supposed to be a clue, the only thing we need in order find him."

Dane held the picture up in order to best catch what remained of the fading daylight. Bones pulled his chair closer in order to get a better look.

"This isn't the original," Kaylin said. "I left that with the police. I took my own picture of it before handing it over to the authorities, and I had a print made on the way down here."

It was a painting of a lean, angular man with a beard and a handlebar mustache seated in a Victorian-style armchair. His close-set eyes seemed to burn into Dane. It was a busy image by the standards of the time. The man held a book in his left hand, and a painting of a steamship hung prominently in the background over his right shoulder. A seascape, a dark island looming in the midst of a stormy sea, hung on the wall over his left. Exotic plants in amphorae framed the image.

"That dude looks familiar." Bones took the picture and gave it a closer look before handing it back to Dane. "Not sure where I've seen him before, but I know he's somebody famous."

"It's Percy Fawcett," Dane said, passing the picture around so everyone could have a look. "He was probably the most famous explorer of the early twentieth century. He disappeared in the Amazon looking for the lost city of Z." His stomach was doing somersaults. As a young man, he had been fascinated by stories of the famed explorer, and the man had always been something of a hero to him. He had a bad feeling about the direction this conversation was about to take.

"I'm sorry, Kay. If the only clue your boyfriend left you is a picture of Percy Fawcett, that isn't going to be enough to go on. Not even close. People have been trying to find him ever since he disappeared. That trail has been cold for almost a century."

"There's a message in this picture," Kaylin insisted. "And there was a code written on the back. Here!" She handed him another picture.

"Numbers and letters. It's not longitude and latitude. We can't punch it into a GPS." Dane truly did want to help her, but he didn't see how they had anything at all to help them even know where to start.

"But, the friend I mentioned, the one to whom Thomas entrusted this, was kidnapped, maybe even killed."

"I'm sorry to hear that, but how do you know that picture is the reason…" Dane began.

"He warned me and then they took him! They wanted me too, but I got away. They searched my apartment. Maddock, you know I'm not a drama queen, and I wouldn't come to you unless I really needed your help."

The need in her eyes took him back to another time and place, and he shook his head to return himself to the present.

"Okay, I understand. So you want us to go to the Amazon to find your boyfriend? I don't know that we're the best men for that job. It's not our specialty."

"I want you to help me solve this mystery, wherever it might lead. That *is* your specialty. Don't deny it." Her eyes bored into him. "I also need someone who can keep me safe." Her voice fell with the admission. "Whoever these people are, they probably don't know I've given the picture to the police. Even if they do, they might want to make sure I can't tell anyone else what I've seen."

Dane rubbed his chin, feeling the stubble that had

cropped up over the course of the day. He felt for her, truly he did, but was he really the right man for the job? And frankly, if it was Kaylin lost in the Amazon, he'd go after her in a heartbeat, but to risk life and limb for her boyfriend? It was… weird.

"You could stay with us," Corey suggested, "and have the authorities search for your boyfriend. You'd be safe here, and there must be people who are better trained for an Amazon rescue."

"It's not that simple. When Thomas first turned up missing, everyone's attitude, the police, the university, was he'd probably just been delayed, because that's fairly normal down there. Now that it's been a while and still no word from him, I'm getting subtle hints that he's probably not coming back. No one really wants to help. If he's going to come out alive, I've got to make it happen."

Bones took the picture from Kaylin, took a long look at it, and dropped it into Dane's lap. "You know we're going to do it, Maddock. You might as well save us all some time and go ahead and say yes."

"Please, Dane," Kaylin's eyes glistened on the verge of tears. "There's no one else in the world I can trust. I need you."

"All right." His voice was hoarse. "I'll do it, and it sounds like Bones wants in."

"Hell yes, I do." Bones pumped his fist. "Gonna' lasso me a kangaroo and ride it clear across the jungle."

"They don't have kangaroos in South America." Willis looked at Bones as if he wasn't quite certain if Bones was kidding or not.

"Seriously?" Bones face fell. "Well, I'm not going. I was only in it for the kangaroo rides." He gave Kaylin an evil grin and she laughed.

"That's another reason I need you guys to help me. You can always make me smile no matter how bad the situation gets."

"Maddock's the best at making a woman laugh." Bones spoke behind his hand in a mock stage whisper. "Just not on purpose."

"Hey, I'm not the one whose nickname was 'Mister Shrinkage,'" Dane retorted. The others guffawed as Bones sputtered an explanation about gossiping women and the temperature of a particular hotel pool.

When the laughter subsided, Corey spoke up. "I take it that, once again, the three of us will be left to finish up the job here, while you guys do your thing."

"That's pretty much the size of it," Dane said. "Look on the bright side. You have a boss who trusts you with every aspect of the business."

"Riiight." Matt downed the rest of his beer in two gulps, belched, and tossed the bottle back into the cooler before fishing around in the ice for another. "You know, such trusted employees just might deserve a raise."

"Seriously," Dane said, his voice sober, "if Kaylin needs help, it's probably going to take all of us. We'll have to do some research on the front end, but if I'm going into the Amazon, I'd like to have all you with me. There's no better crew in the world."

"I'm there." Willis raised his bottle and nodded.

"Me too," Matt said.

All eyes turned to Corey, who sat staring down at the deck. Unlike the other members of the crew, he was not a combat veteran, and didn't get the adrenaline rush from dangerous situations that his friends often did. He sighed and shook his head. "I guess it would get lonely around here if the rest of you jerks were off saving the world, and left me to swab the deck. I'll do whatever you need me to do."

"That's settled then." Dane stood and knuckled the small of his back. "Bones, Kaylin, and I will follow up on this... clue." The simple picture scarcely merited the title, but it was all they had. "You guys shouldn't need more than a few days to finish up here. If we aren't back by then, we'll meet you at home."

Home was the Florida Keys, where Dane had been planning to spend a couple of weeks after this job fishing and being generally useless. That would have to wait. If he was honest with himself, though, the prospect of trying to solve another mystery from the past had his heart racing.

"Well," he said to Bones, trying to keep the excitement from his voice. "I guess we need to pack."

CHAPTER 6

"That's the last one." Bones tossed another book onto the table. "There's not much relating to Fawcett in this library. I did find a freakin' awesome book about cryptids of the Amazon, though. I wonder if they'd let me have a library card."

"Bones, what kind of luddite are you that you're actually looking at books?" Kaylin grinned and returned to the library computer. "I wish I had my laptop, but I didn't want to go back home. Not after, well, you know." Lapsing into silence, she looked around as if danger might lurk behind any shelf.

"I'm going to pretend I know what that word means," Bones replied, "and we'll skip to the part where I tell you to kiss my…"

"A little quieter, you two," Dane said, making an apologetic wave to the two scandalized-looking old ladies who sat at the next table. He was reading an article online about The Lost City of Z, the subject of Fawcett's alleged obsession. It made for interesting reading, but mostly consisted of speculation founded on rumor, with very little substance to it. "And Kaylin, you don't need to look so nervous. The real danger begins when we head to the Amazon. I think we're safe in the library."

"So, what did Jimmy say when you asked him to help us out on this?" Bones asked. Jimmy Letson was an old friend and a high-level computer hacker. His system, NAILS, could access secure databases all around the world, and he had assisted them with key research on their previous adventures.

"Well, he used a few phrases that curled the hair on my toes, and then he told me he didn't do fairy tales or dime store novels, and to call him when we had something real for him to investigate." Dane chuckled. "When he finally took a breath, he explained that, while he could probably turn up plenty of information on Fawcett, it wouldn't be anything we can't find ourselves, and a lot of it will be junk. He's a subject of historical interest, and an important explorer, but it's not like there are secret government documents about the guy."

Kaylin sighed as she clicked on another link. A website opened, filling the screen with old photographs of Fawcett. "I can't find anything relating to this Fawcett painting. What few portraits he posed for are pretty ordinary—nothing as busy as the image Thomas left for us." Her shoulders sagged and she took her hand off the mouse. "I'm already getting discouraged here, guys. Tell me something that will lift my spirits."

"You know," Dane said, "I think what you've found is actually helpful, in a way. If all the other portraits for which Fawcett sat are plain and ordinary, that actually reinforces the idea that our painting is special. I'll bet you that every detail in that picture is critical to understanding Thomas's message, whatever it might be." Dane turned away from his computer and looked at Kaylin and Bones. "What do you say we take each element of the picture separately, and see where each leads us?"

"What do you mean?" Bones had abandoned his book on cryptids, and was now hunched over an old book, trying to erase Fawcett's huge mustache from a black-and-white print. Kaylin snatched it away from him, shooting him a reproving glance.

"We take each item in the picture one at a time, and try and figure out how it relates to Fawcett. Take the ship, for example. Did Fawcett make a voyage on that particular ship, or one like it?"

"We'd have to know her name," Kaylin said. "But I think you might be on to something." She took the picture out of its envelope and slid it onto the table where they all could see it.

"Amphorae," Bones mumbled. "Could be Greek, or, really, any of several Mediterranean cultures."

"I always forget you're not as dumb as you act." Kaylin shook her head.

"Thanks, I guess. Anyway, I don't think I've ever heard of Fawcett doing any explorations connected to the Mediterranean, but it won't hurt to check."

"Let's see what we can find." Kaylin typed a few words into a search engine. "We have a couple of hits." She frowned as she read. "There's speculation that Fawcett's lost city of Z might have actually been an ancient Greek city."

"Wait a minute. A Greek city somewhere in the middle of South America?" Bones frowned. "How does that make sense?"

"It doesn't." Kaylin turned a knowing smile upon him. "But you and Maddock, of all people, should know something doesn't have to make sense in order to be true." She turned back to the computer. "Kephises is a legendary lost city of Amazonia, settled in ancient times by the Greeks. Nothing else of substance, though."

"Do you think that might be what Thomas was searching for?" Dane asked.

"It doesn't sound like him. He's a scientist, so I can't envision him searching for lost cities. I could see him searching for Bigfoot before he went after a lost city." She shook her head. "Then again, I wouldn't have expected him to have any interest in someone like Percy Fawcett, either. I guess I didn't know him as well as I thought."

"Okay, so we have the possibility that Thomas was looking for the lost city of Z. That's not much to go on." Dane cracked his knuckles and picked up the picture. "If he truly believed this picture was enough for someone to come after him, there's got to be much more here than meets the eye." He gazed intently at the picture, as if the famed explorer could speak to him. "How about the book? Is there a connection between Fawcett and…" He took a close look at the picture, turning it so he could make out the title on the cover. "*The Lost World* by Arthur Conan Doyle?"

"I loved that book when I was a kid." Bones smiled and, for a moment, his eyes took on a faraway cast. "Seems like the connection would be obvious, though. That book was written around the time Fawcett was exploring. What other book would you put in his portrait?" Then his eyes lit up. "Dinosaurs! Kaylin, you said Thomas might go after Bigfoot. What if he believed dinosaurs still live somewhere in the Amazon? Would that be something he'd go off in search of?"

"I… suppose." Kaylin frowned. "It doesn't feel right, though."

"I agree," Dane said. They were thinking about this all wrong. They were looking at the picture from the perspective of a Fawcett scholar, deepening the mystery about his quest for Z. What they should be doing, however, was put aside what they thought they knew about Fawcett and Z, and instead, treat this image as a set of bread crumbs that would lead them to Thomas. "Look up Fawcett and *The Lost World*."

Kaylin typed the terms into the search engine, and the screen filled with hits. "Wow!" she whispered. "Look at all of these." Dane and Bones scooted closer to the monitor. "It appears that Fawcett and Conan Doyle were friends. Some of Fawcett's explorations inspired the story, and the main character in *The Lost World* was even modeled after Fawcett." She continued reading. "Conan Doyle presented Fawcett with a signed copy of the book, and…" An excited smile spread across her face as she went on. "Percy Fawcett took it with him on his next-to-last expedition in the Amazon. Members of his party said he used it as sort of a personal journal, making notes in the margins."

"That's got to be it!" Bones pounded his fist into his palm. "Thomas must have found something written inside that book that told him where Fawcett was headed on his final expedition. Find the book, find Thomas."

"But why wouldn't someone have discovered it before now?" Kaylin looked as if she was afraid to believe it could be true.

"Maybe it's in code or something, like what was on the back of the picture," Bones said. "We don't have any better ideas, do we?"

"Does it say where this book is kept?" Dane's heart was racing. This felt right. "Is it in a museum somewhere?"

"It's kept in the headquarters of the Royal Geographical Society in London."

"Did Thomas make a trip to England at any time in the last few years?"

Kaylin frowned, her brow furrowed. "He actually did, shortly after we started dating. I remember thinking it was odd because he was gone much longer than he had planned, but I didn't want to be nosy. We weren't serious at the time. You know, he seemed excited when he got back, and he stayed that way. I assumed it was because he and I were getting along so well, but maybe it was something else." Her face flushed and she hastily called their attention to a thumbnail-sized image of the book inside a glass display case.

"Here's the book." She clicked on the image and the snapshot filled the screen.

There was nothing remarkable about the book itself, but something else had caught Dane's eye.

"Go back to the previous screen for a minute." Kaylin clicked the back arrow. "Click on this picture here." He pointed to a thumbnail image farther down on the page. Kaylin clicked it, opening an image of one of the rooms in the Royal Geographical Society.

"Look at the picture hanging on the wall in the background." The resolution was low, and the image blurred, but there was no mistaking the portrait.

"It's the same picture," Kaylin whispered. "Thomas's picture. Our picture!"

"You know what this means." Dane smiled. "Time to

pack our bags for England."

"Well, I have mixed feelings about this." Bones frowned, looking disheartened.

"What's wrong?" Kaylin asked.

"I've been to England," he said. "The beer's okay, but the food sucks."

CHAPTER 7

"You are telling me that this is the sole piece of evidence you have collected?" It was only with the greatest of effort that Salvatore Scano kept his voice calm. He found cold serenity to be much more intimidating than anger or annoyance. Let them wonder what was going on behind that calm façade, and they would always fear that you were about to do something rash. "With all the resources you have at your disposal, the best you can offer me is nothing more than a poor quality photograph of an early twentieth-century painting?"

Silence reigned in the conference room as everyone exchanged sideways glances. No one wanted to be the first to speak. Finally, Alex, his son, cleared his throat. "That is the only piece of evidence there is, Father. Thornton left no other clues regarding his plans." He fell silent, wilting under his father's cold gaze.

Shane Kennedy took up the explanation from there. "We searched everything, sir. Thornton's office, his apartment, even his girlfriend's apartment. Nothing that would tell us where he's going. We were thorough." Few men could meet Salvatore's stare for very long, but, when it came to Kennedy, nothing seemed to intimidate the gritty former Marine, a quality that Salvtore both appreciated and found annoying.

"Details." He reached for his cup of espresso, his eyes never leaving Kennedy's.

"Breaking the encryption on his office computer was

child's play, but all the files dealing with the Amazon expedition pertained to the trip he was *supposed* to take with his students—not the one he actually took. He had no computer at home. It's either hidden, been destroyed, or he's taken it with him. No paper trail, either. He cleaned up after himself nicely."

"What about his phone records, credit card charges and such?" Salvatore took a small sip of the hot, dark liquid, its bitter taste a perfect match for the information Kennedy relayed.

"Nothing helpful in the phone records. We believe he used a disposable cell phone for whatever calls he needed to make. We're still working on obtaining the rest of his credit card information, though what do we have doesn't reveal much." He drew a sheet of paper from a manila envelope and slid it along the table to Salvatore, who eyed it dispassionately. It was a copy of a credit card statement with a charge for a round-trip ticket to London highlighted. "Thornton went to London several months before his expedition. While this doesn't tell us anything specific, it suggests that the painting is of significance. Percy Fawcett was from the U.K. after all."

"Anything else?"

"Not yet, sir, but we are still working."

"I expect nothing less." Salvatore nodded and returned his attention to his son, Alex, who sat chewing his lip and staring daggers at Kennedy. "And what of the man we have in custody? Thornton's colleague?"

"A waste of our time." Alex's voice was scarcely audible across the long conference table. "He knows nothing."

"What *did* he tell you?" Salvatore took another sip and waited.

"Thornton gave him the picture with instructions to use it to find him should Thornton not return from the Amazon. The man's a Literature professor, a school teacher, he didn't know what to do with it, so he passed it off first chance he got."

"And he confirms that this picture is the only piece of

evidence Thornton left behind?"

"Yes." Alex feigned a yawn. He thought his reticence made him look strong and aloof, but it served only to make him appear childish. More and more, Salvatore had considered the likelihood that Alex would not be a suitable choice to take the reins of ScanoGen. Alex was not half the man his brother had been. If only…

"You're sure of this?" Noticing Salvatore's distraction, Kennedy had taken over the questioning. "He's not hiding anything?"

"He is a worm." Alex's twisted frown suggested a hint of something foul in the air. "He broke under questioning in less than ten minutes. I worked on him several other times just to be certain. He knows nothing else." Alex actually smiled, something he seemed to do only when he was inflicting pain on someone, or thinking about doing so. How was it possible he was Salvatore's progeny?

"Very well." Salvatore resumed control of the conversation. "What about the girlfriend?"

"We are still working on that as well, sir." Kennedy consulted his notes. "Our contact with the Charleston Police Department tells us she left the hotel they put her up in, and now she's disappeared."

"She is completely off the grid?" David Romani was ScanoGen's Chief Operations Officer, and Salvatore's best friend since college. "You can find no trace of her anywhere?"

"Our contact confirms that she hasn't used her credit card at all in the past two days, and hasn't drawn out any cash since shortly after she disappeared." Kennedy consulted his notes once again. "She made two calls to a cell phone number in southern Florida. That's all."

"Our guest insists that the girl knows nothing. She was shocked to learn her *boyfriend*," Alex sneered as he spoke the word, "had hidden so much from her. She was quite heartbroken over it. Such a tragedy." He breathed on his fingernails and polished them on his shirt. "I don't think she is of much concern to us. As soon as Thornton's friend gave her the picture, she headed straight to the police station and handed it over to them."

Salvatore turned his attention to Mitchell Vincent, an agent who was reasonably bright, but severely lacking in the backbone department. "Returning to the topic of Doctor Thornton. I assume your inquiries in the Amazon region have not uncovered any helpful information?"

Vincent shook his head.

"I am sorry Mister Vincent, I did not hear you."

"No sir." Mitchell's face reddened. "We located the town where he and his students began their expedition, but we don't know where they went from there. No one admits to having seen them."

Salvatore rose to his feet and looked down the table. "We invested a great deal of time and money on the Pan project. Doctor Thornton has clearly betrayed us. If we cannot locate him and force him to deliver on his promises, the project is dead in the water, and ScanoGen is in serious trouble." He paused to let that sink in.

"Mister Vincent, you will continue the search for Thornton." He next turned to his Chief Research Officer, Julius, who had remained silent thus far. "Mister Julius, I want you to take all the information we have on Thornton's work and have our people conduct their own research. Perhaps we can discover his secrets independently." Julius nodded, but the look on his face mirrored Salvatore's thoughts. It was unlikely they could replicate Thornton's work—they knew too little of what he had discovered, and much of his information was comprised of nuggets sifted from heaps of myth and legend. "David, Kennedy, you two stay with me. The rest of you are dismissed."

Everyone except Alex hurried out of the conference room.

Salvatore fixed him with a blank expression. "Do you require something of me, Alex?"

"No sir." Alex scowled and flashed resentful looks at Kennedy and David. He was ever envious of their place in his inner circle, but he did not understand that their places had been earned. Alex, however, was content to rely on his family name, indulging his sadistic urges as needed while he waited for the day he would take over ScanoGen. A day that likely would never come. "I mean, what do you want me to do with Thornton's friend?"

"I shall think on it and let you know. You may go now."

Salvatore turned his back on his son and moved to the window overlooking President's Park. Reston, Virginia wasn't the most picturesque place in the world, but the view from Salvatore's office always calmed his nerves.

He waited for the sound of the closing door before he turned back to face the two who waited at the table, still in their seats. He first addressed himself to Kennedy.

"Tell me how you intend to proceed, considering what we have to work with."

"Obviously, we are researching Percy Fawcett and any connection he might have to the items in the painting. We think the book is important. I've got men on their way to England as we speak, with orders to search any places connected with Fawcett, and try to find and obtain anything pictured in this painting. Until we can figure out what exactly this painting is telling us, the least we can do is make sure that if any of the items pictured in it are important, no one else can get their hands on them."

"That is a good start. Anything else?"

"Not at this time, Sir."

Salvatore dismissed Kennedy with a flick of one finger, sank into his chair, and closed his eyes. Only in front of David did he ever let his guard down. "Can you believe that dirtbag Thornton screwed us over like this, David?"

"Relax, Sal, we'll get him." Now that Salvatore's wife had passed, David was the only person in the world who dared call him by his nickname. "Odds are, the guy's dead anyway. What was he thinking, going into the Amazon with nothing but some college kids?"

"That doesn't make me feel any better, David. If we don't find Thornton, we might not be able to complete Pan, and then what?"

"The company will get through it like we always do. So we piss off some defense contractors, and we lose a little money…"

"It's *my* money!" Salvatore slammed his fist down on the conference table, rattling his empty espresso cup and the phone that sat to his left. *And there's more money at stake than anyone knows,* he thought. "Never mind that. We have another problem. I received a call today from a Reverend Felts."

David sat up ramrod straight and frowned. "That idiot with the cable show? The one who blames everything from hurricanes to hangnails on our *'sinful, humanist government?'*"

"One and the same. He wants to meet with me this afternoon."

"Pardon the expression, but what the hell for? Is he on another of his anti-cloning crusades, and accusing us of…" David froze in the midst of running his fingers through his thinning, gray hair. The color drained from his face as he slowly turned to look at Salvatore, his hand falling to his side. "Does he know?"

"He knows something. He wouldn't lay all his cards on the table, but he said enough to convince me it's no bluff."

"You want me to take care of it?" David's features hardened.

"Please do. I'm thinking, though, if he knows, it's because someone let something slip. What I need you to do is find out if there is a leak. And if there is, plug it… permanently."

"I'll do it. Anything else you need from me?"

Salvatore shook his head. As David left the room, he closed his eyes, rubbed his temples, and groaned. "My head is killing me," he said to no one in particular. Opening his eyes, he tapped the call button on his phone.

"Yes, sir?" Tam's rich voice filled the room.

"I need you."

"I'll be right there, Mister Scano." In ten second's time, Tam Broderick, his personal assistant, was coming through the door carrying a glass of Wild Turkey with two ice cubes, just the way he liked it. "I could tell by the sound of your voice that you needed a little something for your headache. She smiled, her teeth pearly white against her rich, chocolate complexion. Her big, brown eyes radiated motherly concern as she moved behind his chair and began massaging his scalp with her strong fingers.

Kennedy had found her in training for the Washington D.C. police force, and persuaded her, with a little help from Salvatore's bank account, to come to work at ScanoGen. She had a well-organized mind and a gift for details. She was also cute enough to be believable as a secretary, but that petite body packed a wallop. She'd done a bit of kickboxing and Brazilian jiu-jitsu, and could handle a gun as well as anyone in the organization outside of Kennedy. It was little wonder she had risen so rapidly up the company ranks. At times, he had been tempted to expand their working relationship, but pragmatism always won out in the end. Tam was too valuable an asset for him to risk affecting her job performance for the sake of a little entertainment.

"You are aware that I have a late lunch scheduled this afternoon with Reverend Felts."

"Yes, Sir. Two o'clock at the Bastille. I have a private table reserved for the two of you, your car is ready. In fact, you leave in ten minutes. You'll have the usual security, plus two of our people in plain clothes dining a few tables away." Her fingers traced circles across his scalp, her thumbs pressing firmly in the indentation at the base of his skull. The dull pain seemed to flow into her hands, draining him of all tension.

"Very good." He was referring to her thorough planning, but his words could have applied to the scalp massage as well. Was there anything this woman could not do? "I need you to take care of one more detail." Her hands worked their way down his neck, her thumbs working deep into the muscles. "Reverend Felts will not be able to make it to our lunch meeting today. I don't want my time to go to waste, so schedule someone of consequence to dine with me. I trust you can line up someone suitable on short notice."

"I'll see to it right away." Tam gave his shoulders a firm squeeze before departing. "Don't forget your drink," she called back over her shoulder.

Salvatore smiled as he raised his glass in a silent, mocking toast to Reverend Felts's health. He brought the amber liquid to his lips and closed his eyes as it warmed his insides. If only all of his problems could be solved so easily.

CHAPTER 8

Traffic was sparse on Kensington Gore as Dane, Bones, and Kaylin approached the red brick mansion that was the headquarters of the Royal Geographical Society. Dane could not tear his eyes away from the massive chimneys, the many gables, and the steep, multi-leveled roof.

"Freakin' cool!" Bones took out his digital camera and snapped a few pictures. "Why don't we have office buildings like this in America?"

"Lowther Lodge." Kaylin sounded mesmerized. "It was a private mansion before the Society bought it in 1912. That section over there," she indicated a nondescript wing of plain red brick adorned with a pair of statues set back in alcoves high in the wall, "was once the stables, but was converted to a lecture hall."

"Who are the stone dudes?" Bones squinted and aimed his camera at the statues.

"Ernest Shackleton, Antarctic explorer," Kaylin said, "and David Livingstone."

"Doctor Livingstone, I presume?" Bones mimicked a British accent.

"Bones, I'll give you five bucks if you can tell me anything about Livingston besides that quote." Dane didn't bother to reach for his wallet.

Dane's phone vibrated and he was surprised to see Jade's name on the screen. The last time they spoke had been four days ago and she expected to be away from any kind of service for a week or more. Feeling more than a little bit weird about talking to Jade with Kaylin standing right next to him, he walked off to the side as he answered.

"Jade! Didn't expect to hear from you for a few more days. How are you?"

"Ugh. It was a disaster, Maddock. We got all the way out to the dig site only to find out Charles hadn't filed all the proper paperwork. Two days hike in, another two out for nothing."

"I'm sorry about that. You should treat yourself to a massage." *"Already on the docket. You know me too well. I wish you were here, you're actually pretty good at back rubs, but you really suck at rubbing feet."*

"That's because I don't like to rub feet. If I was any good at it, you'd want me to do it all the time." The banter felt good and he realized how much he missed her.

"So, what are you up to? Still down in South Carolina finding sunken Spanish gold?"

"Actually, Bones and I are in London." He gave her a quick run-down of the mystery and what they knew.

"Oh, Maddock, you suck! I want in on this!" Her voice was a mock-wail. *"You're going to find a lost city while I'm sitting here waiting for Charles to get his pen out of his orifice and get us some permits."*

Dane laughed. "It probably won't come to that. We just want to find my friend's missing boyfriend and come home."

"Oh, so it's a female friend you're helping out?" she teased. "Who is she? She'd better not be prettier than me."

"Um," Dane felt like he was a kid again, about to confess to his mother that he'd broken a prized family heirloom. "Kaylin Maxwell." Her silence was so complete that he thought, hoped actually, that he'd dropped the call. "Jade, you still there?"

"Yes. I'm just waiting for you to say 'psyche' or for Bones to get on the phone and tell me I just got punked."

"Jade, there's nothing going on. It's her *boyfriend*."

"Even so, it's inappropriate, Maddock. You know that. She's your ex-girlfriend."

"She doesn't have anyone else, Jade."

"Fine. I just don't get why you always have to be the knight in shining armor, always rescuing people. Can't you just be a little selfish every once in a while?"

"You didn't mind so much when I rescued you."

Jade gave an exasperated sigh. *"I know, and you're right. It's one of those things I hate and love about you. I just… Look, I gotta go. I'll text you when I know when we're heading back out into the field."*

"Okay. Be safe."

"You too." She ended the call without a goodbye.

Dane closed his phone with a sick feeling in the pit of his stomach. Jade was so confusing. Was she mad at him or not? Did he really care?

"Yo, Maddock! If you're done with girl talk, how about we go inside?" Tucking his camera into his pocket, Bones sauntered past the black wrought iron gates framed by tall brick columns, and up to the front door. To the right of the arched doorway, a black, marble bust of a man of late middle years sat on a white stone pedestal.

"Churchill!" Bones exclaimed. "I love this dude! Let's rub his head for good luck." He turned toward the bust, but Kaylin took him by the elbow and pulled him back.

"That's not Winston Churchill; it's one of the former presidents of the society. Let's just go inside."

"President? Shouldn't he have been Prime Minister?"

"You keep proving you're smarter than you look, Bones." Kaylin gave him a playful elbow to the ribs.

"Don't tell him that," Dane said. "He prefers to lower people's expectations so he can catch them by surprise with his occasional flashes of brilliance."

He opened the door, held it for the others, and stepped through. The interior of the Royal Geographical Society smelled of books, lemons, and age. The years seemed to emanate from the walls, ghostly echoes of the many great men who had walked these halls.

"Welcome to the Royal Geographical Society. How may I help you?" The speaker was an attractive woman of early middle years dressed in a business suit. Her white shirt was unbuttoned a bit farther down than was strictly professional and, as she leaned toward Dane, elbows propped on the counter, she pushed her breasts up for full effect. Bones stifled a cough and turned away, but not before Dane saw him grinning.

"Yes," Dane said, glancing at her name tag, which read *Sarah Richards*, and quickly redirecting his gaze to the woman's eyes, which were actually a very pretty bluish-green, "we're hoping to do some research on Percy Fawcett. Do you…" he broke off as Kaylin ran her fingers along his forearm. What was she playing at? And after he'd just assured Jade there was nothing to be jealous about. Struggling to suppress the heat that was rising up the back of his neck, he recovered his train of thought and started again.

"Do you have a Fawcett section, or anything like that?" He hoped that if he played the polite, but uninformed, American, he might gain a little extra helpfulness from the woman at the counter.

"We have many documents pertaining to Fawcett." Her eyes flitted toward Kaylin for only a fraction of a second, but Dane did not miss the disapproval, if not outright anger, that burned there. "Might you be looking for something in particular?"

"Yes, we particularly want information on his last expedition." She pursed her lips and her eyes narrowed, doubtless wondering if he was one of the many whack jobs seeking Fawcett's legendary lost city, so he hurried on. "Also, we're looking for a particular painting. It's a portrait of him seated, holding a book…"

"Of course." The smile was back. "That portrait hangs in the room just up the staircase and to the left. For your research, you should go to the Foyle room. Ask for Benjamin and he will be happy to assist you. He is our resident Fawcett expert." After checking their identification, and entering their names into a computer, she pointed them to a grand staircase, its ornately carved banisters polished to a high sheen.

Dane thanked her for her help, and as they turned to

walk away, Kaylin hooked her arm in his and laid her head on his shoulder.

"What are you up to?" He kept his voice low.

"Ditch me," she whispered. "And make it obvious."

"Say what?"

"I want to know if Thomas was here. That lady's got the hots for you. Make an excuse, go back and flirt with her a little bit, and then ask her to check and see if Thomas was here."

"You are one wicked woman." Now her flirtatious behavior made sense. As they reached the stairwell, he pulled away from her. "I'll meet you up in the reading room," he said to Kaylin, his voice loud enough to be heard in the quiet lobby, but not so much as to make it obvious that he wanted to be overheard. "I have a few more questions I forgot to ask. I'll be there in a little while."

Kaylin pouted and shot an angry glance toward the front counter before flouncing away up the stairs. Dane had to hand it to her. She was quite the actress when she needed to be.

"Your girlfriend seems upset," Sarah observed as Dane headed back in her direction. The smile on her face said that she, by contrast, was anything but unhappy at this turn of events.

"Not my girlfriend." Dane leaned easily against the counter and grinned. "My ex. It's complicated though. We still have to work together, which isn't exactly easy. You saw how she is."

"Some women just don't know when it's time to let go." Sarah ran the tip of her tongue across the bottom of her upper lip. So ostentatious was her attempt at flirtation that Dane nearly choked. "So," she continued, "what *else* can I do for you?"

Why couldn't Bones have been the one to hit on her? He was a natural with this stuff. Nothing to be done for it now, so Dane plunged in. "I need a recommendation of a nice, intimate place for dinner tonight, and a phone number for someone to join me."

He flashed his most winning smile, feeling all the while like a buffoon. Surprisingly, it worked. Sarah hastily jotted her name and number on a slip of paper and tucked in into his pants pocket. He forced himself not to react when her fingers roved a bit too far afield. *This girl would be perfect for Bones, but then again…* Realizing his thoughts were drifting, he refocused his attention on the task at hand.

"I do have one other, much less important, request. Can you tell me if a friend of mine visited here sometime in the last year or so?"

"I'm not supposed to do that." Sarah looked at him uncertainly. "Those records are private."

"And I'm not supposed to make dinner dates with beautiful women when I'm supposed to be conducting research." He gave her a wicked grin. "I don't want any private information; just tell me whether or not he was here."

"All right, but if you get me sacked, you owe me two dinners. What's the name?"

"Thomas Thornton." He watched as she typed in the name. She was actually kind of cute in a lush, full-figured sort of way. Perhaps he *should* make time for dinner tonight. What was he thinking? He already had one girl mad at him. He didn't need any more complications in that area.

"Ah! Here he is. Thomas Thornton. I can't tell you exactly when he visited, but I can confirm he was here."

"That's perfect. You've been a big help. I'll just head up and meet my friends." He turned and headed back toward the staircase.

"Dane?" He glanced back at her. "I get off at five o'clock. No pun intended."

"Gotcha." He hurried up the stairs, already wondering if he should make an excuse, or just not call her at all.

He found Bones and Kaylin checking out the original painting of which Thomas had left them the picture, which hung between two more traditional portraits of the famed explorer.

"He looks like he's made of old leather," Dane observed. "Hard to believe he never came back from his last expedition. He always seemed like the kind of guy nothing could stop."

"Not much to see here, I'm afraid." Bones said. "No small, semi-hidden images that we couldn't see in our picture. No secret codes." He glanced at the other two portraits. "Both of these have little plates at the bottom. Let's see, *Donated by Andrew Wainwright, grand nephew of Percy Fawcett.* No brass plate on our painting, though."

They looked at the portrait a little while longer. Finally, agreeing there was nothing else to be found here, they headed for the Foyle Room.

The Foyle Reading Room was a pleasant surprise—a contemporary oasis inside this classic Victorian structure. Sunlight shone through wide plate glass windows that angled inward, illuminating the counter that ran the length of the wall, wrapping around the bends in the oddly-shaped exterior wall. Workstations were set up along its length, with permanent computer setups in the center and laptop connections on either side. Bookcases lined the wall to his right, and various cabinets, counters, and worktables were arranged throughout the room. It had the feel of a university library.

A short, stocky man, with blue eyes and short brown hair looked up as they entered the room. "What can I do for you?"

"We're looking for Benjamin," Dane said, giving the room a quick scan. "Can you tell us where we might find him?"

"You just did." He smiled and shook hands with Dane. "Expected an old fart, did you?" He didn't wait for an answer, but motioned for them to take seats around a nearby table.

"If you're looking for me," he said with a sigh of resignation as he settled into a chair, "you must be interested in Fawcett. We've had quite a bit of that lately. People looking for the lost city, trying to track his last expedition. Those are the normal ones. Then there are the weirdoes…" He dismissed the thought with a wave, propped his feet on the table, and folded his hands on his chest. "So, into which category do you three fall?"

"Technically, we're searching for someone who falls into the first category," Dane said. "We are looking for information on Fawcett's last expedition, but only in order to find a friend who went off in search of him."

Benjamin's face remained impassive.

"We're not making this up." Kaylin showed him a copy of the missing person's report she had filed with the Charleston Police. He scanned it with bored eyes, made to hand it back to her, then snatched it back.

"This chap looks familiar." He held the paper close, scrutinizing the photo of Thomas which Kaylin had paper-clipped to the report. "I remember him. He didn't want to look at any of the usual Fawcett documents. He only wanted to see Fawcett's copy of *The Lost World*."

Dane sat up a little straighter. "Did he find anything in it?"

"Couldn't say." Benjamin shrugged. "Truth be told, he seemed a bit disappointed. Looked at it for over an hour. He wasn't reading it, mind."

"How could you tell?" Dane didn't understand. What else would Thomas have been doing?

"He was flipping through too fast, looking at the margins and the spine through a magnifying glass. Even turned it upside-down a few times. I don't know what he was hoping to find, but whatever it was, I don't believe he found it. Left here quite down."

Dane felt hope draining away, but as long as they had come this far, they might as well take a look at the book. "Could we see it? Is it still on display?"

Benjamin frowned, the lines in his forehead deepening. "Sorry, but it's gone missing. It was gone from its display when I arrived yesterday morning."

"Someone stole it?" Kaylin's voice was soft with dismay.

"I assume so. Odd, though. No alarms, nothing on the security cameras."

Dane's heart sank. "Can you tell us; was there anything… unusual about the book? Was there anything written inside of it?"

"It is one of a kind. It was inscribed to Fawcett by Sir Arthur Conan Doyle himself. Beyond that, I couldn't say. It's not like I handled it on a regular basis." Benjamin frowned. "As long as you're here, is there anything else you want to take a look at?"

A cool sense of conviction flowed through Dane's mind. This was no coincidence. It couldn't be. Someone had gotten here first and taken the book.

"Did Thomas say anything about where he might be going, or what he had planned?" Bones had reversed his chair and sat with his chin resting on his arms. "Maybe the dude had something more in his head than just following Fawcett's last expedition."

"Not that I recall. As I said, I only remember him because I thought it odd that an American would come all the way to London simply to look at a copy of one of Fawcett's personal possessions." He flashed them a knowing grin. "But I see now that it's not as unusual as I had thought."

"Is there anything…" Kaylin bit her lip. "Sorry, I don't exactly know how to ask this. We think this might be more than just a simple matter of someone getting lost in the Amazon. Are there any stories that connect Fawcett to something that might interest people today? I mean, interest them enough to…" She swallowed hard.

"I understand what it is you're asking. There are more legends surrounding Fawcett than I care to know. To call them far-fetched would be an understatement. Fawcett found Z and lives there as a white king like Prester John. Fawcett found a lost white race that has preserved the secret knowledge of the ancient civilization of your choice. Even if one of them were true, it would be of great academic interest, but nothing more." He raised his head and pondered the ceiling for the span of three heartbeats. "If your friend has gone chasing after Fawcett, and has not returned, the most likely explanation is that the same thing happened to him that has happened to too many Amazon explorers in the past. I am sorry."

Dane ground his teeth in frustration. The stolen book couldn't be the end of the line. The book was significant—he was certain of it. But Benjamin had said that Thomas had examined the book, yet seemed disappointed, as if he had not found what he was looking for.

"Do you know of any museum or library that has Fawcett's personal items on display?" Dane asked.

"There is no Fawcett museum. Most of the items of interest relating to Fawcett are here. Is there anything aside from the book that I can show you?"

"I don't suppose so," Dane said. For some reason, he did not feel comfortable asking about the Fawcett painting, and, in any case, it was the book they wanted, and the book was not here.

"You might look up Andrew Wainwright and give him a ring."

"The guy who donated the portraits downstairs?"

"Yes. He's a descendant, and has probably forgotten more about Fawcett than I've ever known. At any rate, good luck with it."

They shook hands with Benjamin, thanked him for his time, and made their way back to the entrance.

"Bummer," Bones said as they descended the stairs and passed through the lobby. "I thought we'd get a little farther than that."

"Me, too," Dane agreed.

Sarah hailed them as they approached the exit. "That was a short visit. Did you find what you were looking for?"

"Benjamin was a great help," Dane said.

"You'll call me about dinner, then?" She eyed him like a tigress contemplating exactly how she wanted to play with her food before eating it.

Before Dane could answer, Bones sidled up to the counter.

"*You* didn't steal the Fawcett book, did you Sarah?" He grinned lasciviously. "We really wanted to see it. Maddock might have to frisk you…"

"Thanks, Bones!" Dane grabbed his friend by the arm and steered him toward the door. "I'll talk to you later, Sarah. Thanks again."

As soon as they were out the door, Sarah left the front desk and hurried to the nearby break room. Terry looked up as she entered, and gave her a hopeful smile. Sooner or later she would have to break down and go on a date with the poor tosser, but for now, the occasional flirtatious smile or touch on the arm was enough to make him as helpful as she needed him to be.

"Terry, would you be a dear and mind the front for me? I need to phone someone, and it's rather private."

"Not a boyfriend, I hope." He tried to play it off as a joke, but failed.

"No, it's nothing like that." She forced a laugh. "I just need a chat with my doctor—female stuff, you know."

Red-faced, Terry assured her that he understood completely. She doubted he knew much of anything about female anatomy or the issues relating to it. In fact, she harbored a suspicion that he still lived with his mum, but he could be counted on to do what she asked of him, and that was what mattered.

She hurried back to her office, took a card from her purse, and punched up the number on her cell.

"Yeah?"

"Hi, this is Sarah from the R.G.S."

"Yeah."

Not a great talker, this one. "You asked me to call you if anyone came around asking after Fawcett's copy of *The Lost World*."

Silence.

"Are you there?"

"I am."

Five hundred pounds, she reminded herself. She could put up with rudeness for that. And it wasn't as if she was doing anything wrong—just passing along a bit of information. She quickly gave the man on the other end the names of the three visitors, and a brief description. She felt a pang of guilt when she mentioned Dane's name. She rather liked him and he was quite handsome.

"Okay, good. Are they still there?"

"No, they just left." She looked out the break room window, and was surprised to see that the three were standing on the pavement, engaged in a serious discussion. "They're just outside the building, though."

"Good. Keep an eye on them until I get there. There's another five hundred in it for you."

The call ended. Sarah took a deep breath and peered outside again, hoping Dane and his friends had departed, but no, they were still there. She had a sinking feeling that she had just made a terrible mistake.

CHAPTER 9

They had almost reached the street when Dane hesitated. Something was bothering him—a feeling that he was right on the verge of making a connection. But what? He was sure it was important, if only he could put a finger on just what it was.

Turning back to look at Lowther Lodge, his eyes fell on the entrance and the bust next to the door.

And it struck him.

"Kaylin, what was it that Thomas wrote on the back of the picture?"

"Let me see." She fished in her purse, looking confused. She pulled out a sheet and handed it to him.

There were five letters at the top, and then a series of number pairs.

MRKHM
2-5 1-17 1-1 2-13 4-10 3-3 1-10 1-22 1-12 3-3 1-19
1-23 1-6 1-8 4-6 4-11 6-9 7-1 7-10 8-16

Could it be that simple?

"Did either of you catch the name on the bust by the front door?"

"Markham!" Kaylin's eyes widened as realization dawned on her face. "Do you think it could refer to the bust?"

"I think it's worth a look. Let's go."

They hurried back to the front door and Dane read the

inscription aloud.

"This monument to the memory of Sir Clements Markham, KCB, FRS, and for 12 years President of the Royal Geographical Society, was erected in the year 1921 by the Peruvian Nation in gratitude for his services as historian of their country."

"And this means… what, exactly?" Bones rubbed his chin and peered doubtfully at the sculpture of Markham.

"I wonder," Dane said, looking again at the numbers Kaylin had written down, "if these pairs of numbers correspond to lines and letters in the inscription." He knelt to take a closer look. "If I'm correct, the first letter would be…" He consulted the paper, and then counted over to the letter *L*. The next number pair gave him the letter *E*. As he continued, his certainty that he was on the right track grew. His heart beat faster as he called out each letter. When he was finished, he stood to look at the paper on which Kaylin had recorded the letters, though he already knew what the message said.

"Let Albert be your guide."

"Great," Bones said. "Now we just need to find this Albert dude and ask him where to go next. Any idea where to start looking?"

"Across the street."

At first, Dane thought Kaylin was joking, but her expression was deadly serious. She arched her eyebrows in an *'Are you doubting me?'* look, and put her hands on her hips.

"Okay," Dane said. "I'll bite. Who or what is Albert?"

"Just across the street, in Kensington Gardens, is a well-known memorial to Prince Albert."

"Seriously?" Bones crowed. "Is he in a can? Do we need to let him out?"

"I'll wager that's what the message is referring to," Kaylin said, rolling her eyes at Bones's weak attempt at a joke.

"Sounds good to me. Let's check it out."

The Albert Memorial consisted of an ornate canopy, nearly two hundred feet high, set above a gilded statue of a seated Prince Albert. Mosaics decorated portions of the exterior, and sculptures devoted to the arts and sciences sat atop the pillars and in corner niches. Around the base was a marble frieze, and at each corner a sculpture representing one of the Victorian era industries: Agriculture, Commerce, Engineering, and Manufacturing. Steps on each side led up to the memorial, and ringing the base were decorative railings, with even more elaborate sculptures at each corner. It was this set of sculptures that caught Dane's eye. Each displayed a group of figures on and around a beast of burden, and was named for a region of the world: Africa, Europe, Asia, and America.

The America sculpture featured a bison, with three figures, one male and two female, all rendered in the classic style—European facial features, flowing robes and, as Bones put it, "topless." Each wore a headdress that reflected Native American stylings, and two of the figures held stylized spears.

"It's got to be the America sculpture, right?" Bones asked, walking over to lay his hand on the bison's head. "I mean, we're looking for connections to the Amazon, so what else could it be?"

They scrutinized the sculpture with care, examining every last detail, but none of them could infer even the most tenuous connection to Fawcett or his expedition. Finally, they were forced to conclude they were on the wrong track. They circled the base of the memorial, first examining the other sculptures, then stepping back and taking in the memorial as a whole, hoping something would leap out at them. It did not.

"I don't understand." Kaylin, usually so positive, hung her head. "It says to let Albert be our guide. How could it not be this memorial? It's right across the road from the R.G.S., and there's Albert just sitting there. This has got to be it."

Dane agreed with her. He was convinced a clue of some sort was right there for them all to see, but, for the life of him, he could not see what it might be. He looked up at the gilded figure of Prince Albert, as if the answer lay in his lifeless gaze.

And it struck him like a slap in the face!

"Bones, I need a big diversion." To his friend's credit, he did not so much as bat an eye.

"How long?" He was frowning thoughtfully, the mental gears obviously turning at a rapid pace.

Dane took another look at the memorial— the rail, the steps, and the sculpture itself—and did a quick calculation. "Two minutes ought to do it. Can you handle that?"

"Are you kidding, bro? I thought you were going to give me a challenge. I got this."

As Bones turned away, Dane slipped off toward the opposite side of the memorial. Thankful for the sparse assemblage of tourists, he quickened his pace, reaching the far side just as Bones began to shout.

"Ladies and gentlemen, may I have your attention please? I need everyone over here for just a moment!"

Dane stole a glance in his friend's direction. Bones was holding Kaylin's hand and calling out for everyone to join them, beckoning to the recalcitrant ones. Judging by the look on her face, he had not clued her in on whatever it was he was about to do. A few curious people were making their way toward the couple, but several more hung back, uncertainty painting their faces.

"That's it! Just gather around right here!" Bones called. He spotted the few who were hanging back near Dane. "You folks as well, please! I want to make this a moment that my lovely lady will never forget." At these words, the confusion in the crowd melted away, and everyone hurried toward Bones and Kaylin. Wishing he could spare time to watch the spectacle, Dane took a last look around, took a deep breath, and vaulted the rail that surrounded the memorial.

"That's right! Video it for us. You can even put it on the internet. I want the world to know how I feel."

Dane grinned and kept moving.

"When I first met this beautiful young woman, I knew

then and there that someday she would be my wife!" Everyone had gone silent, listening raptly to Bones as he proclaimed his love for Kaylin.

Dane sprinted toward the monument, closing the distance in a flash.

"Of course, when I asked her out, she told me she wouldn't go out with me if the world was covered in 'my dung,' to put it delicately, and I had the last roll of toilet paper." The crowd laughed and jeered as Kaylin, playing along, protested that she had said no such thing.

Dane took the steps two at a time, and soon found himself beneath the canopy where Prince Albert sat gazing off into the distance.

"As you can see, she didn't hold to her vow, and I'm the luckiest man in the world for it. And so…"

A sigh escaped the spectators gathered around Bones and Kaylin, and Dane was certain the Bones had gotten down on one knee. An unexpected feeling of envy crept up inside of him. There had been a time he had envisioned the day when he would propose to Kaylin. Of course, that was a long time ago, and they had both moved on. He shoved the thought out of his mind and clambered up onto the statue of Prince Albert. He hoped no one was watching, but if so, it was too late now.

Bringing his head level with Albert's, he stared out across the lawn, trying to follow the prince's line of sight. In the distance, he could clearly see an old brick building. It was as if someone had cut a passage through the sparse trees so that the structure was framed by wooded patches on either side.

"Kaylin, you have made my life worth living. And I have never minded that you're transgendered."

Dane choked down a guffaw and almost fell off of the statue. Internally cursing and laughing at Bones, he moved his head directly above Albert's, just to be certain his line of sight was correct. It was.

"You know I never wanted kids anyway. So…"

His heart pounding with excitement, he sprang down,

and dashed down the steps.

"Will you marry me?"

As Dane sprang over the rail, he heard polite applause ring out, and knew that Kaylin must have said 'yes.'

"Thank you!" Bones shouted. "And I was kidding about the tranny thing. I took one home once, but that was beer-related." More laughter, and a deeper round of applause.

Dane felt a tug at his elbow. He looked around to see a freckle-faced young boy looking up at him.

"What were you doing up there?"

"Oh, I was checking for… rust."

The boy considered this for a moment before nodding sagely and walking away. Breathing a sigh of relief, Dane made his way through the dispersing crowd, and back to his friends.

"Congratulations," he said. "When's the big day?"

"Oh, we haven't set a date yet." Kaylin was looking at Bones with an expression Dane knew all too well. It was her 'I'm pretending to be happy because we're in public, but you will pay later' look. In the time the two of them had dated, she had only given him that look twice, and he had forgotten neither incident. Both had been caused by Dane giving his honest opinion on her friends' artwork: one a so-called sculpture titled "Patriotism" that consisted of strips of the American flag wrapped around toilet paper rolls; the other a performance art piece that he still could not wrap his mind around, though he did remember a country song played backward, and lots of grunting.

"I think I'm onto something," he said. "Follow me." He headed off in the direction of the building he had spotted. Bones and Kaylin strolled along in his wake, holding hands and doing a reasonably good job of acting as if they'd just gotten engaged. When they were back on the main street, Kaylin yanked her hand away and rounded on Bones.

"Tranny? How'd you like to be a eunuch? I dare you to go to sleep…"

"Not now!" Dane hadn't intended to bark an order like that, but he'd been a military man, and some old habits die hard. "We don't need you calling attention to us," he said in a calmer voice. "Yell at him later, if you need to."

Kaylin directed a contemptuous glare at Bones, but said nothing.

"The statue of Albert looks directly at that building right there." He pointed across the street to their destination.

"What is that place?" Bones asked, stepping out into the street and almost being run down by a passing car. He ignored the blaring horn and kept walking.

As they drew closer, Dane could read the sign by the front door. "Royal Institute of Navigation. No way! My dad talked about this place. He visited here when he and Mom were still dating. She spent the day seeing the sights, and finally had to drag him out at closing time." After all these years, the memory of his parents, and of their tragic deaths, was still bittersweet.

"My father came here as well, looking for information on the *Dourado*," Kaylin said, her voice thick with emotion. Her father, a former officer and friend of Dane and Bones, had been murdered a few years before, and the three of them had completed his quest for the lost ship and its unbelievable cargo.

"So what do you figure we'll find here?" Bones asked. "Doesn't seem like a Fawcett kind of place."

Dane and Kaylin suddenly exchanged excited glances, each arriving at the same conclusion. "The ship in the picture," they said in unison.

Dane drew the picture from his pocket and looked at the portrait of the ship hanging in the background. The two-master, with its single smokestack, was the only possible link between their single clue and the Institute of Navigation. Hope rising anew, he led them inside. As he stepped through the front door, Dane was actually relieved to see an elderly man working the front desk. He didn't think he could handle two cougars in one day. The man greeted them warmly, and when Dane asked if anyone on staff was versed in early twentieth century British ships, he directed them to the Cundall Library of Navigation, where shelves strained under the weight of aging tomes. The smell of old paper pervaded the room.

"Good afternoon. How can I help?" The speaker was a plump woman of middle years, with silver-streaked brown hair and a sharp nose that contrasted with the dull look in her eyes. She pushed a pair of black-rimmed reading glasses up onto her head, where they joined the two matching pairs that were already there. She did not quite meet Dane's eye when she looked at him. All told, she gave off an air of casual disinterest.

"Yes," Dane said. "We're doing some research and I was hoping we could find something out about this ship." He handed her the picture and held his breath. Unless this vessel was famous, he was searching for a single grain of sand on a seriously large beach.

The woman squinted at the photograph, held it out at arm's length, and began patting her pockets.

"Bugger it all! Where did I leave my glasses? That's the third pair I've lost today."

Suppressing a smile, Dane pointed to the top of her head. Neither thanking him nor noticing the two other pairs of glasses atop her head, she pulled them back down over her eyes, and held the picture up again. "Ah! *Quest!*" she proclaimed.

"Not exactly a quest," Bones said. "We just want to find out about the ship."

"That's the name of the ship. *Quest*. It belonged to Ernest Shackleton."

"The polar explorer?" Dane asked sharply.

"One and the same." She narrowed her eyes as she looked down at the picture. "Odd that it would be Fawcett in the painting. You would think it would be Ernest."

"Do you know of any connection between Fawcett and *Quest*, or Fawcett and Shackleton, for that matter?" Excitement was rising in Kaylin's voice, and with it rose Dane's spirits. "I'm sorry; we didn't ask your name."

"No matter." She waved away Kaylin's apology as if shooing a fly. Still gazing at the picture, she took a second pair of glasses off of her head and began tapping her lips with them. "Fawcett and Shackleton," she mumbled. "The only connection I can recall is Fawcett went on an expedition with…"

"James Murray!" Dane exclaimed.

If she was annoyed with Dane for finishing her sentence, it did not show.

"Yes. Murray was part of the Nimrod expedition." Bones suppressed a laugh, but he need not have bothered. The woman, who still had not given them her name, seemed blissfully unaware of most of what was transpiring around her. "Shackleton, of course, led that one. Two years later, Murray joined Fawcett on an Amazon expedition. It went badly and Murray hated Fawcett after that. I don't think they ever settled that grudge."

"Interesting," Kaylin said, though her tone said otherwise. This connection was tenuous at best.

"Do you have any information on *Quest* that we could take a look at?" Dane asked.

"Of course." She walked between Dane and Bones, both of whom had to step aside to avoid her bumping into them. Dane watched her disappear between two heavily laden shelves. She had not instructed them to come with her, but who knew if that was intentional? With a shrug, he followed after her. After a moment's pause, Bones and Kaylin came along. They wound through the shelves, coming out at a small wooden table next to a tall window giving them a view of Hyde Park and the Albert Memorial.

"Wait here," their guide instructed. Feeling like schoolchildren, they took their seats around the table and waited. She returned in short order, bearing an armful of books. "These," she laid two books on the table, "are specifically about *Quest*. These three," she laid more books on the table, "contain chapters or sections referencing her, and this," she dropped an oversized tome down in front of Dane, "is a collection of entries and clippings about Shackleton. Leave them here when you are finished."

Dane thanked her, but found himself talking to the back

of her head, as she had already turned and was walking away. Shaking his head, he pulled the large book toward him and opened it up. He soon found himself absorbed in the details of Shackleton's exploits.

Bones and Kaylin also took books and began reading. It was not long before Bones spoke up.

"Dude, it sank."

"What?" Dane looked up from a clipping of an interview with Shackleton. "Where? When?"

"Back in 1922, near a place called Ascension Island. Cool name, huh?"

"Seriously?" Kaylin asked. "Or do you have some kind of pulp adventure book hidden in there?"

Bones laid the open book flat on the table so all three of them could see it.

"I'm serious. It was Shackleton's final expedition. He died of a heart attack and, on the way back, *Quest* sank."

Dane pondered this new bit of information. Could the shipwreck be of significance? "Does it mention any connection to Fawcett?"

"Let me see… Fawcett…" Bones turned the page and he suddenly did a double-take. "Yes! Right here!" He read on for a moment, and then spun the book around so Dane could see. "It says Shackleton and his friend Rowett were on their way to the Antarctic, and they stopped in Rio. Shackleton had what they thought was a heart attack, but he refused treatment. There, they met up with Fawcett, who was returning from a trek in South America, and he joined them on their expedition."

Kaylin snatched the book away, found the spot where Bones had left off reading, and took over the explanation.

"Shackleton suffered another heart attack, died, and was buried in South Georgia. They tried to continue the expedition, but failed. *Quest's* engines were not powerful enough to battle the tough Antarctic waters, and she had a serious leak. They finally turned back, but the ship foundered and sank off the coast of Ascension Island. Fawcett is credited with keeping them alive until help arrived. He spent long hours exploring the small island, brooding, keeping mostly to himself, and cursing the "infernal birds," but he did make sure they had adequate food and water." She continued turning pages until she finally declared that there was nothing more to be gleaned from that particular book.

With a renewed sense of purpose, they focused in on Shackleton's final expedition, searching for more references to Fawcett. Dane found the next clue.

"Listen to this," he began, his pulse throbbing in his temples and his skin electric with excitement. "Fawcett said he lost something valuable in the shipwreck. He never said what it was, but he tried to recreate it, whatever that means, but feared his effort was incomplete." He continued reading, and suddenly came upon a passage that gave him such a start that he almost dropped the book.

"Sorry," he said, finding his place again, "but you have to listen to this." He lowered his voice, though no one seemed to be about. "Fawcett was quoted as saying he was thankful he managed to at least save his copy of *The Lost World*, which he treasured."

"But we already knew that," Kaylin objected.

"Just wait." Dane's voice trembled with excitement. "He said that it was the most treasured of all of his books, and he'd sooner lose the first edition Arthur had given him than lose his personal copy."

It took Bones and Kaylin a moment to comprehend the full implications of the statement, but then Bones whooped and pumped his fist.

"The stolen book is the first edition given to him by Conan Doyle!"

"So the real book is still out there somewhere." Dane thought about it for a while. "Let's take Benjamin's advice and look up this Wainwright fellow."

They had scarcely passed through the exit doors when Kaylin glanced up and her face went pale. "That's one of the guys who kidnapped Thomas. I'm sure of it."

Dane looked up to see a tall, thick man with ash blond hair striding toward them. "Bones, get Kay out of here right now. Go!"

Bones didn't have to be told twice. He took Kaylin by the arm and ducked back into the building.

The man was almost on top of Dane, and as he reached inside his jacket, Dane sprang into action. He leapt in close and drove an uppercut into the man's chin just as he was drawing a pistol from underneath his jacket. The man grunted and stumbled back, but Dane stayed on him. Grabbing the man's wrist in both hands, Dane drove his forehead hard into the taller man's mouth, and heard the satisfying crack of breaking teeth. Still controlling his wrist, Dane swept his legs out from under him, and rode him to the ground. He punched him once, twice in the temple, and banged his head on the pavement for good measure. The gun slipped from the stunned man's limp fingers. Dane picked it up, tucked it his belt, then relieved the man of his wallet before getting to his feet and giving him a solid kick in the temple to keep him down. Keeping an eye open for more potential attackers, he untucked his shirt in order to hide the gun.

"Say! Did that bloke just pull a gun on you?" A paunchy man in a suit stood at the corner, looking at Dane as if he was radioactive. He held a cell phone, but appeared uncertain if he should use it.

"Yes, he did. Call the police." Not waiting for the man to grow bolder, Dane turned and dashed back inside the building after Bones and Kaylin.

"Did you happen to see which way my friends went?" he asked the frightened desk clerk. "The blonde girl and the tall Indian."

"Through that door." The man pointed a shaky finger down the hall. "And another man came in after them while you were… fighting outside."

As he dashed through the door the clerk had indicated, he heard a loud crash, and turned a corner just in time to see Bones punch a man in the throat, grab him by the back of the head, and drive a knee into his face. Kaylin, her face pale, but her expression resolute, hurried out and took Dane's hand.

"What was the crash?" Dane asked as they turned away from the front desk and headed down a narrow hallway, following the sign that read 'Emergency Exit.'

"Bones knocked down some books." Kaylin raised her eyebrows. "I don't know why."

"I was trying to push the freakin' bookshelf over on the dude." Bones sounded defensive, almost hurt by her criticism.

"Those are huge shelves, and they're anchored to the floor. You can't just push one over." Dane couldn't help but grin, despite their perilous situation.

"In the movies, one shove and the whole library goes down like a bunch of dominoes."

"Yes, Bones," Kaylin said in a patient voice, as if speaking to a child, "but real life isn't always like the movies."

"Sure, you tell me that now," he said in a sullen voice, "after I almost got us killed. We could see the guy through the shelf. He had a gun, and looked like he was up to something, so I tried to knock the shelf over on him. All I managed to do was hit him in the side with a few books."

"Some of them were big books," Kaylin said, "with lots of pages. Who knows? Maybe he got a paper cut."

Bones muttered something Dane was certain was obscene, but Kaylin owed Bones for the tranny comment.

Outside, they hurried across the street and tried to blend in among the tourists in Hyde Park. After five minutes' walking, they felt safe enough to stop and talk. Dane took out the wallet and looked at the driver's license. It belonged to a Cyrus Wallace of Manassas, Virginia. The credit cards bore his name as well.

"Why did you take his wallet?" Kaylin frowned and looked at him in confusion.

"One, I wanted to know who he is. Two, having no cash, credit cards, or identification might make it harder for him to come after us." Spotting a garbage can nearby, he hurried over to it and stuffed the wallet down to the bottom. "Screen me," he instructed. While Bones and Kaylin moved in close to block him from view, he took out the pistol, removed the clip, and hastily wiped it down.

"You can't have a handgun, here!" Kaylin gasped. "It's against the law."

"Yes, but bad guys don't always follow the rules," he said, stuffing the pistol down into the garbage and pocketing the clip. He would ditch it elsewhere.

"I know," she mumbled, her cheeks pink. "And our next step is?"

"Now," Dane said, "we pay this descendant of Fawcett a visit."

Chapter 10

The first thing Cy was aware of was a faint, quavering voice in his ear.

"Just lie still there. Help is on the way."

He didn't know the voice. In fact, he wasn't sure where he was. All he knew was he hurt. A lot. Groaning, he rolled over and spat blood on the ground. Running his tongue across his teeth, he counted two chipped, and one that was broken. Muttering a curse, he climbed to his feet. Damn! Now he remembered.

It was that Maddock guy he'd been warned to look out for. The chick from the R.G.S. had called to let him know that Maddock and his friends were asking about Fawcett. She'd lost sight of them as they headed toward Hyde Park, but once he showed a picture around, people remembered the big Indian, and had pointed him toward the naval library. He groaned as the memories returned. They'd warned Cy not to underestimate Maddock and Bonebrake, but neither had looked like much to Cy, and he'd had the element of surprise on his side, or so he'd thought.

The world swam into view and resolved into an image of a portly man peering down at him. Cy snarled and climbed to his feet. He grabbed the man by the tie and pulled him close.

"Which way did they go?"

"Uh, the fellow who… who kicked your arse? He went back inside the building there."

Cy shoved him away and barged through the front door,

hoping, praying someone would try to stop him. Inside, a frightened old man warned him that the authorities were on the way.

"You listen to me, you old fart." Cy reached across the counter and took hold of the man's lapel. "If they get here before I'm gone, you tell them I ran into the park. You do anything else, I use my gun on everyone I see. Got it?"

The man nodded.

"Now, what were those three looking for?"

"I don't know. They went to the Cundall Library. That way."

Cy hurried up the stairs. The average police response time in London was seventeen minutes, and a call about a fight that was already over probably wouldn't be considered urgent. A glance at his watch told him he'd been out for three or four minutes, and had wasted another minute with the fat guy and the old man. If he made this quick, he should be okay.

Inside the Cundall Library, he met a chunky woman with two pairs of reading glasses on top of her gray hair, and another pair perched on the end of her nose. She blinked at him like an owl.

"May I help you?"

"Yeah, you can help. The people who were in here earlier: the guy, the girl, and the big Indian. What were they looking for?"

"Looking for?" She looked around, a dazed expression on her face, and stared at a nearby table as if she had never seen one before. He had a mind to shake an answer out of her, but then she seemed to wake from her trance. "Oh, the Fawcett people."

"Yes, that would be them. Why did they come here looking for information on Fawcett? This is a naval library."

"Why, yes, I know that." She smiled faintly, as if pleased by the thought.

Where did they find this crackpot? Cy tried again. "Do you know if they found anything? Did they write down anything? Make any copies?"

"No copies. No notes."

"All right, lady, listen to me." He reached for his gun... it wasn't there. Where was it? He patted himself all over. It wasn't in his front pockets, nor his back... Wait a minute! Where was his wallet? Hell! He had lost it in the fight. Who was this Maddock, anyway? Kennedy had probably given him a bio in his email, but Cy had skimmed it. He wasn't much of a reader.

The old lady was looking at him like he was the one who was nuts. The expression on her face infuriated him.

"All right, you crazy old cow. Listen to me very carefully. I want to know what they learned and I think you can tell me. Now start talking."

"All I heard was something about an item that Fawcett treasured." Her voice was serene, as if she was unaware of the danger she was in. Her eyes seemed to be focused on a point somewhere just above Cy's head and, for an instant, he thought about looking behind him, but he could not act nervous. He needed to intimidate this loony toon if he could.

"What else did you hear?"

"They also mentioned Shackleton," she said, "and I heard the phrase 'buried in South Georgia.' I did not hear anything else."

"Who is Shackleton, and what part of Georgia?"

"Shackleton is the famed polar explorer, a contemporary of Fawcett. And South Georgia is an island. I believe Shackleton is buried there."

"Nothing else? They didn't say what this thing is that Fawcett treasured?"

"No. I do not eavesdrop." She folded her arms and tapped her toe. "I only happened to overhear a few snatches of conversation as I went about my work."

"Did they seem... excited? Like they found what they were looking for?" She just stared at him. "Fine." Cy let go of her and gave her a shove toward the table. "You just sit tight and don't tell anyone about any of this. You don't want me to come back, do you?"

"No. You are much too loud for a library."

A thought occurred to him. "Did they look at any books?"

"Yes. They seemed particularly interested in that one right there." She pointed to a battered old tome with a gray cover.

Cy picked it up, tucked it inside his jacket, and turned to leave.

"I am sorry, but we do not permit patrons to check books out. I will have to ask you to remain here if you wish to read it."

Unbelievable. Ignoring the old cow, Cy barreled toward the exit, keeping his eyes open for Maddock and his friends. Of course, if they had his gun, he had to be extra careful. He wondered if Jay had gone after them.

Jay! Cy had forgotten he hadn't come here alone. His bell must have been rung hard for him to lose track like that. He made his way down the stairs and through a side exit just as a siren wailed in the distance. Good response time, but not good enough.

He still had his phone on him, so he dialed up Jay's number.

"Yeah?" Jay sounded as groggy as Cy felt. "Where are you?"

"On Kensington. Where are you?"

"I'm in the car. I'll pick you up." Jay broke the connection, and Cy kept walking, trying to look interested in the sights. A police cruiser flashed past him, skidding to a halt in front of the institute.

Moments later, a metallic green Ford Fiesta pulled up to the curb. Habit led him to take two steps around the front of the car before Jay waved him back. Cursing any country that would put the driver on the right side of the car, the car on the left side of the road, and him in a Ford Fiesta, he threw open the door and folded his frame into the compact vehicle.

"You forget again?" Jay grinned as he pressed the accelerator.

"Screw you. What happened to Maddock and the other two?"

"Don't know," Jay said. "That Indian sucker-punched me. He knocked me clean out. I haven't been hit like that since I…"

"Yeah, I know. You boxed in the service. You're a regular Brown Bomber."

"Is that supposed to be a racist comment?" Jay regarded him out of the corner of his eye.

"No, I just can't think of any other boxing nicknames at the moment."

"C'mon, man. There's Sugar Ray, Iron Mike, Smokin' Joe, Gentleman Jim. Lots of great nicknames."

"So, what should I have called you?" Cy had no interest in boxing, but he wasn't in any hurry to admit what had happened to him.

"The Motor City Cobra." Jay savored the words, saying them almost like a prayer.

"But you're not from Detroit."

"Forget you, man. You don't know boxing." Jay glanced in the rear-view mirror. "Don't seem to be any cops following us. So, what happened to you back there?"

"I gotta call in." Cy took his phone out again and scrolled down to Kennedy's name. He took a deep breath, steeling himself, and hit the call button.

Much to Cy's chagrin, Kennedy answered on the first ring. *"Cy, what's the status?"*

"I think I've got something." He filled Kennedy in on the enticing clues regarding Fawcett, Shackleton, and South Georgia, as well as his having procured a book that was of interest to Maddock. He was careful to make it sound like he and Jay had arrived after Maddock and party had departed, and had gleaned these kernels of information through solid detective work. He omitted the part where the two of them got their asses kicked, and Cy got his gun and wallet lifted.

Kennedy was silent for a long time—longer than Cy could stand it.

"It's good, isn't it Kennedy? I mean, we are after Fawcett, and if..."

"We'll follow up on it," Kennedy said in a clipped voice. *"Anything else?"*

"I've already shipped Fawcett's copy of *The Lost World* to you like you asked. Fastest available post."

"Fine. Send the book you found today along to us, and then lie low until you hear from me."

The call ended. Kennedy wasn't much of a people person.

"Thanks for not telling him about… you know." Jay stared straight ahead, his expression blank.

"No problem." Now it was Cy's turn to feel like an idiot. "Say, I'm going to need you to spot me some cash for a few days."

"What? How come?"

"Maddock sort of stole my wallet." Cy would have given anything to be somewhere else at that moment, as Jay threw back his head and laughed. "And when I see him again," Cy muttered, "I'll kill him."

CHAPTER 11

Dane parked the car in front of a modest, two-story, detached brick house in Blackheath, a suburb southeast of London. Despite the pleasant surroundings, he couldn't help looking up and down the street, searching for potential danger, wondering if the guys who attacked them at the naval library would track them down again. He'd given the name and address of the man with whom he'd fought to his friend Jimmy, in hopes he could shed some light on exactly who these people were of whom they'd run afoul.

A tiny man with a shock of unkempt white hair answered the door. He eyed them through thick glasses that gave him the appearance of a snowy owl.

"Mister Maddock and party, I presume?" If his body was small, his voice was huge. He could have done voice-overs for NFL films.

"Yes. Thank you for seeing us, Mister Wainwright." They shook hands, and Dane introduced Bones and Kaylin.

"Bloody hell," Wainwright said, craning his neck to look up at Bones, "are all American Natives your size?"

"They wish. My mother just fed me good."

"Fifteen stone, I'll wager." Wainwright cupped his chin, looking Bones up and down with a critical eye.

"Dude, I haven't been stoned since I was a teenager."

Wainwright did a double-take, laughed and ushered them into a living room overflowing with books. Every wall was lined with floor-to-ceiling shelves, with volumes stacked two deep and tucked into every open space: aging hardcovers, old pulp novels, and textbooks of varying age and subject. Four overstuffed chairs circled a round table, also stacked with books. Books were even piled haphazardly in the corners, and a basket stuffed full of newspapers, magazines, and mystery novels sat next to one of the chairs. He urged them to make themselves comfortable, and returned a few minutes later with hot tea, sandwiches cut in small triangles, apple slices, and sugar cookies.

"Hold this, young man." He handed Dane the tray, then bent down and cleared the coffee table of books with one sweep of his arm. "Ordinarily I would not treat books so," he said, placing the tray on the table and pouring a cup of tea for each of them, "but they are romance novels my late wife's sister thought I would enjoy reading. Perish the thought! If I want pornography, I shall search for it on the internet."

Bones choked on his tea, and Kaylin's eyes were suddenly wide as saucers at the comment. Dane merely grinned and nodded.

"You have quite an impressive library," Dane said, looking around the room.

"Thank you. I fear this is, as they say, only the tip of the iceberg. All of my rooms, save the kitchen and bath, are in a similar state. I have always had a fascination, and perhaps an obsession, with books."

"You know, I'll bet you could put all of these on one e-reader." Bones cocked his head, as if performing the calculations in his head. Kaylin frowned and nudged Bones's leg with her toe, but Wainwright laughed.

"I have one of those as well. Most of my books, however, are too old and obscure to be available electronically. If you would like to scan them for me, I'm certain it would not take you more than a few decades."

"You don't want Bones touching your electronics." Dane took a bite of a sandwich and forced down a grimace. It tasted like cream cheese and cucumber, or something like that.

"I scanned my butt once and emailed it to *Playgirl.* They didn't write back, though." Bones stuffed two of the small sandwiches into his mouth at once.

"I'm sorry, Mister Wainwright." Kaylin laid a hand on the man's arm. "We are not as crazy as we must seem. Well, Dane and I aren't."

"Nonsense. It is a delight to have young people in the house. I was a university professor for many years, and I miss the absurd humor of youth."

Dane couldn't remember the last time he'd been categorized as young, much less youthful, but he'd take it. "The reason we are here is actually in regard to a book. One that belonged to Percy Fawcett."

Wainwright gave him a shrewd look. "What book might that be?"

"A copy of *The Lost World.* A personal copy in which he took notes. It was supposedly one of his most treasured personal possessions."

"I see." The temperature in the room seemed to drop ten degrees. Wainwright sat up straighter, his posture stiff. "May I ask why you are interested in this book?"

Dane sensed he would have to tread carefully. His instinct also told him that anything short of the truth would not suffice. Wainwright impressed him as a sensible, perceptive man.

"We are searching for a friend who disappeared in the Amazon. From what we have learned so far, we believe he was on the trail of Fawcett's final expedition, and we think he found information in this book that guided him on his search."

"He has been missing for some time now." Kaylin sat her cup on the table and folded her hands together in a supplicating gesture. "He is not some crackpot—he is a college professor, like you were. We need to find him."

"What is his name?" Wainwright still eyed them with suspicion.

"Thomas Thornton." Kaylin took a photograph from her purse and handed it to Wainwright, who looked at it for a long moment, and then seemed to sag.

"I warned the lad. He was here, I don't recall for certain, perhaps a year ago, if that. I let him look at the book, and told him what I know, and what I suspect about my granduncle's final expedition. I'm sorry. I tried to dissuade him. Truly I did."

"Thomas was here!" Kaylin's face and voice were filled with hope. "Did he show you this picture, or a picture like it?" She handed him the image of the Fawcett painting.

"Ah! The portrait that hangs in the Institute. No, he did not show this to me, though I am familiar with it. It is, in fact, the final portrait Fawcett commissioned of himself."

"Thomas left this for us as a clue to his whereabouts," Dane said.

"Did he? Well, it certainly ties several things together. Fawcett, *The Lost World*, the island, *Quest*, and, of course, the amphorae." Three seconds' tantalizing silence followed the statement. Dane's heart raced, and he found himself inching forward in his seat, as if the old man's words would reach him sooner. Finally, Wainwright shook his head and continued.

"I fear Fawcett was losing his mind prior to his final expedition. The story has been passed down through the generations of my family. It is said that he paced the floor, muttering to himself about something he lost on the shipwreck. He spent long hours poring over his copy of *The Lost World*, works of ancient history, and the Bible."

"The Bible?" Dane was puzzled. "What was the connection there?"

"No one knows. At any rate, something happened on his next-to-last expedition into the Amazon that made Fawcett more certain than ever that the lost city of Z was real, and that its inhabitants were descended from the ancient Greeks. Hence the portrait he had commissioned and donated to the Institute just before his departure. He knew he could not make public what he believed about Z. He was already a subject of some skepticism because of his beliefs. To share the conclusion he had come to would have held him up to public ridicule."

"But if this portrait represents what he thought he was going to find," Bones began, a look of deep concentration on his face, "he could come back later and tell the world, *'See, I knew it all along. In your face!'*"

"That is one way of saying it." Wainwright smiled. "Fawcett was a proud man, and it would have been important to him to prove that he had not simply stumbled upon the lost city by happenstance, but had set out to reach it, already knowing it was there."

"What exactly happened on the previous expedition that affected him so?" The familiar feeling of anticipation that always came when he was on the verge of a breakthrough, surged through Dane. Bones and Kaylin also sat in rapt silence, waiting for the answer.

Wainwright, clearly enjoying his captive audience, took a sip of tea, and carefully placed his cup and saucer atop a stack of books before beginning his tale.

"Understand, what I am about to tell you is conjecture, partly supported by cryptic phrases jotted in the margins of Fawcett's copy of *The Lost World,* and partly based on family legend of the things he supposedly said during his final months at home."

Dane nodded, and Wainwright continued. "Fawcett was just completing an extended trek through the Amazon. Supplies and morale were low, and he and his party were making their way out of the jungle, when a young man stumbled into their camp one evening. He was in bad shape: weak from hunger and dehydration, eaten up by insects, and nursing old wounds. He looked, according to Fawcett, decidedly Mediterranean, and he spoke an odd language, containing enough words familiar to Fawcett and his native guides that they could piece together bits of his story. Some of his words, however, sounded Semitic to Fawcett. He recorded a few of the words, spelling them phonetically, and eventually concluded they were Punic."

"You lost me there," Bones said.

"Punic was the language of Carthage," Dane said.

"Oh yeah! Hannibal and the war elephants. Cool!"

"They were descended from the Phoenicians," Dane said, "the first great sailors in the ancient world. Some say the Phoenicians reached the New World centuries before Christ." Dane wondered if this could possibly be true, or had Fawcett fallen prey to hope and wishful thinking?

"Precisely." Wainwright took another sip of tea. "From what they could gather from the young man's ravings, he and a young woman had fled their home, a place he called 'Keff Sess.' You have, I presume, heard the legend of Kephises?"

Dane nodded and motioned for him to continue.

"The young woman was lost along the way, the victim of what the young man called 'the Dead Warriors.' He offered, as proof, fragments of pottery Fawcett believed were Mediterranean in origin, as well as some sort of plant material that the young man said had strange, mind-altering properties. He also gave Fawcett a map carved in stone. It was very old, and showed the path his ancestors had taken to Keff Sess. His home, he said, was 'in the air,' and could only be reached by taking a secret path—the Path of Five Steps. These steps, Fawcett wrote in his copy of *The Lost World*."

"What about the map?" All thoughts of rescuing Thomas were forgotten. In his mind, Dane was already trekking through the Amazon, following Fawcett's last journey.

"Lost when *Quest* sank, along with the only copy Fawcett made of it. The pottery and the strange plant material were lost as well. Only *The Lost World* was saved."

"So, when he went on his final expedition, what did he do? Just go by memory?" Bones asked.

"It is odd, that. After the shipwreck and the loss of his maps, he grew paranoid. He claimed to have made a map from memory shortly after the wreck, and he said he put it where no one could get to it. When he set off on his final expedition, he left his book behind, presumably after copying the five steps, and whatever other information he needed. And, as the story goes, he was never heard from again." Wainwright folded his hands in his lap and gave them a small, sad smile.

"Why has none of this ever been made public?" Kaylin asked. "It could have shed light on Fawcett's final expedition."

"My dear, you can't possibly believe the story to be true. Fawcett had clearly let his dream of finding Z overcome his good sense. To his mind, the raving young man's Kephises was his fabled city of Z. He was already believed to be… eccentric. The family could not reveal the story of his last months to the rest of the world. It would have sullied his memory and cast a shadow over all the good work he did in his life. He was perhaps the most important explorer of the twentieth century." Wainwright sat up a little straighter as he spoke the last. "He did not deserve to be remembered as a fool who believed in myth and superstition."

"But, couldn't the family have used the information to search for Fawcett?" Kaylin persisted.

"If the map had been available, perhaps, but all the family had were the five steps. As it stands, many have searched for him and failed."

"Mister Wainwright," Dane began, "could we please see the book?"

"Young man, you seem a sensible sort. Don't tell me you would actually set off on this fool's errand."

Dane had seen enough strange things in his life that he had little trouble believing Fawcett's tale, though he sensed this was not what Wainwright wanted to hear.

"We aren't looking for the lost city; we're looking for Thomas. If he believed in the lost city, maybe there's something in the book that will help us find him."

Wainwright stared at him, and finally, hung his head. His voice was rough with regret. "How can I possibly show it to you after what happened to your friend? I fear I encouraged him by letting him read it, and now he is gone."

"Bones and I are highly capable. We have spent more than our share of time in hostile environments and dangerous situations. I assure you, we are also going into this with eyes wide open. You have made it clear to us that this is, in your opinion, a wild goose chase, and a potentially deadly one. To us, this is a rescue mission, not an adventure, and we need your help."

The old man took his time considering Dane's request. He sipped his tea and stared into the distance. Finally, he nodded. "Very well. As long as we are clear that I am actively discouraging you from this quest. Make no mistake, that's what it will be. I can see it in your eyes. You have the same spirit that my ancestor had. You might begin by searching for your friend, but sooner or later, the longing will overcome you, and you will not be able to rest until you have solved the mystery, or at least tried. Don't try to deny it." He held up a liver-spotted hand. "I would have no lies between us." He eased himself out of the chair and shuffled off into the adjoining room, returning a few minutes later with a tiny flash drive, which he handed to Dane.

"After your friend visited me, I worried that the story might get out, and what it would do to Fawcett's legacy if it did. I have not decided what should become of it after my passing, but it is in a safe deposit box for the time being. I have scanned all the pages with his notes on them. I trust that you will do me the courtesy of not sharing these with the world."

"You can count on us." Dane tucked the flash drive in his pocket and shook hands with Wainwright. "I should warn you. Someone else is on the trail of Fawcett's last expedition, and they could be dangerous."

"I will take all necessary precautions," he said. "I have considered taking a holiday outside the country. Perhaps now would be a good time."

They all thanked him profusely and bade him goodbye. As they piled into the car and drove away, a sense of excitement filled the air.

"So, what next?" Bones asked.

"First, we give Jimmy some more homework. We need him to see what he can do to help us pinpoint *Quest's* location." He grinned. "We are going to find a lost shipwreck."

CHAPTER 12

Tam rapped twice on Salvatore's door. She was the only person whom he permitted to do so because he knew she would only interrupt him if it was important.

"Come!" he called.

"Boss, we have a problem. Two men fitting the description of the bumbling idiots Kennedy sent to London are wanted for questioning." She laid a folder in front of him and went on. "It seems they confronted Maddock and Bonebrake at the Royal Institute of Navigation. Cy was caught on a security camera getting his ass handed to him by Maddock. Jay apparently didn't make out any better with Bonebrake. Jay, at least, had the good sense to get out of there, but Cy stormed inside, threatened the staff, and told them he had a gun and would kill everyone if he had to."

"I would love to ask if this is a joke, but I know better." Salvatore closed his eyes and took a few deep breaths. "Tell me, what do we know about Maddock and Bonebrake?"

"Ex Navy SEALS. Now they find shipwrecks, search for sunken treasure, that sort of thing."

"Why did Maxwell reach out to them in particular?"

"There's a history there. Her father was their commanding officer at one time. She and Maddock also had a relationship a few years back."

"Interesting. She asks her old boyfriend to help her find her new boyfriend. What else can you tell me?"

"About Maddock and Bonebrake? Not a great deal, except for rumors. Sketchy stuff related to archaeological finds. Nothing firm." She wasn't sure what to make of what she had heard about them.

"Anything else?"

"I think Cy lost his wallet. It appears Kennedy had to scramble to secure new identification and a passport for him, as well as a credit card. Now I.T. tells me someone hacked into the personnel files looking for information on…"

"Cyrus Wallace." Salvatore slammed his fist down on the table. "Get Kennedy on the phone. I want Cy on the next plane back here. I'll flay that idiot." He stood and walked to the window. "The hacker, how far did he penetrate?"

"Not very deep, as far as we can tell. Just the basic personnel files."

"How did he get past the firewall?"

"The techies are working on that as we speak. They understand it means their jobs if they don't find that breach and seal it. I took the liberty of suggesting it might mean their balls, too."

Salvatore didn't smile, but Tam thought she saw a hint of a twinkle in his eyes. "Did they back trace him?"

"Couldn't. Whoever it is, he or she is good. We'll keep trying, of course."

"I know you will. Now, get Kennedy in here."

Kennedy frowned when he saw Tam seated at the conference table. He took a seat across from her and waited for Salvatore to speak.

"I want a full report on Cy and Jay." Salvatore's voice was ice.

"Of course." As always, Kennedy was unflappable. "They acquired Fawcett's copy of *The Lost World*, but there was nothing in it, except for an inscription from the author to Fawcett. I'm having it checked for invisible ink, and the inscription reviewed for any irregularities that might suggest a code of some sort, but nothing so far. They almost got themselves into trouble with the authorities, but we got them out of England, and they're now following up on a possible lead." He glanced at Salvatore's face and didn't wait for a follow-up question. "I've sent them to South Georgia Island to check out Shackletons' burial site. Cy thinks there might be a connection there."

Salvatore grunted a subdued, mirthless laugh. "Good. That will get them out of the way for a while, at least. So, you are telling me that England was a complete failure?"

"Perhaps not." Kennedy grinned and opened his brief-case.

Tam kept the surprise from her face. What had Kenne-dy found that he had kept so well hidden?

"Dane Maddock was reading this book." Kennedy made a funny face as he said Maddock's name. He placed an aged volume on the table. "It makes reference to a voyage on which Fawcett embarked prior to planning his final expedi-tion. The ship he was traveling on sank and Fawcett lost something important. We don't know what it was, but it's not inconceivable that it's connected to our situation. I think we should find the site of this sunken ship and see what, if anything, is there."

Sal looked at Tam. "What do you think?"

"It's thin," she said, "but it's a possibility, which is all we have right now. I haven't yet read the passage, since Kenne-dy has kept this to himself." She paused, hoping Kennedy was at least squirming on the inside, since he never showed anything on the surface. "I don't, however, see any harm in following up on it. We have the resources to get the help we need." She thought for a moment. "If Kennedy isn't mista-ken, which is possible, since his information comes from Cy, Dane Maddock will probably be coming for whatever is in-side this wreck. Do we want to go for it ourselves, or simply wait for him to get it, and take it away from him?"

"I don't like waiting around for anything," Salvatore said. "Kennedy, I want you moving on this immediately. We have to assume that we're in a race with Maddock; a race you will win, or we shall have a conversation." He dismissed Kennedy with a flick of his finger.

Kennedy rose, nodded to Sal, and spared a steely glance at Tam before striding out, his phone already to his ear. He would not soon forget that Tam had questioned him in front of Sal. That did not matter now. The two of them would have it out one day, and he had no idea what he was up against. Some people resented being underestimated, but Tam found it a useful tool in her arsenal.

"I'm going to roll the dice here," Sal said, his eyes boring into hers. "We need to go after Thornton, and quick. Assemble a team and be ready to move on my command. You have your choice of the agents. If Kennedy finds something, that is well and good. If not, use what information we have about Thornton and about Fawcett, and begin the search. We can't put this off any longer."

"Sir, are you saying…" She didn't dare let herself believe it could be true.

"I'm putting you in charge. You might not have Kennedy's experience, but you're a hell of a lot smarter than him, and you haven't screwed up… yet. Choose your agents, outfit your team, get down to Brazil, and await my instructions."

Heart pounding, and dizzy with triumph, Tam stood and gravely nodded her head. "I won't let you down, Salvatore."

He rose to his full height, and looked down at her with a ghost of a smile on his lips. "I know you won't, *figlia mia.*"

CHAPTER 13

Sea Foam sliced through the gently rolling sea, its rising and falling barely noticeable. Dane sat on the bed in his below-deck cabin, scrolling through the latest report from his hacker friend, Jimmy Letson.

"The guy who attacked me works for a company named ScanoGen. Sound familiar?"

Kaylin shook her head. "No, why should it?"

"Because, according to Jimmy, they made a substantial transfer into Thomas's bank account a few months before he left on his expedition."

Kaylin's entire posture changed. She sat ramrod-straight in her chair, her lips pursed. "He never said anything to me. Not about ScanoGen, and certainly not about any money." Her shoulders sagged. "Of course, all of this came as a surprise. It's hurtful to know that he had a whole part of his life that he wouldn't let me into." She suddenly looked right at Dane, and then something passed across her face, and she turned away.

When the two of them had been a couple, she had accused him of locking her out of various parts of his life—mostly memories of his time in the service, and of his deceased wife. That was probably what was on her mind now, but he was not about to go there with her. Not now, at least.

"I'm sure he had his reasons." He tried to make his voice soothing, but his throat was dry, and his words lacked conviction. Trying to make an ex-girlfriend feel better about her current boyfriend was not his thing. The sadness in her eyes, however, convinced him to try again. "Look, he obviously knew these were dangerous people, and he wouldn't have wanted you mixed up with them."

"Well, I *am* mixed up in it, in case you didn't notice."

"Yeah, I think I noticed. I'm in the middle of it, too." He held up a hand, forestalling her retort. "The guy tried to keep you safe. That's what guys do for the women they care about. He probably figured he could do for ScanoGen whatever it was they wanted done without involving you, and then the two of you could enjoy the money he made off the venture."

"He just… the lying…" She stood and began pacing the room, which only required a few steps, but she moved to-and-fro, fists clenched, until he couldn't look at her without feeling dizzy.

"If you're that upset with him, we can call this thing off if you like. You can lie low with us until ScanoGen gets off your case, and then you can go back to your life."

Kaylin froze. Slowly, she turned to face him. The anger on her face melted, replaced by an amused smile.

"Right, Maddock. You've waded knee-deep into a mystery, and you'd just turn back and walk right out again without seeing it through to the end?"

He had to laugh. "Fine, you know me too well. Now shut up and let's finish going over this."

The ice broken, she plopped down beside him on the bed and leaned against him. The closeness should have been uncomfortable, but its familiarity was welcome and natural.

"ScanoGen is a bioengineering firm. Most of their money comes from military applications. That's not a big surprise, considering the Amazon is believed to hold countless species of plant life that could have properties previously unknown. People have searched the rainforests for everything from recreational drugs to a cure for cancer." For a moment, he was sadly reminded of their mutual friend, Franklin Meriwether, who had joined them on one of their adventures. Another place to which he didn't want to let his thoughts drift.

Kaylin seemed to know what was on his mind, and she slid her arm around his waist and laid her head on his shoulder. "So Thomas found something, or believed he would find something, that ScanoGen wanted. It's the whole Fawcett connection that doesn't make sense to me. In all the research we've done, there hasn't been any mention of Fawcett going after some super plant, or whatever it is they want."

"You remember the story Wainwright told us. The young man had with him a plant that had some sort of great power." Dane tried to ignore her closeness, the softness of her hair against his cheek. "That's the only way I can see how a company like ScanoGen fits in."

Kaylin looked up at him, her green eyes sparkling.

"What is it?" Dane dropped his papers on the bed and met her gaze.

"You know, you never would let me all the way in, Maddock, but when we were together, you were never dishonest with me."

Before Dane could reply, her arms were around his neck and her lips pressed firmly against his. His surprise dissolved in the familiarity of the moment. It was as if the two of them had never broken apart. He returned her kiss, pulling her tightly against him.

"Ahem."

They jerked away from each other like two teenagers caught parking. Kaylin smoothed her clothing and Dane sat up straight.

Bones leaned in the doorway, grinning. "Sorry to interrupt, but I thought you'd like to know, we've found *Quest*."

Unable to contain his excitement, Dane bounded to his feet, offered Kaylin a hand, and followed Bones out of the cabin. Bones arched an eyebrow at him and grinned, but Dane ignored him.

Above deck, Willis was already suiting up. "It's about time we got into the water. Man, I hate this searching stuff."

Inside the cabin, Matt and Corey were looking at a small monitor.

"Uma's down there right now," Matt said, his eyes not leaving the screen. Uma was an unmanned submersible camera, so nicknamed by Bones, who was a big fan of Uma Thurman's character in the movie *Pulp Fiction.* On the screen, the outline of *Quest*, blue-gray in the deep water, suddenly filled the screen. She had settled on her port side, the bow resting on a rocky formation on the seabed, and the ship's distinctive profile made her easy to recognize.

"She's in great condition," Matt observed. "Smoke-stack's still intact and everything."

"According to Jimmy's information, Fawcett's cabin was most likely in the aft section on the starboard side," Corey said, scrolling down through a document. "Take her in that direction and let's see what we can see."

"Are you going to send Uma inside the ship?" Kaylin asked, leaning forward to get a better look. She touched Dane's arm, a detail not missed by Bones, who smirked.

"Not a good idea," Dane said. "She could get tangled, or the ship's hull might cause us to lose our signal. There's higher-tech equipment out there, but Uma's usually all we need for our work."

"Maddock, take a look at this." Matt sounded surprised, and not in a good way. He pointed at a dark spot on *Quest's* hull. Growing larger as Uma came closer, the image resolved into a square hole cut in the ship's side."

"Sorry to state the obvious, but that's not natural." Bones said.

"Look at the edges. They're sharp and clean. The cut is fresh, too." Mat shook his head. "Somebody got here before us, and not too long ago."

Dane stood up straight, clenching and unclenching his fists. "It has to be ScanoGen. As far as we know, they're the only other player in this game, and I'm sure they have the resources to pull it off fast."

"So what do we do?" Bones enunciated each word. When he spoke like that, he was right on the verge of breaking something or someone.

"We go through with the dive. Maybe they missed

something. It would be crazy to come all the way here and not even take a look."

"Then what?" Matt already sounded defeated.

"I've got something up my sleeve," Dane said. "We'll talk about it after the dive." Really, all he had was a nugget of an idea buried deep in his mind. He didn't know if it would pan out, but they'd find out soon enough.

Dane plunged into the water, letting the cool depths envelop him. Down here he could put thoughts of Kaylin and Jade out of his mind, and focus on the dive. This was the one place in the world that always felt right. Bones swam on his right, Willis his left. They glided through the water like three phantoms, slipping down into the semi-darkness. If only he had gills, he thought, he'd never leave the water. He'd felt that way since the first time his parents had taken him to the beach. Dane, just a toddler, had slipped his hand from his father's grip and wobbled toward the surf as fast as his legs would carry him. He had two memories of that day: the salt spray on his face, and his parents' laughter as they trotted alongside him. Smiling, he kicked harder, plunging toward the sunken *Quest.*

The hole in the ship's hull was exactly as Matt described it. It had clearly been made very recently, and the clean, straight cut indicated the use of the modern tools. It was large enough for two men to swim abreast through it, but they took it one at a time, just to be safe.

Dane took the lead and found himself in a small room that fit the description of the cabin in which Fawcett had resided during his voyage on board *Quest.* He gritted his teeth. ScanoGen had done their homework, all right, and the likelihood of Dane and his crew finding the missing artifact, whatever it was, was now even smaller.

Bones and Willis followed him in, moving with caution, so as not to stir up too much silt. As planned, the two of them exited the room to explore other cabins in case Jimmy's information had been incorrect.

Dane scanned the cabin. Though *Quest* lay on her side, one of the advantages to being underwater was that he could easily orient himself, creating the illusion that the ship still sat upright. Everything in the cabin had gradually slid to one corner, so he began his investigation there. A few items were scattered about, probably by ScanoGen's divers. Dane sifted through the crumbling remains of what had once been personal items belonging to the legendary Fawcett. Aside from crumbling bits of furniture, most of what remained had been reduced to silt and muck, and was no longer recognizable, though he did find a broken mug, a few buttons, which he stashed in his dive bag, and a corroded spoon, which he also kept. He searched every inch of the cabin, but found nothing else of interest.

Discouraged, he checked his watch. Two minutes until time to head back to the surface. Bones and Willis would be returning any moment. With no time to check out any other section of the ship, he returned to the pile of accumulated detritus in the corner and slid his hand down below the pile of muck. He ran his fingers along the seam where the cabin floor met the wall and was rewarded when he felt something hard that had wedged into a crack.

Exercising care, he slowly worked the thing back-and-forth until it came free. Holding it close, he grinned as his dive light shone on a fragment of pottery. He'd seen enough of these to know what it was. Feeling a little bit more positive about things, he secured it in his bag as a glimmer of light appeared in the darkness beyond the cabin door, telling him that his friends were on their way back. Dane gave each of them the "thumbs up" sign as they passed through the cabin, indicating they should head back up top.

Back aboard *Sea Foam*, Dane wasted no time in showing the others what he had found.

"It's a fragment of pottery, and it's definitely Mediterranean in origin. This at least confirms part of Fawcett's story."

"So," Bones began, "that probably means that Fawcett really did have a map carved in stone that showed the way to

Kephises."

"And now, ScanoGen has that map," Matt finished. "So, where does that leave us?"

Dane thought about all they had learned of *Quest's* sinking, and the aftermath. He gazed out at the ocean, his eyes drifting to one of the small islands near Ascension. He wondered…

"I have an idea." Dane pointed to the small, rocky island in the distance. "Matt, take us there, as close as you can get."

"What are we looking for?" Bones gave him a speculative look, the amused twinkle in his eye showed that he could tell Dane was up to something.

"I'll know it when I see it."

Kaylin frowned. "But Maddock, what is the point…"

"Don't bother," Willis interrupted. "When he's like this, there ain't no point. *That's* the point. He'll tell us when he's ready. Me, I'm gonna get a beer and wait for the big reveal." He headed below to retrieve the beer cooler from the galley.

"What is that place?" Kaylin asked as Matt took *Sea Foam* in the direction Dane had indicated. Out here on the water, with her blonde hair flying in the breeze, she was as beautiful as Dane had ever seen her. He looked into her green eyes, so open and honest, and thought how different she was from the dark, exotic Jade. One was his seemingly perfect match, the other his perfect counterpoint.

"Did you hear me?" Kaylin grinned. "Typical man. I'd ask you what you're thinking about, but I know how much you hate that."

"Sorry. It's called Botswain Bird Island."

"Interesting name."

"The name comes from all the birds that nest there. We've been assuming that Fawcett and the others took refuge on Ascension Island after *Quest* sank, but I noticed before we made the dive that Botswain is closer to the spot where she went down. Also, remember what we read in the naval library, about Fawcett complaining of 'the infernal birds' that annoyed them while they waited for rescue."

"Okay, so how does that help us?"

"You'll see." He met her annoyed look with a roguish grin, and headed into cabin where Matt was piloting the ship in while Corey kept one eye on the depth readings and the other on a navigational chart.

"Are you looking for anything in particular?" Matt asked, keeping his eyes trained on the water.

"Yep. Just get in as close as you can and circle the isl-and. I'll tell you when to stop."

"It shouldn't take long," Corey observed. "The island's small enough."

His words proved to be correct. Within five minutes, they were circling the shore of Botswain Bird Island. The tall, gray rocks gave it the appearance of a giant molar rising up from the sea. Dane kept his eyes on the shore as they circled, *Sea Foam* plowing through the chop. Time crept by, and he was about to admit that he had been wrong, when they found what he had been looking for. A natural stone arch rose up from the water, joining the steep, rocky cliff at the water's edge.

"Does that look familiar?"

"It's the island in the painting!" Kaylin had joined them in the cabin. "You think it means something?"

"Matter of fact, I do."

CHAPTER 14

Tam sat in the shade of an umbrella in an outdoor café in Cuiabá, the capital city of the state of Mato Grosso, Brazil. Under different circumstances, she would have found it a delightful place to visit. The city was tourist-friendly, and boasted a rich local culture of music, dance, and cuisine all reflecting African, native American, and Portuguese influences. At the moment, though, she was focused on the job at hand, and anxious to get started.

Her sat phone rang and she answered immediately. It was Salvatore.

"How are things?"

"We're ready. I've got three guides lined up. Just say the word and we're off."

"I am pleased to hear it. I knew I made the proper decision in sending you. You shall begin very soon. It also seems that Kennedy was successful in his efforts to find the sunken ship." Salvatore did not try to keep the satisfaction from his voice.

"That's wonderful." She wasn't sure how wonderful it actually was. On the one hand, she didn't like Kennedy and never cared to see him succeed. On the other hand, if he found something that helped her complete her part of the mission, good on him. "What did he find?"

"A map carved in stone. After all this time in sea water, the images were faint. Our people were, of course, able to make laser scans of the carvings and create enhanced digital images. We are now cross-referencing it with existing maps of the Amazon region. It appears, however, that the map has no particular scale, and little is known

about the region into which you shall be traveling. They tell me that, assuming Fawcett followed this map, it appears that what the world knows about his final expedition is wrong."

"Interesting, but not surprising. That certainly would make it difficult for anyone to have followed his trail, much less find him."

"Indeed. I shall send whatever they come up with along to you as soon as it is ready."

Tam's heart beat faster. It was really happening. *Don't blow it,* she told herself. This was her first assignment and she could not afford to fall out of Scano's good graces by blowing it. She had worked too hard to get where she was in the organization, and it would be a serious blow indeed if she slipped up. "Very good. When can I expect it?"

"Soon. But you be patient. I'm sending a few…disposable items your way."

"Sir?" She did not like the sound of this one bit.

"Thomas Thornton's colleague, the one whom we questioned about Thornton's only clue, has proved useless. The Charleston Police Department has been investigating his disappearance. We could go to the trouble of doing away with him and making it look like a crime, but it would be much cleaner if you would simply lose him in the Amazon. Besides, there is still a possibility he knows something useful, though I doubt it. Assess him, and eliminate him when you deem he is of no use. It should not be a problem."

"No sir, it will not." Tam felt a weight in her stomach. Damn! Another loose end to tie up. "You said 'items,' as in more than one." *Not Alex,* she prayed. *Don't send me your snotty, psychopath son.* That was one distraction she could live without.

"Yes. Cyrus and Jason have outlived their usefulness as well." Tam had to remind herself that he was referring to Cy and Jay. *"They seemed to think it a good idea to exhume Shackleton's remains. Getting them off South Georgia Island and covering their tracks was a close thing. I cannot afford to have men with so little sense in my employ. Kennedy will arrive tomorrow with all three expendables. He knows your orders, but I fear he might grow sentimental about Jason, in particular. See to it that the job is done."*

"Kennedy's coming here?" Her stomach was in a twist. Kennedy posed a problem of an entirely different sort.

"You need not worry. He understands that the command is yours. He's a good soldier and he'll follow orders." She doubted that. *"Kennedy is one of our best."*

She didn't know what to say to that, so she kept her silence. A quiet ensued, enduring for so long that she wondered if the connection had been lost. Finally, Salvatore continued. *"Our investors have grown anxious for Project Pan to get underway. They are growing impatient. We do not need them to take a direct hand."*

Tam's heart raced. "You've never told me who our investors are, Mr. Scano."

"Nor will I." His voice was sharp with implied rebuke.

"Forgive me. I only wonder what I might come up against should they decide to get involved."

"You need not worry about it." Salvatore's voice had regained the fatherly, reassuring tone he often took when talking to her about a difficult situation. *You and Kennedy have a head start, and you are well-equipped. Finish the job, and finish it soon, and we won't have to concern ourselves with anyone else."*

"Yes sir."

"Good luck, *figlia mia."*

The call ended and Tam sat staring at the wall. The last thing she needed was Kennedy and two of his lackeys, no matter how moronic, interfering. She was close, she could feel it. But if they interfered…

She ordered up another Baden Baden Stout, the signature beer of the Brazilian microbrewery of the same name. Beer was seldom her drink of choice, but this particular beverage complemented the spicy food nicely. She took a sip, enjoying the rich, smoky flavor with a suggestion of dark chocolate and burnt coffee. She let the cool drink and calm atmosphere sooth her jangled nerves. She was a professional, and she would face whatever came her way.

She took another drink and smiled.

A complicated job had just turned into a Gordian knot. Oh well, a knotty problem required a bold stroke, and she had plenty of those up her sleeve. She wondered for a moment if Salvatore would still think of her as "daughter" when this was all over.

CHAPTER 15

As they drew closer to the arch, Dane's certainty grew. This was the same place shown in the painting. It had to be significant.

"So, now will you tell me all about your brilliant idea?" Bones asked, leaning on the rail and gazing intently at the stone formation.

"It was Fawcett's complaints about all the 'infernal birds' that got me thinking. I believe they took refuge on Botswain Bird Island, not on Ascension."

"The book did say it was a small island," Bones agreed. "I get it. You think the arch in the painting was more than just a signpost to Botswain Bird Island. You think the arch itself is important."

"Yep. And we're told that Fawcett tried to recreate the map to Kephises. I think, while he was off keeping to himself and brooding over their situation, he carved a new map from memory, or at least tried to."

Bones thought for a while. "You know, Maddock, you could be right. Didn't the book say that Fawcett screwed it up, though?"

"He said it was an incomplete map. Fawcett was a perfectionist. If he felt he'd left out even the smallest detail, he would have been unhappy with the finished product. I'm wagering he did a reasonably good job of replicating what the native had given him. It's the best hope we have, in any case."

They anchored *Sea Foam* a safe distance from the shore

and began their search. Willis and Matt headed for a spot that looked like a likely place for the crew of *Quest* to have taken refuge. They would head out from there, scouting out any possible pathways Fawcett might have taken. Dane and Bones went to take a closer look at the arch itself.

It wasn't spectacular, by any stretch, but it was impressive in its own way. It was a thick column of stone rising up from the churning surf, curving in to meet the imposing cliffs of Botswain Bird Island.

They inspected the base of the arch, then used binoculars to scan its surface on either side, but they saw nothing that looked like a map, or even a hiding place where one might be secreted. A search of the island in the immediate vicinity of the arch proved fruitless as well. They checked in with Willis and Matt, but the two had not had any luck either. Discouraged, they sat down on a stone slab in the shade of the arch, letting the salt spray cool them.

"I'm thinking we're going to have to expand our search area." Bones didn't sound disheartened, but neither did he seem pleased at the prospect. "Of course, covering every square inch of this island might suck, but it's better than the alternative."

"Which is?" Dane was only half-listening. He gazed up at the underside of the arch, turning the problem over in his mind.

"Scouring the entire Amazon basin looking for Thomas. I don't know about you, but I want to be done with this and back home in time for football season."

Dane had to laugh. "You know there's nothing in the world you'd rather be doing than what we're doing right now."

Bones look affronted. "What? Sitting on a rock in the middle of nowhere getting our butts wet?"

Dane grinned and stretched, working the kinks out of his head and neck. "Maybe we should get back to the search," he said, tilting his head back and popping his neck. And then he spotted something. It was only a shadow, a pool of black below the spot where the arch met the cliff face, but as his eyes fell on it, a bird took flight from somewhere inside its dark depths. He stood transfixed, keeping his eyes on the spot as if he feared it might disappear if he looked away even for a moment.

"What is it?" Bones craned his neck to see. He spotted it almost immediately. "No freakin' way! Do you think it might be?"

"Only one way to find out." Dane turned a conspiratorial glance his way. "Race you to the top."

The first fifteen feet of the climb were a challenge. Here the edges of any cracks, protrusions, or irregularities in the stone had been rounded off by the surf, but the way grew easier as they ascended. Dane reached their destination first and hauled himself up into a cave just wide enough for two men to squeeze inside. He turned and gave Bones a hand, hauling his friend in behind him.

"You cheated, dude," Bones grumbled. He prided himself in his climbing ability and hated not being the first one somewhere.

"Your arms and legs are just too long," Dane replied, unhooking his mag lite from a clip at his waist and shining it around.

"Tell me how that makes any sense at all." Bones took out his own light and together, they inspected the cave. The passage cut straight back into the rock, with no end in sight. "Do you really think Fawcett could have found this place? I mean, we almost missed it."

"I think Fawcett could do just about anything." Dane was confident in his assessment. "He was maybe the greatest explorer of the twentieth century, and he was stuck on this pile of rock with nothing else to do. I think he would have explored every nook and cranny. Let's just hope you don't get stuck in here."

"I'd better go first in case it gets narrow farther back," Bones said. "Anywhere I can fit, we'll know you can get through, too. If I'm behind you and get wedged in, it could get ugly."

"Oh, I'd just kick you in the head until I jarred you

loose, but if you want to go first, be my guest." The two switched positions and Bones headed off into the darkness, Dane right behind him. They had only gone about twenty feet when he stopped short. "Whoa, dude!" The passage came to an end at a deep crevasse. They shone their lights down to reveal a fifty foot drop onto jagged rocks. "Not fun."

"See that?" Dane trained the beam of his light on a tangle of bone and decaying fabric amongst the rocks below. "We're not the first to come this way." He wondered who the person was and what had led them up to this place. Another adventurer on the track of Fawcett, or just an unfortunate soul who had gotten a bit too curious or too careless?

"You want to try to jump across?" Bones shone his light to the spot across the way where the tunnel continued on the other side of the chasm.

"I don't think this would have stopped Fawcett, do you?" Dane gauged the distance. It wasn't too broad a leap. It was the consequences of failure that made it a bit more interesting.

"No, but I don't think your little legs will carry you that far, do you? It's a good ten feet. That's a long way for an old man like you"

"I'm a month older than you." Dane arched an eyebrow at Bones. "You've already lost a climbing contest. Do I need to beat you in long jump, too?"

"Just don't beg me to climb down and get you if you fall. I hate it when a grown man whines."

They both made the leap with ease and continued their search. The way grew wider as they progressed and soon they could walk side-by-side. It was slow going, as they kept a careful eye on the stone walls all around in case Fawcett had hidden the map somewhere, or perhaps carved it directly onto the wall. They came upon two side passages, but neither led anywhere, each of them narrowing until they were impassable. Finally, the passageway came to an end. No twists and turns, only stone.

"Oh, no way." Bones cursed and kicked at the pile of loose rocks at the base of the wall. "To come all this way and find nothing. This is crap."

Dane sidestepped as a rock bounced off the wall and rebounded his way. He felt like picking up one of the rocks and bashing something.

And then a thought struck him.

"Bones, help me move these loose stones." Holding his mag lite in his teeth, he leaned down and hefted the largest one, setting it off to the side. Bones didn't ask what Dane had in mind, but lent a hand. They had only moved about five of the biggest stones when cool air flowed across their arms from somewhere behind the rock pile.

"Maddock, you are the man!" Bones clapped him on the back and attacked the rocks with vigor.

At the base of the wall was an opening just high enough for a man to worm his way through. Dane lay down and shone his light into the opening, revealing a small chamber on the other side, and on the far wall…

"A map!" he breathed. "Bones, this is it!"

They squeezed inside and moved to take a closer look. A curved line, presumably a river, snaked across the wall. Tributaries crept down like menacing hands. At various points, distinctive shapes were carved, signifying landmarks. At one bend, a smaller line wended away, perhaps another tributary, ending at a giant question mark.

"This question mark must signify the thing Fawcett couldn't remember," Dane said. "The final landmark."

"Who cares?" Bones began snapping pictures of the map. "If the map can get us that far, we'll figure out the last clue when we get there. After that, we have the five steps from Fawcett's book. Mystery as good as solved."

"Of course, we might not even have to figure out the last clue," Dane said. "We could find Thomas along the way, or find out what happened to him, and then we could go home."

Bones lowered his camera. "Maddock, are you telling me that you would just give up like that?"

Dane thought about it. Kaylin had asked them to help find Thomas, but that mission had taken on a life of its own. The adventure bug had bitten him again, and he knew he would have to see things through. He, like so many others, wanted to know the fate of Percy Fawcett, and to learn what, if anything, lay in the heart of the unexplored Amazon. Dane was no longer on a rescue mission. He was on a quest.

CHAPTER 16

Dane knocked on the door of the tiny house. A tired-looking little woman of late middle years opened the door. She frowned when she saw him, but her expression softened a bit when she noticed Kaylin.

"Hello," Kaylin said. "My name is Kaylin Maxell, and this is Dane Maddock. We're looking for Victor. We were told he lives here."

The frown deepened. "Victor don't talk."

"I see. We are looking for someone who we think might be lost in the jungle, and we were told that Victor might be able to help us."

The woman frowned and shook her head.

"Could you at least tell us if you have seen our friend?" Dane asked. Kaylin took out a photograph of Thomas and handed it to the woman.

She stared at it for a long time, her sour expression curdling.

"I seen that man. Long time ago. Many weeks."

"Are you sure?" There was a note of excitement in Kaylin's voice.

"He came with a pretty girl and two young men. He was a teacher."

Dane's heart leapt. This was the first solid lead they'd had on Thomas, and if he'd been seen here, in this tiny frontier town, the same one to which Fawcett's map coupled with Jimmy's research had led them, that confirmed that Thomas was on the same trail they were.

"Do you know where he is now?" Kaylin looked like a bubble that, at any moment, would either soar into the air or burst, depending on the woman's reply.

She nodded vigorously. "They go into the jungle. The river, then the jungle. They don't come back. Only Victor come back." She shook her head. "They hire him to…" Unable to find the word, she made a motion with her hand like a snake slithering through the grass. "… into the jungle."

"And Victor came back without them?" Deadly scenarios played out in Dane's mind. What might this Victor person have done to Thomas and his students? Had he led them astray and abandoned them? Or had it been something worse?

"Yes. But he is… not right. He does not talk since he come back."

"Could we please see him? It's important." Kaylin bit her lip. "We're just trying to find out if he and the others are all right."

The woman shook her head. "I think they don't come back."

"Ma'am," Dane said, "could we please see Victor? Maybe he could tell us where they went. If they are still in the jungle, we will need to go in after them. If Victor was their guide, perhaps he can tell us which way he took them."

"He don't talk," she said again, but she opened the door and motioned for them to come inside. The tiny home was sparsely furnished and smelled of coffee. Dim light filtered through a small window, giving the room a gloomy, oppressive feel.

A man a little younger than Dane sat on the floor, staring at the wall. He did not acknowledge their presence. In fact, he did not seem to register they were there at all. The old woman nodded at him, indicating that this was Victor.

Kaylin sat down cross-legged beside him. "Victor," she began, in a gentle voice, "my name is Kaylin. I'm looking for someone who is lost. You guided him into the jungle a few months back, and I am hoping you can help me find him again."

Victor continued to stare straight ahead. It seemed like the man was in a catatonic state. Dane glanced at the old woman, who looked at him with sad eyes.

"He hears. He don't talk."

Kaylin tried again. "Would you please take a look at this picture and tell me if you remember anything at all about this man or the people who were with him?" She held out the picture of Thomas.

Victor let out a screech and crab walked as fast as he could away from Kaylin. When he banged into the wall, he rolled over into the fetal position, covered his face, and wailed. Both Kaylin and Victor's mother tried to calm him down, but he continued to cry and shiver, and refused to remove his hands from his face.

Finally, they were forced to give up. They apologized to the woman, who, Dane realized, had never given her name, and left.

Kaylin looked like a deflated balloon, so thoroughly defeated was her posture as they walked along the street. Dane nudged her.

"Hang in there. At least we know we're on the right track. Thomas was here, and it looks like he was headed in the same direction we're going."

"I suppose that's true." Kaylin sighed. "It would be much worse if we didn't at least know we were headed in the right direction." She glanced at Dane. "Now what?"

"Now," he said, "it's time to begin our jungle adventure."

The flat-bottomed aluminum boat slid through the dark waters of the Kuluene, the largest of the headwaters of the Xingu River in the Mato Grosso, or "Thick Woods," region of Brazil. The third-largest state in Brazil, the western state featured diverse ecosystems, including the Pantanal, the world's largest wetland, in the south, and the Amazonian rainforest in the north. Piloting the craft through the debris that choked the surface, Dane could not help feeling a thrill at the thought that they were actually on the trail of Percy Fawcett's final expedition. He had fantasized about this as a youth, wandering the forests near his home, imagining deadly creatures, dangerous tribesmen, and lost cities, but now it was real.

Bones and Kaylin sat in the boat with him. He had not wanted to bring Kaylin into this dangerous place, but she had informed him that, should he leave her behind, she would mount her own expedition, and probably get herself killed doing it. He knew she was serious and had relented, though he had briefly contemplated marooning her on Botswain Bird Island until this was over. If he was honest with himself, he wanted her with him. He felt guilty about that, but it was what it was. He'd sort out his women problems later... much later.

Up ahead, Simáo, their guide, piloted a craft identical to the one in which they rode. Willis and Matt rode with Simáo. Only Corey had remained behind in the city of Cuiabá. He had protested, but not too vehemently. Everyone agreed he would best serve them as their link to civilization via sat phone, and could also be a go-between to Jimmy, should they need his assistance.

It had not been easy to secure a guide. There were plenty of cons in the region who would get a party lost and then demand payment to lead them back out, or who would conspire with friends to rob or even kill a party of explorers. Dane and his crew could take care of themselves, of course, and given the information Jimmy had assembled by cross-referencing Fawcett's map with satellite imagery, could probably find their way to their destination, but an experienced guide could get them there much faster. Since they had to assume ScanoGen had a good lead on them, they needed to move as quickly as possible.

It was a shame that Victor had not been in any condition to provide any helpful information which might have sped up their progress, though. After leaving his home, they had gone about hiring their guide. A priest in Mato Grosso's capital city of Cuibá had given them the names of three guides whom he knew to be reliable men, and directions to the frontier town where they could be found—the same one in which Victor and his mother resided. The first two had been interested at first, but had flatly refused when Dane had shown them a map with their probable destination marked. Neither had given a reason for his refusal, but had simply walked away.

The final candidate, Simáo, had been hesitant at first, but finally agreed, saying his wife was pregnant and he needed the money.

"Are you watching where you're going?" Kaylin's voice cut through his thoughts. Her hair was pulled back in a ponytail, and a few loose strands whipped across her face in the gentle breeze. "You look like you're in a trance."

"Just thinking about things. How about you?"

"I was just wondering what's waiting for us out there. What do you think Simáo meant when he said the 'Dead Ones' live in the area where we're going?"

"It's probably just a nickname for one of the native tribes, but it might even be one that has avoided contact, and thus legend has grown up about it. That happens here. Mato Grosso is basically the size of France and Germany put together, and very little of it has been touched by modern man."

"That's fine by me," Kaylin said, looking out at the dense greenery that lined the river.

"Me, too. The fact that such a huge place has seen so little exploration means that there really could be undiscovered people or places hiding right under the noses of modern man."

"So you think there really could be a Kephises out there waiting to be discovered?"

"Crazy as it sounds, there just might be. More likely, there's a more mundane explanation for it. Perhaps a tribe with a higher than usual prevalence of albinism sparked the legend of a lost civilization of European origin."

"That would be boring." Kaylin winked to show him she was kidding. "Whatever is out there, I hope Thomas found it, and we find him. I can't explain it, but even though I'm no longer sure he and I have a future together, I need him to be okay. Does that make sense?"

It made a lot of sense to Dane. He already felt guilty for playing both sides of the coin with Kaylin and Jade. If the situation was reversed, and something were to happen to Jade, his having feelings for Kaylin would make it feel a thousand times worse.

"You do realize you're doing way more than you're obligated to? Thomas can't possibly have expected a college art professor to go trekking into the Amazon after him."

"We've already had this discussion, Maddock. Yes, he probably imagined I would sort out the clues and then send someone in after him, but I don't care. I'm already on the expedition with you. There's no point in arguing about it now."

"That's not my point." Why did she always take his words and turn them in an entirely different direction than he intended? "What I'm saying is, no matter what happens, you've done all you can do, and then some. You have nothing to feel guilty about. Life is too short to live with guilt. Besides, there are no guarantees. It can be over in a flash. Thomas had a dream, something that drove him, and he went for it. If the news is bad, don't beat yourself up for the rest of your life. Don't let guilt stop you from being happy."

Kaylin looked surprised and a little upset, but then her expression softened. She was about to say something when Bones called back from the bow.

"Hey Maddock, are there piranha in this river?"

"Some. Why?"

"Because if I have to listen to one more minute of this relationship talk, I'm swimming for it." He pulled the brim of his Washington Nationals baseball cap down low over his eyes, folded his hands across his chest, and leaned back against a sack of provisions. "Besides, it annoys me that you obviously don't understand irony."

Kaylin flashed a wicked grin, gave Dane a satisfied look, and turned to look downriver. "How far do you think we'll have to go?"

"I don't know. The Xingu runs north all the way to the Amazon. Could be a long way." He thought about it. "Thanks to modern transportation and roadways, no matter how badly in disrepair, we've already covered a distance that took Fawcett a month or more to trek. We'll just see how it goes."

The sun beat down on them as the day wore on and the heat of the Amazon shrouded them like a blanket. Dane kept a close eye out for danger, especially the human sort. According to Simáo, the natives in the area through which they would initially travel were usually easy to deal with, provided one treated them with courtesy and respected their lands. Dane was more concerned about the threat posed by ScanoGen. He had no doubt they too were following Fawcett's trail, and he wondered what resources they might bring to bear.

By late afternoon, however, the only potential threat he had spotted was the occasional black caiman peeking up out of the water, dark eyes and black, scaly skin gleaming in the sunlight, but the deadly reptiles all kept their distance from the boats.

Up ahead, in the lead boat, Matt waved for him to pull up alongside of them. Dane brought his craft around to their starboard side and slowed to match their speed.

"Simáo says he thinks the first landmark should be up ahead. If we're reading the map correctly, we'll have to make a short portage."

"No problem," Dane said. "I'm ready to stretch my legs anyway."

When they rounded the next bend, everyone sat up straighter. Bones raised the bill of his cap and took off his sunglasses to get a better look.

"Dude, is that the ruins of some lost city?" He turned to Simáo. "How long have you known about this place?"

Their guide laughed. "Many people are fooled. It is natural formation in the rock. I can no say how it happen."

As they passed alongside the rock formations, Dane

could see how someone could mistake this place for the site of ancient construction. The natural rock lay in regular, even layers, giving the impression of stone work. Vertical shears created the illusion of corners and right angles. One shape even resembled an arched doorway.

"Man, this is unbelievable." For the first time all day, Willis actually laid down the Mossberg 501A1 shotgun he carried, and looked on in fascination. "And you're sure this ain't the real thing?"

"Is real, yes. Made by man? No."

Following Jimmy's application of the Fawcett map to modern maps, they left the river just beyond the stone formation. Dane thought they might have to search for the hidden branch of the Xingu to which they had to portage, but Bones solved that problem immediately.

"Someone's been through here. Several someones." He squatted down to inspect the ground about ten paces from the river's edge. "I see scuff marks and some bent grass."

"How long ago were they here?" Kaylin knelt down next to Bones and squinted in the direction he was looking, as if she too could see the signs.

"I'm not that good, but I appreciate your confidence in me, chick. There are a few plants back home that, if they're broken off, I can make a fair guess by the amount of wilting, but not here. I can tell you, though, that they went thataway." He pointed off into the distance, like a general commanding his troops.

Leaving the others behind, Dane and Bones scouted ahead, making sure they had a clear path for the boats. The trail snaked through a dense patch of jungle growth, leading them back toward the rock formation, where they passed between two high walls of stone that Dane, despite knowing their natural origin, still could have sworn were wrought by human hands.

They emerged on a bluff overlooking a waterfall that poured out from an underground channel below their feet, feeding a narrow river that churned its way into the jungle and out of sight.

"Somewhere back there, the Xingu runs underground and comes out here," Dane said, looking down. "And with this branch of the river being so narrow, it's no wonder it escaped the notice of map-makers. It didn't even show up on Jimmy's satellite images, though, thanks to Fawcett, we knew it was here. I'll wager not many people outside local natives even know about it."

"Dark and dangerous. Sounds like my kind of place." Bones cracked his knuckles. "So, are we ready to haul all those freakin' supplies and the boats over here?"

Dane would have groaned in mock-complaint, but just then, something caught his eye. Twenty feet away, almost completely hidden by undergrowth, a body lay face down on the ground. Dane drew his Walther and dropped to one knee. Glock in hand, Bones was at his side in an instant, looking all around.

"What are we looking for?"

"Probably nothing," Dane replied. "See that body over there?" Bones cursed at the sight. "Not a local, unless the tribes around here are African-American with a buzz cuts, t-shirts, and camo pants."

He looked around. Obviously, if anyone had a gun and meant them harm, they'd already be dead, or at least have been shot at. Besides, from the looks of things, the dead man's head had been bashed in, which meant he'd probably been attacked by a local. After they'd waited long enough to satisfy themselves that no one was about to attack them, they went for a closer look.

The back of the man's skull was crushed. Dane didn't have enough experience with such things to know how many times he'd been hit, or with what type of object, but he definitely had not been shot. He rolled the man's body over onto his back and his eyes widened in surprise.

"That's one of the dudes that came after us in London," Bones said, kneeling to check the man's pockets for identification. He came up empty. "I guess a local killed him and took whatever he was carrying."

"If he's from ScanoGen," Dane said, looking around,

"where is the rest of his group?"

"I guess they left him behind. Those are some cold characters, bro."

"Another reason I'm going to keep my eyes open and my guard up," Dane said. "Let's get those boats down to the river and see if we can't ruin their day.

CHAPTER 17

"There's the second landmark." Kennedy pointed straight ahead, where a large, gray object rose up out of the water. It was a dome-shaped rock at least ten feet high, and it looked to Tam like a giant tortoise cutting through the water as the river rushed past it on either side of it. Centuries, millennia of erosion had worn away a few inches of the base on either side, adding to the tortoise-shell illusion. Faint lines carved into its surface indicated that, at some point in the past, humans had also seen the resemblance and sought to augment it by carving a tortoise shell pattern into the stone. Had she been a tourist, she would have stopped to take pictures, but time was a luxury she did not have. In fact, it bothered her that these stray thoughts even entered her mind. What was wrong with her? She had a job to do.

"That's a relief," she said, though she hated speaking to Kennedy at all. "I was hoping the map-maker didn't intend for us to take a right at the first turtle that came swimming up to the boat."

The corner of Kennedy's mouth turned up in a false half-smile, but that was the only response. He was angry about Jay's death, but if he knew the truth, he'd kill Tam, or at least, try to. She had a feeling the two of them were headed for a reckoning sooner or later, but for now, she needed him.

"Go right at the fork," she told the guide who piloted their boat. Now that two of the landmarks had proved to be real, her confidence was bolstered, and she was eager to press on toward their destination.

"When can we stop and eat?" Even riding in a different boat, Cy managed to get on her last nerve. Despite his recent spate of screw-ups, and the death of his partner, he seemed to believe he was only a notch below Kennedy in the pecking order, and in his mind, Kennedy was at the top of the food chain on this expedition. He bullied their guides and condescended to the three ScanoGen security agents, all of whom were ex-military men Tam had brought along for extra muscle and firepower. Add in the fact that he made no bones about his belief that Tam was in charge in name only, and she was seriously considering going ahead with Salvatore's orders regarding Cy, no matter what her conscience might tell her.

"Later," she snapped. "Keep a lookout on both sides of the river for something that looks like an open mouth. Once we find it, there's a side channel somewhere around it that we'll need to take."

"Shut up and look," Kennedy snapped, not looking back at Cy. Perhaps Tam should have appreciated the support, but she knew it was simply Kennedy trying to assert some authority over the only man on this trip who was clearly loyal to him.

"If *you* say so." Cy made it clear that the "you" to whom he was referring was Kennedy, not Tam. He took off his cap and fanned at the cloud of mosquitoes that swirled around his head.

Biting and stinging insects were just a few of the minor perils of the Amazon. They all wore long pants and long-sleeved shirts, and frequently doused themselves with the finest insect repellent money could buy. Cy, however, still managed to draw a cloud of swarming pests. They hovered around him, seemingly waiting for his repellent to wear off so they could suck him dry. He complained about it incessantly, pointing out that no one else received similar treatment from the flying nuisances. She could not help but laugh at the man's petty annoyance, which was far less than he deserved.

Seated in front of her, Smithson, one of her hired guns, leaned back, let his arm hang over the edge, and trailed his fingers in the water.

"Don't do that!" Her tone was harsh. He jerked his hand back immediately and gave her a look that was a mix of annoyance and embarrassment. "You can lose a finger that way, or worse. There are piranha, caiman, snakes, even electric eels in these waters. Unless you want to lose your trigger finger, keep your hand inside the boat."

Smithson lost the annoyed look, nodded, and turned around to face forward. At least the security guys were willing to take orders from her. Rather, they had been willing up to this point. She worried that Kennedy would insinuate himself in-between her and the men. She would just have to deal with that as it came.

Shafts of late afternoon sun bathed the river in a burnished orange glow when they finally spotted it. The river twisted sharply to the left, and directly in front of them loomed the arched outline of a dark cave. Its façade resembled a macabre face. The cave was the mouth, a stone jutted out directly above the opening, forming the nose, and jungle growth hung like thick hair up above it.

"If that's our landmark," Kennedy said, "where's the side channel?"

"I think we're supposed to go inside the cave." A deep sense of foreboding filled Tam. She didn't like the look of this cave, but she knew she was right. She could tell by the flow of the water that the cave was not a dead end, but a passage leading… somewhere.

Kennedy turned to her. "Have the third boat take the lead."

She understood his thinking. The third boat held supplies, a security agent, a guide, and Andy, the professor of whom she was to dispose since he had no useful information to offer. To Kennedy's way of thinking, they were the most expendable.

To her mind, however, she was at least a little more certain of the loyalty of her handpicked members of the expedition than that of Cy or Kennedy, though the guides frequently gave her dark looks, and muttered under their breath when she gave them orders. Besides, it wasn't his place to give orders to her, even if he had almost made it seem like a suggestion. At least he hadn't given the order outright, a sign that he, too, thought the guides and security men might properly acknowledge her as leader.

She decided to split the difference. *She* wasn't expendable, but Cy was. She instructed the guide piloting his boat to take the lead. Cy probably should have been annoyed, but he quickly rummaged for a flashlight, drew his side arm, and crouched over the bow like an eager pirate ready for plunder.

Kennedy gave her a dirty look, which she met with a smirk. "You know what Salvatore's instructions are in regard to our friend Cyrus," she said softly. "Maybe something in there will do the job for us."

Kennedy looked, for a moment, like he was about to argue, but he held his tongue. He turned around and fixed his eyes on their destination.

The cool, moist air of the cave was a welcome relief from the oppressive heat on the river. Nonetheless, Tam did not relax. Weapon in hand, she played her light back and forth in the darkness, wondering what might lay in wait. Her mind conjured images of vampire bats, or the glowing eyes of a jaguar lying in wait.

Her pulse quickened as they penetrated deeper into the darkness. The low ceiling gave her the feeling that the world was pressing down upon her. As they passed through the tunnel, the water was filled with sharp rocks that had to be carefully skirted, lest they damage their boats. Several times the boats hung up on the shallow bottom, and they were forced to get out and drag them, all the time worrying about the dangers that might lurk in the dark water just out of sight.

She breathed a deep sigh of relief when they finally emerged unscathed into a mist-shrouded lagoon. It was nearly sundown; the waning light and the thick canopy of the jungle cast the place in sinister shadows.

She spotted a clearing on the far side of the lagoon and directed them to go ashore there to set up camp. The jungle was silent here, and when they cut the engines and let the boats glide the last few feet to shore, the discomfort she felt in the cave filled her again.

Her grandmother had taught her that some places were "just bad," and were to be avoided. She hadn't meant dangerous places, like bad neighborhoods, but wicked places, places where evil resided so strongly that one could literally feel it. Tam had never believed her, but now she did. This was a bad place.

It happened in the blink of an eye. There was a sudden blur of motion as something sprang up from underneath a low-hanging branch. The guide in the lead boat had only a moment to cry out in surprise and pain before something clamped down on the back of his neck. Tam's mind registered only a flash of olive and yellow before the man was snatched down into the water.

"Anaconda!" she cried, springing to her feet and almost capsizing their boat. Her Makarov was in her hand and her head was on a swivel, searching for a target.

Kennedy, cursing like a sailor, fired blindly into the water. The lagoon was filled with shouts as the two remaining guides called their friend's name, while Cy cried out in panic and dove for the unattended motor. All the boat engines suddenly roared to life as everyone tried to get to shore as fast as human possible.

Tam wobbled as their boat struck ground, but she kept her feet and sprang nimbly onto shore. Their guides scrambled out of their boats and fled blindly into the jungle. Everyone else stood watching and waiting.

"Over there!" Cy shouted as, on the far side of the lagoon, the water roiled and a mass of coils surfaced for an instant. Only the man's left arm was visible, desperately tugging at one of the coils. Cy and the two agents sent a flurry of bullets in the anaconda's direction, but if they hit it, there was no sign.

"Stop!" Tam shouted. "You're wasting ammunition. There's nothing we can do for him now, and we don't know what else we might run into." Deep in her bones, she knew her words to be prophetic. Something told her their troubles had only just begun.

CHAPTER 18

This place was wrong. Everything about it sent up warning flares in Dane's subconscious mind. He scanned the shore of the lagoon, but saw no obvious threats. Of course, in the Amazon, the unseen threat was often more dangerous than the one you saw coming.

"I don't know, dude." Bones was searching the trees with the same intensity as Dane. "There's some serious wrongness here. It's too quiet, and I don't know what else, but I feel it."

"Man, check out that snake." From the other boat, Willis pointed to a spot along the bank where the biggest anaconda Dane had ever seen lay sunning itself.

Bones cursed and reached for his Glock, but Dane grabbed him by the wrist. "Don't bother. Looks like it's already eaten."

Bones's eyes went wide when he saw what Dane had already noticed. The middle of the snake's body was swollen and distended almost beyond recognition, but it was evident that its last meal had been a human being.

"He won't be going after anyone for a while. He'll be too slow, and won't have much of an appetite. What we need to do is make certain there are no brothers and sisters ready to make a meal out of us."

All eyes went to the surrounding trees, scanning the branches for the giant predators. Matt hefted his Heckler and Koch MP5 submachine gun and his expression made it clear he was ready to shred anything that moved. Willis kept his Mossberg trained on the sunning anaconda, his finger on the trigger. He despised snakes, and all manner of what he termed, "squiggly things."

"Come on Maddock! Let me take care of this thing." In the shadowed lagoon, Willis's eyes seemed to glow against his dark skin. "It ain't hungry now, but it just might be by the time we come back this way."

"No. The ScanoGen people might be somewhere close by, and they'd hear the gunshot. If it can be helped, I don't want to warn them that we're catching up to them." They had taken a risk and traveled through the night. One person in each boat took a turn piloting the craft while the other two slept in the bottom of the boat, using mosquito netting for a blanket.

They had not let Kaylin take a turn, a decision about which she vigorously protested. Dane reminded her that she was on this expedition against his better judgment, and that her carping was liable to draw the attention of unfriendly natives or worse. Now she satisfied herself with the occasional resentful look, or an "I told you so" stare whenever Dane or Bones yawned.

"Fawcett claimed to have killed an anaconda that was sixty-two feet long." Kaylin gazed at the snake in admiration. "He was generally ridiculed by scientists, but I think he might have been telling the truth. That thing has got to be close to that long." She raised her camera and snapped a few pictures. "Hey Bones, why don't you swim over there and stand next to it so I can get some scale perspective?" She winked at him.

"Will my middle finger be enough scale for you?" The anaconda chose that moment to slither away at a glacial pace, slowed no doubt by its heavy burden. "See that? It's camera shy."

The banter ceased as Dane's boat slid gently onto the bank, followed moments later by the second craft. Willis and Matt sprang out of their boat like commandos storming the beach, alert for danger.

"You're not fooling anybody," Bones told them as he

helped Kaylin to shore. "You two think if you stand there like you're on guard duty, you won't have to help unload the boats."

"True that," Willis said. "But I got out first, so guess I'm gonna be the guard." He looked at Matt, who was glowering at him. "What? What? You too slow, ranger boy. Get to work."

"How did I ever get lassoed into hanging out with a bunch of SEALs?" Matt slung his MP5 across his back and turned to help Simáo unload their boat, while Dane and Kaylin unloaded the other. In a matter of minutes, they had divided their provisions and loaded up a backpack for each person. Matt and Willis hid their boats within a thick stand of trees, camouflaging them with foliage. Bones, meanwhile, scouted the jungle nearby. He returned just as the rest of the group was donning their packs and getting ready to move.

"We're definitely in the right place," he pronounced, "and so is ScanoGen. They left plenty of prints on their way out of town. I also found their boats hidden close by."

"Hopefully that means the guy inside the anaconda is one of theirs." Matt bared his teeth in something between a grimace and a grin.

"How many boats did they have?" Dane wondered how many men they'd be facing.

"Three. I couldn't guess their numbers by the tracks they left behind." Bones was thinking along the same lines as Dane. "But if you figure they needed room for supplies, there can't be more than a dozen in their group. Probably fewer."

"Minus the one inside the snake," Matt added.

"All right. Let's move on, then." Dane consulted the map on which Jimmy had projected their path, then re-checked Fawcett's rough map. "It looks like we're headed that way." He pointed in the direction from which Bones had come. "Think we should just follow ScanoGen's trail?"

"As long as they're on the right track, why not?" Bones nodded. "If it looks like they're drifting off course, we'll change directions."

"We'll need to move as quietly as possible." Willis and Matt did not need to be told, and perhaps neither did Kaylin and Simáo, but Dane did not wish to leave anything to chance. He and Bones took the lead, with Matt and Willis bringing up the rear.

The farther they trekked from the lagoon, the denser the jungle grew, with the shafts of sunlight sifting through the treetops fewer and farther between. The unnerving silence continued, with no sounds of any kind, save their soft treads and the occasional rustle of branches up above. He glanced back to check on the others. Kaylin appeared transfixed by the beauty and mystery of this dark place untouched by modern civilization, though her knuckles were white from the tight grip with which she held her M6 Scout, a multi-purpose weapon, an over-under weapon that fired both .410 shotgun shells and .22 bullets. It wasn't a high-powered combat weapon, but it was the right fit for her. Dane had no concerns about her using the weapon. She was the daughter of his and Bones' former commander, and knew how to handle any number of firearms.

Simáo, on the other hand, was trembling and sweating profusely. He periodically stopped short, aiming his bolt-action hunting rifle in the direction of some unseen enemy. The third time he did this, Bones threatened to take the weapon away from him. The guide shook his head profusely and muttered something in his native tongue; but after the scolding, he ceased pointing his rifle at every sound.

They had hiked for hours, following the trail left by ScanoGen, when the path suddenly fell away in a deep trench that had been reclaimed by the native flora. Dane halted at the edge and held his hand up for everyone to stop. It was difficult to discern the lay of the land beneath the dense foliage, but he could make out a series of circular terraces rising up behind the trench. This was not a natural formation, but something many centuries old, or perhaps older.

"It's like a moat," Kaylin whispered, looking down at the circular ditch that wrapped around the terraces. "They've found formations like this in Xingu National Park, though not as formidable as this."

"This must be the next landmark." Bones tapped the paper Dane held in his hand. The image, carved so long ago, looked like a layer cake, and had baffled Dane until this moment.

"Circular terraces, one on top of the other, ringed by a ditch. You're right. This is it." His heart pounded. Despite the perils inherent to the Amazon, he would have been thrilled with the tantalizing possibility of discovery, were they not facing the threat of armed men from ScanoGen somewhere up ahead. "Okay, the map makes it look like we're supposed to go right over the top of this thing. I wonder if we couldn't just go around?"

"Help me!" No sooner had the faint voice floated up from somewhere below than the crack of rifle fire shattered the silence. "Don't shoot! Please!"

Cursing, Bones snatched Simáo's rifle and gave the man a shove. He landed hard on his backside and sat glaring at Bones in bitter resentment.

"Don't you realize there are people out there who want to kill us?" Bones hissed. "If they're anywhere close by, they heard your shot, and they know we're right behind them. Idiot!"

"I thought it was the dead ones." The man trembled, the anger already gone from his eyes.

Dane didn't have time for native superstition. He raised his M-16. "Whoever you are," he called down into the ditch, "come out slowly."

A small, bedraggled man crawled out of the foliage and wobbled to his feet. Dane could not imagine anyone looking more out of place in the depths of the Amazon than this slender, fair-skinned man.

"Andy!" Kaylin gasped. "What are you doing here?"

"You know him?" Dane frowned.

"This is Thomas's colleague. The man who gave me the Fawcett picture! The one who was kidnapped."

Dane gave Andy a hand up the embankment, and the

little man stood trembling as Kaylin hugged him. His quaking finally eased enough that he accepted a drink of water from Matt's canteen before sinking to the ground.

"Tell us how you got here." Dane squatted down so he could look Andy in the eye. Depending on how long the man had been wandering in the jungle, his information might not be reliable. He seemed lucid, however, as he began his explanation.

"The people who kidnapped me brought me down here with them. I didn't understand at first. I mean, I didn't know anything at all about Thomas or what he was up to. They held me forever, it seemed like. They'd interrogate me, sometimes hurt me, but I didn't know anything. Finally, I started making up stuff just to get them to stop, but I think they knew I was lying." He swallowed hard. "I thought they were going to kill me, but one day they told me I was going on a trip, and they brought me out here."

"I don't get it," Dane said. "Weren't they taking a risk bringing you along?"

Andy managed a rueful laugh. "What danger am I? They've got all these fancy weapons, and they all look like... them." He pointed at Matt and Willis. "And you guys." He nodded at Dane and Bones. "They didn't even handcuff me or anything. Just shoved me into the plane, then the helicopter, and so forth. When we got to the edge of nowhere, the girl told me I was free to run away any time I wanted. Everybody laughed like it was some big joke, which it was. I'm useless."

"What girl are you talking about?"

"Her name's Tam, or at least, that's what they call her. She's in charge, but I don't think the guys in her group like that very much. She questioned me at different times along the way, stuff about Thomas. I tried to bluff her into believing I knew some final clue, thinking she'd keep me alive, but she didn't buy it. They kept making little comments about getting rid of me. We'd see a caiman and this one guy, Cy, would say it looked hungry for professor meat, stuff like that. I was starting to wish they'd just go ahead and get it over with. I hate this place." He glanced up at the trees and shuddered.

"So, how did you manage to get away?" Dane could not conceive that this little academic had outfought or outwitted his captors.

"She let me go."

"She let you go. Just like that?" Bones interjected, suspicion heavy in every word.

Andy shook his head. "We got up to the top of that hill, or whatever you call it," He indicated the terraces, "and we found the tunnel."

Bones did a double-take. "What tunnel…"

"That can wait." Dane said. "One thing at a time. Go ahead, Andy."

"So, the others started going down into the tunnel, and the girl told them to give her five minutes, because she had something she needed to do. She took me down into the ditch, fired her gun off into the woods, and then gave me a canteen and told me to stay hidden until she came back for me, and that's exactly what I did until you got here."

"That's odd." Dane rubbed his chin. "Do you know anything about her? Anything at all?"

"She's a killer. She doesn't know I saw, but I watched her bash a guy's skull in with a rock because he put his hands on her. She told the others a native had done it. I don't know if they believed her, or if they just didn't care. Every one of them is cold-blooded."

Dane remembered finding the body of the dead man. "How many of them are there?"

"Eight," Andy said after a moment's thought. "There were eleven, including me. Tam killed the one guy and an anaconda got another." He shivered. "Two of the remaining guys are guides, locals, but they seem as nasty as the rest of the group."

"So, five professionals at most. I'll take those odds." Bones patted his M-16. "Do they have any idea we're after them?"

Andy shook his head. "I don't think so. At least, they

didn't let on that anyone was after them. I heard one of them, Kennedy, say they had the only map, so I'm guessing they think they're in this alone."

"Good." Dane smiled. "Let them go on thinking that. How far ahead of us are they?"

"Less than a day. It was just this morning she let me go. I don't think I'd have lasted through the night, though. I already drank all the water she left me and lost the canteen while trying to get to you."

"It's all right. We're glad you found us." Kaylin gave him a reassuring pat on the shoulder.

Dane disagreed, but there was no point in saying so. Andy wasn't cut out for this environment, and was liable to get himself killed. Dane doubted the professor was even capable of walking quietly in the woods.

"I will not go!" Simáo, like the others, had been listening in silence, but now he was on his feet. "That hole is the… the doorway to the land of the dead ones! You will all die if you go there."

Dane contemplated this turn. They didn't need Simáo. Frankly, they had really only needed his boats, but his services as guide had come with the rental. He had been of some use at the outset, but as soon as they left the beaten path, he had been of little help.

"Can you find your way back to the boats?" The man nodded. "Bones, the ScanoGen boats. Could you hotwire one if you had to?" Bones rolled his eyes, which, coming from Bones, was a strong affirmative. "All right. Give him back his rifle." Bones gave him a quizzical look, but handed the weapon back to Simáo.

"I want you," Dane said to the guide, "to take Andy here back to the boats. If you ration them, your provisions will hold the two of you long enough to get back to your village. Look out for him until we come back, and I'll double what we paid you."

Simáo nodded vigorously. He likely would have agreed to anything that would get him out of this place and away from the "dead ones," whoever they were.

Dane turned to Kaylin, but she waved him away.

"Don't even bother, Maddock. I'm staying with you all the way."

"But we know where the ScanoGen people are now, and we're headed right for them. You'll be safest if you keep as far away from them as possible."

"I'm safest with you." Her tone was hot, but her eyes were soft. "I always have been."

Dane could tell it was pointless to press the argument any farther. They bade Andy and Simáo goodbye and good luck, and headed down into the ditch.

The climb to the top terrace was a challenging one, and they were all scratched and dirty when they reached the top. Dane took a breather and looked around. The mound on which they stood was below the level of the tallest trees. All he could see in every direction was dark green.

Chunks of sod and rotten wood lay strewn about, indicating the opening to the tunnel had been camouflaged prior to the arrival of ScanoGen. *Less work for us*, Dane thought.

The way down was a dark, sloping passage with no obvious steps or handholds. Dane leaned closer for a better look, and crinkled his nose at the dank, musty air.

"Too bad there's no rain," Bones said, kneeling down next to him. "This would make one hell of a waterslide."

Dane chuckled. "Actually, I know we haven't had any luck since we left the main branch of the Xingu, but if we can get a signal, we should try to raise Corey on the sat phone before we go down there. Maybe Jimmy can pinpoint our location before we go in."

"What's the matter, Maddock?" Bones elbowed him. "Afraid we're going to get us a little Jules Verne action going on underground? Maybe slide to the center of the earth?"

"Afraid we'll get to the bottom and have no way back up is more like it. I'm surprised the ScanoGen people didn't secure a rope before they went down, in case they had to climb back out."

"Well, we can't all be as smart as you, Maddock."

Matt tried, but was unable to get any connection with

the sat phone. Dane wondered what Corey was thinking right now, sitting and waiting for them to check in, and hearing nothing. Everyone took a moment to secure their packs and get ready to move.

Dane stood, looked down into the waiting darkness, and then back at his friends.

"All right, who wants to be the first one down into the creepy, dark tunnel?"

CHAPTER 19

"Everything is going as planned, gentlemen. My team is in the process of completing the job as we speak. I estimate we shall be able to move on to the next stage of the project in less than two weeks time." Salvatore stared across the table at the two smartly-dressed men in power suits and forced a polite smile.

Senator Nathan Roman of Utah, member of the Senate Arms Committee, sat back, a condescending smile painting his face. "You understand, Mister Scano, that we can tolerate no more delays. There are deadlines to be met, and you are far behind the promised timetable. If we are forced to start over somewhere else, I fear our armed forces will choose to do business elsewhere. In fact, the government might be forced to dig deeper into some of ScanoGen's more questionable practices."

The man did not intimidate Salvatore in the least. A Senator, no matter how powerful, derived his power from the consent of the governed, a fickle lot at best. One scandal and the good senator just might find himself back in Utah selling real estate. In fact, the groundwork for such a scandal had already been laid in the form of a young lady who would soon be leaking cell phone pictures of the senator engaged in some very embarrassing costume play. And that was just the tip of the iceberg. He glanced at David, and saw a shadow of a smile cross the man's face. Senator Roman would play ball soon enough. It was the other man who worried them.

"Now, now, Nathan. There is no need to bandy threats. Mister Scano and ScanoGen have always been reliable business partners, and doubtless that will not change. I have every confidence in them." The man turned an icy smile toward Salvatore.

Frederick Hadel was an enigma. He was the leading figure in a large, independent religious organization known as The Kingdom Church. What bothered Salvatore was that was all they knew about him. Hadel had clout, there was no denying it, but how much he had, and whom he had under his thumb, had eluded Salvatore and his people. That bothered him.

"Senator Roman simply wants you to understand how important this project is to us," Hadel continued. He paused to take a sip of tea. "It is no longer merely a matter of scientific speculation. The work your people have already done has set an excellent foundation, and major plans have been laid with that work at its core. We must, however, move forward."

"Your concern is duly noted, Mr. Hadel," David assured him.

"Bishop Hadel, if you please. Perhaps it is vanity, but I do prefer to be addressed by my title. I worked very hard to earn it."

"My apologies." David made a placating gesture. "It did take some time, but things have fallen into place. Our people are on the ground as we speak."

"I have people of my own at the ready if you require assistance." Hadel raised his eyebrows. "I can call on them at a moment's notice."

"That will not be necessary, but we appreciate the offer." Salvatore stood and David quickly followed suit. "Your concerns are duly noted."

Hadel and Roman exchanged looks, clearly not appreciating the curt dismissal. Finally, the two stood, and Roman shook hands with David and Salvatore.

"We will talk again in two weeks," Roman added, squeezing Salvatore's hand tighter than was necessary. The imbecile actually believed that, in the twenty-first century, musculature was a sign of power? He would not last long in Washington.

"I look forward to it." Salvatore tapped a button on his phone, indicating that Alex, who was temporarily and unhappily filling Tam's role as receptionist, should see his guests out.

Hadel stepped through the doorway, paused, and turned back to Salvatore and David. "Traffic in the Washington area is dangerous, is it not?"

"It is." Salvatore had no idea where Hadel was going with this, but he was certain the man would not bring it up without reason.

"Perhaps you heard about the death of a dear colleague, Reverend Felts. He was killed in a tragic accident very recently."

"Yes, I did hear something about that." Salvatore kept his tone conversational, but his mind was racing. How much did Hadel know?

"Truly a tragedy." Hadel grimaced. "How Reverend Felts, who was a competent driver without a blemish on his driving record, could have run off the road like that is beyond me." Now he looked Salvatore in the eye. "I wish I could say I was sorry to hear the news, but I fear my friend had lost his way. It is a shame, but accidents do happen." His smile was mirthless and his eyes cold.

"Yes they do," Salvatore agreed.

Hadel nodded and closed the door.

"He knows." David's fists were clenched tight. "He knows we are behind Felts's death, and he obviously approves. Why doesn't he just say so?"

"He's sending us a message." Salvatore pursed his lips. He wants us to think we can't do anything without him knowing about it." Perhaps it was the truth. So much they did not know about Hadel.

"So, do I proceed with our plans regarding the senator?" David eyed him in trepidation.

Salvatore took a deep breath. "Hold off until Tam has

completed her mission. Perhaps it will not be necessary." He hated the feeling that someone else was controlling him, but he had not risen this far by putting ego before wisdom. *Tam,* he thought, *do not let me down.*

CHAPTER 20

Dane was the first into the tunnel. The initial drop was so steep that he was forced to slide down, using his Recon 1 knife as a brake to control his descent. About fifty feet down, the way became less steep, and he was able to stand, though he kept a steadying hand on the ceiling, which was no more than six feet high.

"Come on down!" he called to the others. "Bones and Willis, the ceiling's low, so don't bump your heads when you stand up!"

Kaylin came down, springing gracefully to her feet at the end of her slide. Her eyes widened as she played her light down the tunnel. "Awesome!"

"You sound like Bones." Dane had to grin. Though Kaylin looked like she belonged behind a news desk or reporting from the sideline of a college football game, she was a Navy brat through and through, and wouldn't let something like a dark tunnel bother her.

"Oh well. You're the one who keeps him around. If he rubs off on me, it's not my fault." The rest of the group joined them in short order and they proceeded down the passageway.

The floor was made of stone, but the walls and ceiling were lined with wood, much of it succumbing to various stages of decay. Roots peeked out in various places and Dane wondered if they were strengthening or weakening the structure. He hoped it was the former.

"This whole place looks like it could come down at any

moment," Kaylin observed, shining her light on the ceiling. So engrossed was she in the construction of the passageway that she almost didn't see the pit in front of them.

Dane grabbed her by the arm and snatched her back just as her foot came down on… nothing. He shone his light down on a deep pit. Twenty feet below them, a body lay impaled on a wooden stake. Other stakes lay shattered on the floor, confirmation of Dane's assessment of the weakened condition of the wood due to years of dry rot. One of the stakes, though, had held together, to the detriment of the man who had fallen. He was lying on his stomach, the stake jutting out of the small of his back. His face was turned to the side, and Dane could make out his native features.

"One of the guides," Bones observed. They're down to seven. Sweet!"

"Hey! Anybody got a notepad or an index card?" Willis looked around at the others, grinning.

"What for?" Kaylin cocked her head to the side.

"I want to make a scorecard, like baseball. I know I'll kill more of them than y'all." He elbowed Matt.

"Want to put some money on that? A hundred bucks?" Matt offered his hand to shake on it.

"Hell, Army boy, you don't even *get* to be on the scorecard. You're gonna' carry my backpack and let the SEALs do the killing." Laughter drowned Matt's profane response.

Beyond the pit, the tunnel sloped down and they were again forced to descend in a controlled slide. Dane kept a sharp eye out for more pits or other hazards, all the while thinking that the condition of the tunnel made the whole place a potential booby trap.

Faint light glimmered in the distance and they reached the bottom of the tunnel without incident. Weapons at the ready, they followed the winding passageway toward the glow that grew brighter the farther they progressed.

They emerged in a deep canyon, walled in by sheer cliffs that ran out of sight to the north and south as far as the eye could see.

"No wonder they had to build the tunnel." Dane looked behind them at the wall of stone. "There's no way you could climb down that."

"Speak for yourself," Bones said. "I am Spider-Man on rock walls."

Dane rolled his eyes. "And," he turned back around, "no telling how far this canyon runs. This might be the only way across for miles or more."

"This place has a weird vibe to it." Willis stepped forward, looking all around, his eyes narrowed and his jaw set. "It feels like we don't belong here."

He was right. The canyon was very different from the jungle through which they had trekked thus far. The trees here were smaller and grew farther apart than they had up above. It was as if the valley had once been cleared, but later left to lie fallow. On the opposite side of the valley, a waterfall poured over the canyon rim.

"It's like a lost world," Kaylin whispered.

"Let's hope it's not as dangerous as the one from the book." Dane's eyes scanned the valley, all his senses alive, seeking out any potential threat, but the silence was complete.

"Looks safe to me," Bones said. "Should we keep following ScanoGen's tracks?" He didn't wait for Dane to say yes, but moved ahead.

They had walked only five minutes or so when they came upon an abandoned campsite. Four tents had been slashed and trampled, and camping gear lay strewn everywhere. Dane noticed a spatter of something dark on a tree trunk, and took a closer look.

"Looks like blood," he said to Kaylin, who was peering over his shoulder. "Can you tell anything from the tracks?" He called to Bones.

"Only that everyone scattered in a big hurry." He looked at Dane. "There are about five paths we could follow, and I assume you want to stay together?" Dane nodded. "Good call, I think. So, the question is, which path do you want to follow first?"

Dane pondered the question. They had come to the end of Fawcett's imperfect map. They did not know the final landmark, which left following ScanoGen, or wandering until they found something as their only choices. The first option was out for the moment and the second was unappealing.

A shot rang out in the distance, breaking the silence, and then another.

"That way," he said, pointing toward the waterfall on the opposite side of the canyon. He wasn't sure why he chose it as their destination, except that it would be an easy landmark for everyone to find should they get split up. That, and it just felt like the right way to go. "Everyone stay concealed as much as you can, and be careful."

CHAPTER 21

Cy felt like a bumper car as he careened from tree-to-tree in his mad dash for safety. He had emptied his rifle and hadn't had time to reload before being forced to abandon it. His pistol was gone, dropped in the midst of hand-to-hand fighting with those freakish, silent natives that had swarmed their camp.

They won't die!

He had put bullets in a half-dozen of them at least, and stabbed one in the gut, but they kept coming! What were these things? Zombies? Couldn't be, but he had no explanation for how a man could take a bullet in the chest and keep coming. He had seen Kennedy blow the leg off of one and it kept on crawling forward like it hadn't felt a thing. That's when Cy panicked and ran.

He could hear the sound of the waterfall somewhere up ahead. His only hope was that Tam had been correct in her assertion that the final landmark would be found somewhere in its vicinity. If he could find it, maybe he could get away from these… things.

A limb smacked him across the face and he reflexively covered his eyes. He stumbled a few steps, and then the ground went out from under his feet. He had only a moment to cry out in surprise before he was enveloped in cold darkness.

Water filled his mouth and nose, and he choked. His feet hit the slimy bottom and he pushed up. He emerged gasping and coughing. He vomited a stream of water, and then blew out through each nostril, clearing them.

Eyes burning, he looked around to see he was in a dark waterway surrounded on all sides by thick vegetation. The channel was straight and narrow, obviously man-made, and he could see that it cut a straight path to the waterfall! His feeling of relief was cut short by a rustling in the foliage.

The jungle growth parted, revealing two of the natives armed with primitive stone axes. They were broad-shouldered with glossy black hair and weird orange body paint with black spots, like a giraffe. What made them frightening were the blank, inhuman eyes that gazed down on him as if he were no more than a fly to be swatted. He heard a sound behind him and whirled to see another of the zombie-like warriors emerge, pointing a spear at Cy's chest.

Cy slowly raised his hands above his head. There was no fighting, no running, only the hope of surrender.

"Please." He was so frightened that he didn't know if he had said the word aloud or not. The native pressed the tip of his spear against Cy's throat, and Cy felt his bladder release.

Excruciating pain, the like of which he had never imagined was possible, erupted not in his throat, but his groin. He screamed in pain and staggered back, clutching his burning genitals.

Perhaps taken by surprise, the native drew back his spear, leaned down for a closer look at him, and then looked at his companions. Was it possible that a ghost of a smile played across his stony face?

A fragment of a memory flashed through Cy's mind as his body crumpled down into the water in sheer agony. Something he had learned about the Amazon and its native fish.

Candiru.

Enters the urethra.

Locks its spines in place.

Agonizing death.

He screamed again, staggered backward, and found himself facing the two club-bearing warriors. "Please," he wailed. This time he was not begging for his life, but for release from this agony.

Still staring at him with empty eyes, one of them raised his club and brought it down in a swift motion. The world fled, and with it, the pain.

Tam ducked down in the shadow of a thick shrub, her Makarov at the ready. Kennedy crouched beside her, his eyes gleaming with the thrill of battle. How had she gotten stuck with him? This would be a good time to put a cap in him, but she probably needed all the allies she could get against this swarm of seemingly-unstoppable natives. Well, that wasn't entirely accurate. They'd killed several, but they were nigh-impossible to bring down, and didn't seem to feel pain the way a normal human being would.

"See if you can raise ScanoGen on the sat phone," Kennedy barked. "Maybe they can get a read on our position and send help." The tone of his voice said it was futile, but they were in a desperate situation.

"Already did," Tam lied. "They said they'd do what they could for us, but it would take some time."

"That's not very promising." Kennedy scowled, still searching the surroundings for the natives.

"It is what it is. We can't count on anyone but ourselves to get out of this." She bit her lip. How was she not only going to get out of this situation alive, but then get away from Kennedy?

"Have you figured out the final landmark yet?" he snapped. "That would help."

"Yes!" Sudden inspiration struck her and she forced down a smile. "It's that rock formation up there." She pointed to a nondescript outcropping.

"How can you tell?" Kennedy tilted his head to the side and squinted. "It doesn't look like a skull."

"You have to see it from the other side. I was trying to work my way to it when these… things blocked my way, and I had to double-back. That's it though, I'm sure of it. Think we should make a break for it?"

"Why not?" Kennedy sneered. "Even if you're wrong, I'd rather be doing something than hiding here like a scared woman."

Tam didn't know if that last comment was meant as an insult to her, or was simply a reflection of his misogyny. She was just happy to see Kennedy take off at a dead sprint in the direction she had indicated. *Scared woman? How about gullible man?* Hopefully, he'd get himself killed. If not, she had bought herself enough time to get to the waterfall and see whether or not her theory was correct. She raised her Makarov and took a deep breath.

Time to roll the dice.

CHAPTER 22

Dane stopped and dropped to one knee as dark figures appeared from the cover of the surrounding trees, stalking toward them. They were natives, armed with axes, spears, clubs, and wooden sword-like weapons with teeth, probably those of a caiman, set in either edge like the Aztec macuahitl. Oddly, they didn't charge Dane and his party, nor did they halt, but stalked toward them, weapons at the ready.

"Stop! Don't come any closer!" Dane shouted, hoping they would get the gist of his words, despite the language barrier. No luck.

He fired off a warning shot with his M-16 just over the head of the foremost warrior, held up his hand with his palm toward them, and again shouted for them to stop. It didn't do any good.

They charged.

Gunfire opened up on all sides, shredding the line of attacking natives. Some stumbled, some reeled or staggered backward.

But they did not go down.

Bloodied and torn, the warriors kept coming. Some stumbled forward, slowed by their wounds, but none of them stopped.

Willis, pumping and firing his Mossberg at a steady rate, blew the legs out from under an attacker. The man tumbled to the ground, shook his head, and began crawling forward. Willis fired another shot, taking the man in the top of the head, and he lay still.

"No body shots!" Dane ordered. "Legs or head!"

"That's what I'm talking about!" Bones shouted, taking aim with his M-16 and hitting an attacker with a clean head shot. Matt opened up with his MP 5 submachine gun, spraying a thigh-high stream of lead across the line of attackers. The withering gunfire was taking its toll, sending the attackers to the ground, but more were appearing, drawn by the sounds of gunfire.

Dane emptied his M-16, drew his Walther, and opened up on the attackers. "Everybody retreat back to the tunnel entrance!" Dane ordered.

"No can do, boss man." Bones spoke as calmly as if he were discussing the weather. "They're behind us."

Dane glanced back to see an even larger group of warriors stalking toward them. They wouldn't be getting through that way any time soon.

"Scatter and meet up at the waterfall!" he called. "Kaylin, follow me!"

He dashed to their left, where only a few warriors stood in their way. Two shots with his Walther put bullets through two skulls. He trained his weapon on the next warrior who impeded his path, and was about to pull the trigger when Kaylin screamed.

His shot caught the attacker in the shoulder, and he turned to see Kaylin use her shotgun to deflect a spear thrust by a warrior who had just emerged from behind a tree. He had time to fire off a hasty shot that caught Kaylin's attacker in the chest before the warrior whom he'd shot in the shoulder was on him.

Dane ducked beneath the vicious stroke of the primitive sword, and fired off two rounds into the man's chest, emptying his clip. The warrior staggered backward, but before Dane could finish the job, another attacker charged in, from behind. Still holding his M-16 in his left hand, Dane deflected the downstroke of the man's club, but the rifle was battered from his hand. He lashed out with his right foot, sweeping the stumbling warrior's legs out from under him, and delivered a kick to the temple. The warrior groaned and slumped to the ground.

He heard someone coming at him from behind. Dropping his empty Walther, he snatched up the warrior's club, drew his Recon knife, and turned to face the second attacker, who was charging back in despite gouts of blood pouring from twin holes in his chest. They didn't seem to feel pain, but surely loss of blood would take its toll. The problem was, before that happened, the man just might live long enough to finish Dane off.

The warrior, snarling through gritted teeth, swung his weapon in a deadly arc with much more speed and precision than Dane would have expected from someone who had taken two bullets to the chest. Dane dodged the stroke and lashed out with his knife, opening a cut on the man's arm. It might as well have been a mosquito bite for all the difference it made. The tooth-lined sword came around in a vicious backhand stroke. Dane deflected it with the club and stabbed twice for the heart in rapid succession. The warrior staggered backward, clearly on his last legs. He raised his weapon, his arms quaking, but before he could bring it down, Dane leapt in, opened his throat with the Recon knife, and shoved him backward, where he landed atop his stunned tribesman, who was just beginning to rise.

Dane retrieved and reloaded his Walther, then finished each man with a head shot. His life no longer in immediate danger, he looked around for Kaylin. Her shotgun lay abandoned on the ground, but she was gone.

Kaylin fled from the natives with reckless abandon. She didn't know which way she was headed, and she didn't care. All that concerned her right now was getting away from the silent attackers who, despite their usual measured paces, could move quite fast when they wanted to.

She leapt across a fallen log and landed awkwardly. Her ankle rolled over and she went down in a heap, pain shooting up her leg. Something moved behind her, and she reached for her .380, but she was too slow. A sharp blow to the head sent flares of pain through her skull and stars swirled across her field of vision.

Strong hands hauled her to her feet, and she felt someone relieve her of her pistol and knife. She stamped down on the man's foot, eliciting a grunt of surprise, and spun, throwing out an elbow, but she struck only air. Her injured ankle twisted beneath her as she spun, throwing her off-balance, and a blow to her stomach sent the breath shooting out of her in a rush. Before she could recover, her assailant had her by the hair, raising her head. She felt the cold pressure of steel against her throat, and she froze.

"What have we here?" A tall, blocky man with a scarred cheek, outfitted in jungle camouflage stepped in front of her. He had the bearing of a military man, his every move suggesting scarcely-contained danger. "You would be Kaylin Maxwell, Thomas Thornton's special friend."

She finally regained her breath, gasping and coughing, still very much mindful of the blade pressed against her throat by unseen hands. "Who are you?" she croaked.

"I represent the company who paid Doctor Thornton a lot of money to do a job. He didn't live up to his end of the bargain, and I'm here to find out why."

"He's lost out here in the jungle is why, you idiot!" She didn't know where the words came from, because she was more frightened than she had ever been in her entire life. Perhaps she had just enough of her father in her to give her a measure of courage.

The man slapped her, just hard enough to sting. The coppery taste of blood filled her mouth. She spat at him but he sidestepped, and slapped her again, this time on her ear. A loud pop like a bursting balloon made her ears ring.

"No more playing around. I want answers." He drew his knife and moved in close.

"I won't tell you anything. You're just going to kill me anyway."

"Oh yes. But if you tell me what I need to know, we won't make it hurt." He touched the tip of his knife to the corner of her eye. She squeezed her eyes closed and tried to turn her head, but he pressed the blade harder against her flesh. "Open your eyes or I'll cut your eyelids off." He didn't sound the least bit annoyed with her, and that's what convinced her he would do what he threatened. She opened her eyes to meet his cold, impassionate gaze. "Good. Now, tell me how you found this place. Did you follow us?"

"Yes. We tracked you." It was technically true, though not the whole truth.

"How about the river? You can't track us on water."

Kaylin couldn't think of what to say next. Her lips moved, but no sound would come.

"Tell me, or I take out your right eye." The man brandished his knife.

"Fawcett's map," she gasped. "We followed it until we found your tracks."

"You're lying. We have Fawcett's map. You couldn't have followed it." He grasped her right eyelid and yanked it up. She couldn't pull her head away, no matter how she tried. The tip of his knife touched her eyeball and she broke. A swift death might have been one thing, but torture was something she wasn't prepared to endure."

"Okay! Okay! We also found the book."

"The book." The man sounded like something important was falling into place. He didn't take the blade away from her eye, though. "Tell me everything and tell me fast, and you keep your eye."

Tears poured down Kaylin's face as she hastily told the man about Fawcett's other map, and about the copy of *The Lost World* that one of his descendants had preserved. She was ashamed of her weakness, her moment of bravery evaporated in the face of mortal fear. She should have held on to that fighting spirit, but she couldn't. This wasn't like books or movies—the terror was real, the knife was real, and the possibility, no, the probability of her death was real, too. As much as she wanted to hold back information, she was too afraid.

"After you get past the last landmark," she gasped,

"which we don't have…"

"We already have it," the man snapped. "Go on."

Tears trickled down her face. She tried to summon the courage to resist, but the razor sharp knife hovering inches from her eye made that impossible.

"You have to follow the path of five steps…"

CHAPTER 23

Dane heard voices up ahead, and saw someone or something moving away from him. He crept forward, his Walther at the ready.

"Do whatever you want to her," a voice called, "but make it fast. Meet me beneath the stone outcropping."

Her? That had to mean Kaylin. His suspicions were confirmed moments later when he heard her cry out. Moving quickly and silently, he caught a glimpse of blonde hair, and heard her whimper.

"Easy. You don't want me to cut you, do you?" The heavily accented English had to belong to one of the guides with ScanoGen's group. Careful not to be spotted, Dane ducked behind a tree and peered around it.

Kaylin was being held by a tall, dark-skinned man. In one hand, he had a knife pressed to her throat, and was pulling up her shirt with the other. Half of his head was obscured by Kaylin's. It was a small target, but it would be enough if he was fast.

He stepped out, Walther in a two-handed grip. The man spotted him and froze for a split-second. That was enough.

Dane's first bullet took him in the eye, and Kaylin pushed the dead man's body away as he fell. Weeping, she ran to Dane, who swept her up in his arms and held her tight.

"We've got to get behind cover," he whispered, moving backward. "We don't know who might be coming. There's the natives, and now these guys to contend with. Are they

ScanoGen?"

Kaylin nodded. "Maddock, I'm sorry, but I told them about the Path of Five Steps. That guy, he was going to cut my eye out. I'm so sorry."

"It couldn't be helped." He pulled her close. Their one advantage over ScanoGen was now gone, but he couldn't expect Kaylin to hold up under threat of torture. It was stupid to have brought her here in the first place, no matter what she said.

"I did lie to him about one of the steps. The one about Rome. That might help. I just couldn't do more. I was so afraid he could tell I was lying. I'm so sorry." There was a longing in her eyes, and he knew she wanted him to tell her all was forgiven.

He managed a sympathetic nod. "What matters is you're all right. We need to find the others quickly. Did they take your gun?"

"I think the dead guy has it."

Hastily, they retrieved Kaylin's knife and pistol from the dead guide. As she tucked the knife back into its sheath, they heard the sound of many feet shuffling through the underbrush, coming right toward them.

"It's those zombie native freaks," she hissed. "They must have heard the sound of your gunshot."

"Let's go, and be sure to stay with me this time." Dane took her by the hand and together they took off in the direction of the waterfall.

Bones trained his M16 on the figure hiding behind the bush. It wasn't one of the natives, but an attractive woman with short, black hair and skin the color of dark chocolate. She was dressed in fatigues and armed with a Makarov. This must be Tam, the ostensible leader of the ScanoGen group. She was good with a handgun. Bones had already watched her put a bullet through the skull of a charging native at fifty feet.

Of course, she was no SEAL. Bones was now twenty

feet away from her and she had no idea he was there. He could take her out any time, but it suited him to let her waste her bullets taking out the natives while he waited here by the foot of the waterfall for Maddock and the others to arrive.

Also, something told him there was more to this girl than met the eye. He kept coming back to the fact that she'd set Andy free instead of killing him. Also, Andy implied that the ScanoGen crew didn't truly accept her as a leader. Something was stinky in Dodge, or however the saying went. Perhaps there was a rift in the ScanoGen group—one big enough for him to worm his way into. He decided to take a chance.

"Don't move a muscle." He kept his tone low, just loud enough for her to hear. She didn't flinch. She kept her body still and turned her eyes in the direction of his voice. "Don't even think about it, sweetheart," Bones added. "Doc freakin' Holliday isn't that fast."

"I can't see you, but I can tell where you are by the sound of your voice. I put enough bullets in the air, one of them will hit you."

"Look, chick," Bones said, knowing how much women hated being addressed that way. "First of all, we can sit and talk all day and my concentration won't lapse one bit. That's a promise. Second, you'll have a bullet in your skull at the first sudden movement you make. Now, open your hand and let the gun drop."

She grimaced, but did as she was told.

"Good, now put your hands on top of your head.

"I've never let anyone sneak up on me like that," she said as she slowly followed Bones's instructions. "I must be sleep-deprived."

"Don't let it bother you. It's all part of the training." He loved this girl's calm demeanor, but it also made her dangerous.

"I'm guessing you're either Maddock or Bonebrake."

"Why the hell does Maddock always get top billing? I'm the badass."

She smirked. "Look, I know you won't believe me, but

I'm F.B.I. I'm on your side."

"Bull. If you're F.B.I., what are you doing in a foreign country?"

"I'm a plant inside ScanoGen. Have been for a long time. My primary assignment is domestic. My orders were to find out all I can about a shadow organization that's funding them and other groups, but I failed. I worked my way up through the organization and all I got was a name. The Dominion."

"What the hell are you talking about?" Bones's blood ran cold. It couldn't possibly be true, but then again, neither could it be a coincidence. "Do you mean the Deseret Dominion?"

"That's one small segment of a nationwide organization. I'm surprised you've heard of them. That cell has been quiet for a while."

"Maddock and I sort of had something to do with that." He probably shouldn't have made that admission, but he couldn't help himself.

"You're kidding me." Her eyes were wide with surprise. "Is this a joke to mess with me?" He had finally rattled her, though only a little bit.

"Nope. If you convince me not to kill you, I'll tell you all about it when we get out of here." He realized he had already decided to let her live, and he hoped he wasn't making a mistake.

"My cards are on the table." Her voice was calm and he detected no deception. "I've done my job the best I can, and tried not to do too much harm along the way. ScanoGen ordered me to kill a man, Thornton's colleague, but I let him go instead, although he doesn't stand much of a chance out there if I don't get back to him quick."

"We found him and he's all right. We sent him back with an armed guide." Something occurred to Bones. "You said your primary job was to investigate the Dominion. What else were you supposed to do?"

"To find out the truth behind Project Pan," she replied glumly, "and either steal the science behind it for the government, or put a permanent stop to it."

"What is Project Pan?"

"Something the Dominion hired ScanoGen to do. I don't know exactly what it is, but we believe it has a military application, and that it's somehow related to modifying the human brain."

"You mean like turning soldiers into semi-zombies that can't feel pain and keep on coming at you until you blow them apart or blow their heads off?"

"Maybe." She gave a sad smile "All I know for certain is Thomas Thornton claimed that he knew where to find the key, and I'm sure it lies somewhere beyond that waterfall. Look, I can't offer you any proof, but I'm telling you the truth. Take away all my weapons if you like. Do whatever you need to do to feel safe around a little girl like me, but let me come with you. While we're sitting here chatting, Kennedy and what's left of the ScanoGen guys are getting a head start."

"All right," Bones said. He moved to her side, pocketed her Makarov and relieved her of her knife and spare clips. His eyes fell on a strange-looking weapon lying nearby. "What is this?"

"Personal Halting and Stimulation Response rifle. PHaSR for short. Some call it a dazzle gun. It temporarily blinds your enemy. I tried it on the zombie things, but they just stopped and sniffed the air and came after me again like they were hunting dogs or something."

"Sweet!" Bones hefted the high-tech weapon. It was bulkier than a machine gun, and looked a bit like something you'd see in a science fiction movie. "I'll have to save this for Corey. He loves to get his Star Wars on!" He looked at down at his new pseudo-ally. "I am sorry about disarming you. You understand, don't you?"

"Don't worry about it." Tam looked up, turning her large brown eyes and bright smile on him. "I can take my weapons back from you any time I like."

"Bring it on any time." Although he was only ninety-seven percent sure she wasn't going to try to kill him, Bones couldn't help but like this girl. "My friends and I are to meet up here. If they agree to it, you can come along." He had to laugh. He could only imagine what Maddock was going to say.

CHAPTER 24

Dane was not sure what to make of this new development, but he trusted Bones's judgment, and his own instincts told him that Tam was all right. He didn't know what to think about her claim that she was investigating the Dominion. What were the odds that name would crop up again? Until she proved herself, however, he was going to watch her closely.

He heard a rustling over the sound of the waterfall, and turned to see Matt and Willis come into view, the former supporting the latter's weight. Willis's right pants leg was soaked with blood.

"He caught a spear in the thigh," Matt grunted as he helped his friend ease down onto a nearby rock. "It looks worse than it is, I think."

"Says you." Willis winced as Bones ripped open the gash in the fabric in order to get a better look. "How come it's always the black man that has to die first? Tell me that, any of y'all."

"You're not dead. If you were, you wouldn't be so freakin' talkative." Bones chastised. They stood guard as Matt hastily cleaned, dressed, and bandaged the wound. "I'd stitch it up, but that would take a while, and there's no telling when those natives will be back."

"I think we just ran out of time!" Dane had spotted movement in the distance. Shadowy forms were coming their way, and that meant danger, whether it was the natives or ScanoGen who were on their trail. "Let's get to the waterfall. Even if Tam's wrong about that being the last landmark, that will cut down on the approaches they can take to get to us."

They picked their way across the narrow, rocky path that ran between the base of the cliff and the dark pool fed by the waterfall. Cool mist coated their faces and made the way slick. Dane put Tam in the front so he could see if she tried anything. Willis refused further help, and managed the trek reasonably well, though Dane was worried about his comrade. Bones had confided in him that the wound was deep, and would require better attention than the quick treatment Matt had given it.

As they drew close to the waterfall, Dane could see that the cliff face was hollowed out behind it. Hope rising, he urged Tam to quicken her pace before they were spotted. Skirting a head-high boulder, they stepped behind the curtain of water into a cave ten feet across running twenty feet back into the rock. Light filtering through the water cast the place in a flickering glow, and made it easy to see what awaited them inside the cave.

A giant skull was carved into the back wall. The mouth, nose, and eye sockets were all large enough for a person to crawl through. The irregular light sent shadows wavering across its surface, seeming to bring it to life.

"Wicked," Bones observed as he, bringing up the rear, entered the cavern.

"This is it." Tam put her hands on her hips and stared at the huge stone skull. She seemed to have already forgotten her position as a prisoner amongst a group of armed captors. "The problem is, I don't know where we go from here. Fawcett's map only takes us this far. It's entirely possible this is rigged so that someone who doesn't know the trick gets it." She dragged a finger across her throat and made a squelching noise.

"I think, for safety's sake, we should assume that's the case," Dane said. "We can help you here. You see, we found Fawcett's *personal* copy of *The Lost World*." He grinned at Tam's look of surprise. "Now we need the Path of Five

Steps. Kaylin, what's the first one?" He hoped that by asking her to contribute, even in a small way, he could assuage some of her guilt at surrendering their secret.

"All about me I see enemies. Rome, the scent your funeral pyres is the finest perfume."

"Weird." Matt frowned. "Couldn't they just say, '*Push this button and go here*?"

"You have definitely been spending too much time with Bones." Kaylin shook her head. "Remember, this is a combined translation from Fawcett and a native. It's not going to be crystal clear, especially if it was some sort of secret code."

"So what does it mean?" Tam looked and sounded impatient.

"You like what you see, but not what you smell." Dane said. "Sounds like we need to pick its nose." He looked at Tam. "Go for it."

She smirked. "Scared to try it for yourself?"

"Nope, but if I'm wrong, I don't want to lose one of my people."

"Fine by me." She strode over the skull and peered into the hole where the nose should be. "There's a handhold in here." She glanced up at the eye sockets and down at the gaping mouth. "Also one in each of the eyes, but not the mouth. That's just a blank wall." She looked back at Dane. "Mister Maddock, you had better be right about this." Gingerly, she reached into the sinus cavity, set her jaw, and pulled.

Nothing happened.

Tam stepped back, hands on hips, looking at the skull like it was a man she'd just caught with another woman. And then a loud, creaking sound resonated above the sound of falling water, and with a scraping like the opening of a crypt, the wall at the back of the skull's mouth slid down into the floor, revealing deep, impenetrable darkness behind it.

A ragged cheer went up among the group. Dane grinned and tossed Tam a flashlight. "In you go."

They had to proceed on hands and knees through the

mouth of the skull. On the other side, they could stand, though Bones and Willis had to duck down in places to keep from hitting their heads. The tunnel ascended at a steep angle, and Willis, his leg bleeding again, was forced to accept help as they made their way up.

They reached a spot where the path leveled out and the way opened up into a large chamber. Standing before them were two statues: a horse and an elephant. Each stood about four feet tall at the shoulder. They could see no door, nor any other obvious means of egress.

"Now this is a puzzler." Dane scratched his chin. "What's the second step, again?"

"The vile Numidians," Kaylin replied.

"What else?" Tam turned to Kaylin with a quizzical look. "That can't be all."

"That's it." Kaylin nodded insistently. "It was the easiest one to remember. Maddock has them written down if you want to double-check."

"No need," Dane said. Something had clicked into place. "The Numidians were the finest cavalry in the ancient world. The horse would represent them."

"So who is the elephant?" Bones asked.

"Carthage." The more Dane thought about it, the more certain he was that he was correct. "Carthage was known for its elephant cavalry. It used the Numidian cavalry against Rome early in the Punic wars, but the Numidians later turned on them, and things went downhill from there. When you consider that Rome was the bitterest of Carthage's enemies, the first clue also makes sense in that context."

"You think Kephises is a Punic city?" Kaylin suddenly gaped. "Remember what Wainwright said! Fawcett recognized some of the words the young man spoke as being Punic."

"It could be," Tam mused. "They were descended from the Phoenicians, the greatest sailors of the ancient world. There are legends of the Phoenician sailors reaching the Americas. Perhaps the knowledge was preserved and passed down, and someone from Carthage came here."

"That's how I see it," Dane agreed.

"So if these are cavalry mounts," Tam said, "we hop on the back of Carthage's finest." She took two steps and sprang up onto the back of the elephant.

"You see, Maddock?" Bones said. "I did the right thing keeping her around. She's our very own canary in a coal mine."

His words were drowned out by a rumble as the elephant began to sink slowly into the floor. Tam's eyes bulged, but she kept her seat. The girl was brave, no doubt. She disappeared from sight, and the rumbling ceased, leaving them standing in awed silence.

"You can come down!" Tam called. "There's another passage heading back from here."

Matt went down first, and he and Bones helped Willis down. Willis grumbled and cursed the whole way, but did not refuse the assistance. When the last person had climbed down, they took a minute to bandage up his wound again. As they were working, the elephant suddenly rose back up and locked into place with a loud clack, closing them in the tunnel. They could see now that it was supported by a rectangular block of stone.

"How do we get back out?" Kaylin looked the column up and down with nervous eyes.

"We'll figure it out. Don't worry." Dane gave her hand a quick squeeze. "Time to move on."

"This can't be right. Tam lied to me." Kennedy hated to admit he'd been duped, but there was no hiding it from the others. "When I find her, I'll kill her."

"Where do you think she is?" Smithson tapped the trigger of his F88 as if he, too, was eager to dispose of the woman. The three ScanoGen agents were still alive, and had managed to meet up with Kennedy. He'd had doubts about their loyalties, as Tam had hand-picked them for a the mission, but they were all ex-military, and not inclined to take orders from a civilian, even if that civilian was Salvatore

Scano's favored son, or daughter, as it were.

"I don't know, but the mission remains our top priority. We won't seek her out, but should we come across her, your orders are to shoot on sight. Anyone have a problem with that?" No one spoke. "Good. Our first order of business is to find the last landmark, and then see if this Path of Five Steps is for real. I'll bet we find Broderick somewhere along the way."

"Sir, I saw her headed in the direction of the waterfall." Wesley was the youngest of the group, and a bit too eager, but he wasn't stupid. "Should we try there?"

"That's as good an idea as any. Remember to keep an eye out for Dane Maddock and whoever he brought along. Don't underestimate him or his companions. They know what they're doing."

"Same orders as with Broderick?" Brown, a big, red haired brute with a southern twang, grinned.

"Correct. Shoot on sight. But do it right, gentlemen. You are professionals. We want every man, and woman, in their party dead."

He bit the inside of his jaw, relishing the pain and the taste of blood. It always whetted his appetite for action. Despite all that had gone wrong on this mission, it felt good to be back in the field, ready to kill if necessary. And now, with Maddock and Bonebrake on the prowl, he had additional targets. Eliminating them would be a pleasure.

CHAPTER 25

They came to a fork where the passageway to the left was guarded by lions carved in the walls on either side, while wolves stood sentinel on either side of the passage on the right. Dane grinned. He doubted he even needed the clue for this one.

"Time for the third step," Kaylin said. "Rome is forever cursed."

"There's got to be more," Matt objected. "You know, something about wolves and lions. This is crap! If we go down the wrong tunnel, we don't know what's going to happen."

"Don't worry. I got this one." Tam smiled, and Dane could tell she was thinking the same thing he was thinking. "Romulus and Remus were the founders of Rome. They were abandoned as babies and…"

"…nursed by a mother wolf!" Kaylin exclaimed. "So it's a choice between the African lion and the Roman wolf."

"No choice at all, really." Tam smiled and took the passage on the left.

The way continued upward in a steep ascent. They must be nearing the top by now, Dane thought. Just then, the tunnel leveled out, but after only a few paces, Tam stopped and put her hands out.

"Wait!" she snapped. "I think we've come to the next step." She shone her light across the floor. It was made up of square tiles, five wide and at least twenty deep. Each tile had a symbol engraved on it.

"Too far to jump across," Bones observed, walking right up to the edge and looking things over. "Bummer. That would simplify things."

"This step is an odd one." Kaylin knelt down in front of the tiles. "Walk safely across the moon."

"None of them look like the moon to me," Bones mused. "They aren't even round."

"I actually know something about this one from a religions course I took in college." Kaylin bit her lip, like she always did when she was deepest in thought. "At least, I think I do. I'd hate to be wrong."

"Your guess is better than anything else we have to go on," Dane said. "What are you thinking?"

"The main deities of the Punics were the god Ba'al and the goddess Tanit. I remember her symbol because I thought it looked like an angel without wings." She pointed to one of the tiles.

"It also looks like an ankh," Tam added, "except for that strange thing at the top."

"Exactly." Kaylin's voice grew stronger as she warmed to her subject. "That's the moon clue, I think. Tanit is the moon goddess, and that symbol is a crescent moon!" She looked up at Dane with a hopeful expression. "What do you think?"

"Makes sense to me. Anyone else have a better idea, or another suggestion?" He looked around, but the others shook their heads.

"Alrighty then." Tam rose to her feet with a sigh of resignation. "I hope you're right."

"Wait a minute. You've taken enough risks. It's my turn." Dane took of his pack and handed it to Bones.

"No way, Maddock." Bones shoved the pack back into his arms. "We need you. I'll do it."

"We're all needed, Bones. I'm going."

"I'll go," Kaylin interrupted. "I'm sure if I just keep to the tiles, I'll be fine. Besides, I'm the most expendable one here."

"You are not," Dane said.

"Excuse me." Tam moved between them. "How about I just go, while you and your girlfriend argue?"

"She's not my girlfriend," Dane muttered.

"Really?" Tam raised her eyebrows. "She's cute. You should go for it."

"That's what I keep telling him," Bones chimed in. "But does he listen? Not a chance. He's all about figuring women out instead of just chilling and having a good time."

"You two both suck." Dane looked at Bones. "Give Tam back her dazzle gun."

"Are you sure?" Bones and Tam said at the same time.

"No, but let's do it anyway." Bones unslung the gun from his shoulder and handed it to Tam. "You've done everything we've asked, and you could have easily stolen Kaylin's gun or her knife when she knelt down beside you just now."

"You would have shot me." Tam didn't look or sound accusatory, but spoke in a matter-of-fact manner.

"Yep, and I still will if you try anything, but I believe Bones is right about you. You didn't kill Andy, when it would have been easier to do so, and that says a lot. Besides, we're coming up on the final step, and we don't know what's waiting for us. You need a way to defend yourself."

"Thanks." They shook hands and she looked at him with a solemn expression. "I want to finish this as much as you do, and I give you my word. I'm not against you."

"We'll see," Dane said. "Now, I don't care what anyone says. I'm taking the lead on this one."

He focused on each tile, choosing those carved with the Tanit symbol. He could not let go of the thought that these tiles were probably more than two thousand years old. It would be just his luck to be the one under whom they finally broke. One step, then the next. Each stride was uncomfortably long—just enough to make it difficult to maintain his balance. The third tile shifted as he put his weight down, and he froze.

"Hurry up, Maddock!" Willis shouted. "Even the army boy could go faster than that."

Dane kept his eyes on the tiles and saluted his friend with an upraised middle finger. When he finally stepped off the last tile, everyone cheered him with sarcastic applause.

Willis had been resting up, and he went across next. He had been weak and wobbly on his feet, but you couldn't tell it from the confident manner with which he crossed the tiles, each foot firmly set in its proper place. Dane breathed a sigh of relief when Willis was finally across. The others followed in short order, with Bones last.

"Glad you could join us," Dane joked as Bones made a mocking bow.

"I just scouted ahead," Tam said from behind Dane. "It looks like the fifth step is just around that corner."

Dane couldn't help but smile. "We're there!"

Kennedy stood and stared at the two paths— the lions on one side, the wolves on the other. This clue had him stumped, though he hated to admit it.

"What did the girl say, again?" Smithson asked. "Something about Rome?"

"Rome is forever glorious."

"Well, that's easy, then. The lions, the arena, gladiators. We go that way." Smithson gestured to the tunnel guarded by the lions.

"Perhaps, but the wolf is associated with the founding of Rome. Also, the first clue was anti-Roman, saying their funeral pyres were perfume."

"Maybe they're burning the bodies of their enemies," Wesley suggested.

Kennedy thought about it. He couldn't wait too long. Maddock was out there somewhere, and so was Tam. The longer he stood here thinking, they were either gaining on him, or perhaps extending their lead if they had managed to get in ahead of him. Furthermore, indecisiveness instilled no confidence in those who followed you.

"Let's go with the wolves," he finally said. "But keep

your eyes open and stay close to one another."

Wesley took the lead, his eagerness tempered only by Kennedy's order to remain close together. He stalked between the wolf carvings, their bared fangs seeming to portend doom. He had taken only six steps when the floor gave way beneath him. Wesley cried out in surprise as he plunged downward. Kennedy dove forward and grabbed his collar a split-second before Smithson and Brown grabbed Wesley by the arms. A good thing, too, else Wesley's weight would have dragged Kennedy down as well. They hauled the shaken man out of the pit.

"I guess it was the lion," Kennedy said, massaging his shoulder and staring down into the dark hole which had no visible bottom. Now he *really* wanted to kill Tamara Broderick and Dane Maddock.

Dane rounded the corner to find that the passageway ended at a wall carved with a landscape. To the left was a lake, at the center a field, and a wooded ridgeline to the right. An iron ring set in a round plug hung below each image. On the floor in front of each, a seam outlined a six foot square, perhaps a pair of trap doors. A similar outline in the ceiling above each indicated something else potentially dangerous. He had visions of the floor dropping out from underneath him, or a giant block turning him into strawberry jam. He'd better interpret the last clue correctly.

"Here lies victory." He stared at the image until the edges blurred, and the water seemed to ripple. There wasn't any battle going on in the carving. What could it mean?

"If it was me, I'd take the high ground," Bones said. "Of course, they're probably looking for something a little more 'out there' than simple strategy."

"I think you've hit it on the head." Dane smiled as the pieces came together. "Before the Romans destroyed them, Carthage's two greatest military victories were at Cannae and at Lake Trasimene. At Trasimene, they trapped the Roman forces between a ridge line and the lake, and slaughtered them. Some tried to escape by way of the lake and were also cut down. At Cannae, they pinned them against a river, and the slaughter was even worse. The Punic forces gradually gave way until the Romans were stretched out all along the river, and then the cavalry came down from the high ground, encircled, and slaughtered them. Rome's force was so large, and their defeat so complete, that they say many of the soldiers were just waiting to be killed when the forces of Carthage finally cut through the outer ranks to get to them. They even found Roman soldiers who had grown tired of waiting for the inevitable and had buried their heads in the dirt and suffocated themselves.

"That's crazy, dude." Bones shook his head. "So no safety on the low ground or in the water."

"Here goes nothing." Dane stepped onto the square in front of the mountains and took hold of the cold, iron ring. He took a deep breath, turned and winked at Kaylin, and pulled.

The plug slowly gave way and, when it was extended about six inches, it stopped with a loud clunk. The floor began to vibrate and Dane tensed, but nothing dropped out from beneath him, nor did anything come crashing down. Instead, the block on which he was standing sank slowly down into the floor. Sheer, dark stone slipped past, and a new passageway rose up before him. He smelled fresh air, saw a glimmer of light, and he knew they had made it.

When the remainder of the group had reached the bottom, they all stared in silence toward the end of the tunnel, which was partially obscured by hanging vines and low-growing flora. The question seemed to hang in the air. What would they find on the other side?

CHAPTER 26

Dane stepped through the curtain of vines and into the late afternoon sun, then stopped in stunned amazement. Below him stretched a valley teeming with life. A stream ran down the center, wending its way between cultivated gardens on one side and orchards on the other. Giant kapok trees were scattered here and there among the fields. He could see people tending to the crops, but none of this was what shocked him. At the far end of the valley, beyond the orchards and cultivated fields, the jungle grew wild in a thick, dark, tangle, and rising up behind it stood a pyramid. Its dark, weathered stone speaking of age and mystery. Trees and plants had rooted in various places on its surface as the jungle struggled to claim it. What was a pyramid doing in this part of the world?

"Mayan?" Tam asked, staring at it in confusion. "But it couldn't be. This is the wrong place for it."

"Right." Dane continued to stare at the pyramid. It bore some resemblance to Mayan architecture, but something wasn't quite right about it. Something about the angles gave it a different feel than the Mayan pyramids he had seen. "It almost looks like it has some Incan influence, or something, doesn't it?"

"The influence was Egyptian, actually."

Dane was surprised to see a man staring up at them from down the path that descended into the valley. He had wavy brown hair, dark eyes, and a large, curved nose. His skin was deeply tanned, making his teeth seem even whiter when he smiled. He carried a small bow, but he did not have an arrow nocked.

Good thing for him, Dane thought. He was not sufficiently armed to cause them any trouble.

"I am Mago and I welcome you to Kephises." He bowed. "Please put down your weapons. You have my word that we mean you no harm."

"I only see one of you," Matt scoffed.

"That, I think, is the point." Mago's smile widened.

"There's at least two guys hiding in the brush over that way," Bones said, inclining his head to the right. "They've got arrows trained on us. I'm guessing there are a few more I haven't spotted."

"You would be correct," Mago said. "Your weapons, I'm sure, are formidable, but you would be killed."

Dane had to go with his gut. They were in an exposed position, and this man truly did not seem to want to hurt them. Could he blame these people for wanting to protect themselves from intruders in their realm? Besides, what choice did they have? Sure, they could fight, but at least some of their number would be killed, and probably for nothing. They had come this far to find out the truth behind Fawcett's final expedition, and hopefully to find Thomas, and that was what they were going to do.

"All right," he said, laying first his M-16, and then his Walther, on the ground. "But I have to warn you, there are dangerous men after us, who are better armed than we are. We mean you no harm either, and it would be a good idea to let us keep our weapons."

"We shall see," Mago said. When the remainder of Dane's party had laid down their weapons, he made a quick gesture and several figures appeared, as if from nowhere, to collect their weapons. "Now, if you will please follow me."

He led them down the trail into the valley, with his comrades trailing behind, some carrying the confiscated weapons and backpacks, and others keeping arrows trained on their backs.

Dane ignored them, hungry to take in the incredible

scene. This was Kephises, the lost city so desperately sought after by Fawcett. Its very existence defied belief. He understood how this place had gone undiscovered. It was too far off the beaten path, and too well hidden, not to mention protected by the tribesmen below, for an explorer to stumble across it. Furthermore, with the heavy jungle growth all around, and the trees interspersed between the gardens, it would take the most detailed scrutiny of an aerial photo or satellite image to realize this was anything more than another patch of green in the midst of the vast Amazon region.

The people tending the crops stared at them as they passed. They lacked Mago's distinctive Mediterranean features, and instead bore some resemblance to the natives of the area, though their height, eye color, and complexion suggested a mixed ancestry.

"May I ask you a question?" Dane actually had a hundred or more questions he wanted to ask, but he thought he'd start small.

Mago shook his head. "I am not the person to answer questions. When we reach the temple, there are others who will speak to you."

A jaguar emerged from the cover of the trees and slunk toward them. Dane tensed, wishing he had a weapon, but their escort smiled at it as it padded up to him and nuzzled his hand. He scratched it behind its ears and spoke to it in gentle tones, as if it was a favorite pet. It left Mago and sidled up to Dane. He froze, wondering if this beautiful but deadly beast was docile only for its master, but then the big cat rubbed against his thigh and purred.

"Isa likes to be scratched behind the ears and between the shoulder blades," Mago said. "Go on. She won't hurt you."

Dane reached down and scratched the jaguar, whose purr sounded like a Harley revving up. Kaylin knelt down and stroked Isa's back.

"She's magnificent. And she is tame?"

"She will do violence only in defense of her life. All the animals in Kephises are that way." That raised another question Dane wanted to ask, but Mago was already moving again. One of their armed escort motioned with his bow, indicating they should move on.

They entered the shade of the thick patch of jungle that barred the way to the temple. The path wound back and forth, almost like the coils of the Amazon River as it snaked its way across the continent. This was likely the only path through the jungle, and was cut this way in order to slow down invaders. Defenders could hide at each curve to repel invaders. The only alternative would be for the attackers to come through the jungle itself, which he imagined each citizen in Kephises knew like the back of his hand.

The jungle gave way to a sparsely wooded area. Stone houses, built in the style of the ancient Mediterranean world, stood in the center, with huts resembling those of native Amazon tribes scattered all about. The trees, all tall with broad limbs, cast this village area in mottled sunlight.

"This would be hard to spot, even from a satellite," Bones observed, looking up at the massive trees. "And the pyramid, as eroded and overgrown as it is, probably just looks like a hill."

"I wouldn't have believed it was possible for a place like this to exist undiscovered," Tam said. "But it makes sense to me now."

Mago ushered them into the largest stone building, a rectangular structure with small windows and an arched entryway. A fragrant scent, like incense, greeted Dane as he stepped inside. Three men looked up as they entered, one of them springing to his feet.

"Kaylin! Oh my God, what are you doing here?" It was Thomas, and he hurried forward, arms outstretched.

Dane stepped aside, and a spark of jealousy flared in his heart, but it was extinguished almost immediately as he saw the look of hesitation in Kaylin's eyes. It was only there for an instant, long enough for her to steal a glance at him before Thomas crushed her in a tight embrace.

"I didn't mean for you to come," he mumbled, his lips pressed against the top of her head. "You were supposed to send help."

"Things got complicated," she said. "I had to come along for my own safety."

Thomas drew back and frowned at her. "You went into the deepest, most unexplored region of the Amazon for your own *safety?*"

"ScanoGen was after us. Is after us," she added. "I don't know who you need to warn, but they might be right behind us."

"I have taken precautions, Father," Mago said, addressing a broad-shouldered man who remained seated, staring impassively at them. Finally, he nodded, and Mago bowed himself out of the room.

Kaylin introduced everyone to Thomas, who shook each person's hand and thanked them profusely for coming to his aid. She saved Dane for last, and a shadow crossed Thomas's face when he heard the name. Clearly he knew Dane and Kaylin had once had a relationship. He recovered immediately, and gave Dane the same warm thanks he had given the others.

"I imagine you have many questions." A tall, lean man of lighter complexion than the others waved them to sit on a wooden bench that ran the length of one wall. Of middle years, he was lean and athletic-looking, and had about him an aura of abundant energy. "We will answer what we can. You have obviously taken a great deal of personal risk to come here."

Dane frowned at the man. There was something familiar about him. Perhaps it was his eyes, which, though friendly, were lighter than those of the others Dane had seen in Kephises, and burned with an intensity bordering on zeal. His accent was different, too. It almost seemed to have a touch of the U.K. in it.

"Would you care for food or water?" the man asked.

"Actually, my friend has a wounded leg that needs tending to." He nodded to Willis, who waved dismissively, but his smile was a tired one.

"We shall see to it at once." Now it was the big man

who spoke. He rose to his feet and clapped his hands twice. A young man, another of those who looked to be of mixed race, hurried in and dropped to one knee. "Take the Nubian and see to his hurts."

Willis's jaw dropped in surprise, but he was too tired to reply. Tam covered her giggle with a forced cough, and Bones looked like it was taking all he had not to chime in.

"I'll go with him," Matt said, rising to his feet and helping Willis stand. "I have first aid supplies that might come in handy." They followed the young man out the door, Willis leaning heavily on Matt. Clearly, he was in worse shape than anyone had suspected, and the climb up the five steps had taken its toll. Dane had to admire his friend. He was resilient.

"Is that word amusing to you?" The big man had not missed their reactions. "Or is it no longer used?"

"Forgive us." Tam spoke up quickly. "The word is still in use, but it is typically only used when complimenting a beautiful woman. You might call her a Nubian queen or princess."

"Ah." The man settled back into his seat. "Your amusement was not disrespect, then."

"No disrespect was intended," Dane assured him. "I am curious, though. Your settlement has clearly been here for many years."

"Two thousand, one hundred, forty four, to be exact. My ancestors wandered in the wilderness for a long while before finding this place."

"Were your ancestors from Carthage?" Dane had a feeling he knew the answer to that question, but did not want to make assumptions.

"Yes, they were." The man with the British accent spoke up. "You have the honor of addressing Hamilcar of Kephises, descendant of Hannibal Barca, the greatest of the Punic generals."

Hamilcar inclined his head, the expression on his face almost kingly. Under different circumstances, this would have been a stunning revelation, but considering they had just discovered Percy Fawcett's legendary lost city, Dane found it merely surprising.

"So, Kephises was not a Greek city," Kaylin said, half to herself. "The legend was inaccurate."

"The name is of Greek origin, for reasons that have to do with the purpose of my people's journey here so long ago," Hamilcar said.

"May I ask what that purpose was?" Tam's voice was hopeful. Obviously, the answer to this question lay at the core of her, ScanoGen's, and the government's interest in Fawcett's last expedition. Assuming, of course, she had told the truth about her government connections.

Hamilcar shifted uncomfortably in his seat.

"I can show you later," Thomas said. "I owe you all an explanation after you came all this way to find me." He sat next to Kaylin, holding her hand, though she did not look pleased about it.

"If I may ask," Dane began, turning his attention away from the discontented couple, "how is it that you speak English?"

"I'm afraid the fault lies with my grandfather and great-grandfather." The man whom Dane had thought familiar-looking took over the explanation. "I am Brian Fawcett, great-grandson of Percy Fawcett and grandson of Jack Fawcett."

Dane's heart raced. "So Fawcett did make it here!"

"Why, yes he did." Brian smiled, clearly proud of his ancestor. "Mister Thornton, here, tells me my great-grandfather is quite famous, though it is generally believed he died in pursuit of a folly."

"That's true. But now people will know the truth." Dane imagined revealing the true story of the heroic explorer, and validating the man's life's work. But then he imagined what would happen next. The very best scenario he could envision was a swarm of researchers: archaeologists, anthropologists, historians, even geneticists wanting to learn more about this place and its people. They would destroy Kephises as it existed right now. "Sorry, I wasn't thinking."

Fawcett nodded. "I understand. It must be an even greater surprise to you than it was to my grandfathers." He leaned back in his chair and smiled, as if he was telling a story by a campfire. "Of their party, only Percy and Jack reached Kephises. The rest died along the way, or were killed by the 'dead ones' as Thornton tells me they are known to the outside world. The people of Kephises welcomed and honored them, though they were not permitted to leave."

Bones shifted uncomfortably and cast a dark glance at Dane, but did not interrupt.

"I do not think they wanted to leave, frankly. They were treated well, and Jack was even permitted to marry into the Barcid family, which had been kept to a pure Punic bloodline. I have the rare honor to be descended both from the great Percy Fawcett and the legendary Hannibal."

"You would be a famous man in the outside world." Dane smiled. "Have you ever been tempted to leave?"

"No." Fawcett's face darkened. "I have not."

Hamilcar suddenly rose. "You will be given food and drink and a place to stay."

"If I may be so bold." Dane had no idea how to address this man. If there was an honorific due him, he didn't know what it was. "Please do not underestimate the men who are after us. They are well-armed and I seriously doubt they care who they kill as long as they get what they came for." He glanced at Tam, who remained silent. "My friends and I are trained soldiers. We can help you defend yourselves."

"I will consider your words." Hamilcar made a backhanded gesture, like brushing away an insect, and inclined his head toward the door.

"I'll show you around." Thomas stood, nervously brushed invisible dirt from his pants, and ushered them out the door.

The sun was an orange ball perched on the edge of the horizon as they stepped out into the light. Dane looked around, unwilling to relax. He and the others had not put up a fight when they met the protectors of Kephises, but this would not be true of ScanoGen. They would be looking for a fight, and though they would most likely be on the lookout for Maddock's group, if they encountered anyone from Kephises, they would probably shoot first and ask questions later.

"I get the impression they think they're going to keep us here." Bones kept his voice low so that no one else could hear.

Dane nodded. Yet another reason they needed to retrieve their weapons as soon as possible. But how to do it without coming into open conflict with people they would prefer to protect?

Kennedy stood in the shadows at the end of the tunnel, letting the darkness and the vegetation conceal his presence. He could not make out much from this vantage point, but he could see there was some sort of valley or canyon below them, and what looked like a pyramid in the distance.

"See anything?" Smithson whispered.

"Not much, but there's at least two men hiding out there, keeping watch. If I can see them, there have to be more of them I can't see."

"You think it's more of those zombies?" Wesley actually sounded eager for a return engagement with the mindless natives.

"I don't think so. They didn't seem like the type to hide out and guard an entrance. There's something else going on here. I think we've reached the end of the line."

"Well, let's go get 'em then!" Wesley bobbed up and down on the balls of his feet. His near-death experience in the booby-trapped tunnel had not dampened his enthusiasm one bit.

"Not yet." Kennedy despised inaction, but he wasn't stupid. They needed intel. What waited for them out there? How many men? How were they armed? What was the key to Project Pan, and where was it?

"Yes, sir." Wesley's disappointment-soaked words were

respectful. The man might be a pit bull, but he was a well-trained one. Good thing, too. Kennedy didn't tolerate men who could not or would not follow orders.

"We'll wait for dark. Our night vision goggles will give us a major advantage. I'll take one of them alive if I can, and find out just what's waiting for us out there. Then we'll move in." A grim smile crept across his face. He did not know if Maddock or Broderick had reached this place ahead of him. It would probably be an easier fight if they had not, but somehow, he hoped they were here. He had a bloodlust that needed to be satisfied.

CHAPTER 27

"You should see the pyramid. It's really something." Thomas's speech was clipped and his expression grave. He was moving fast, as if he didn't care if they kept up with him or not. When they reached the pyramid, he began climbing. "Watch your step." He didn't look back as he spoke. "It's crumbling in places, but if you stay behind me, you'll be all right."

Dane wanted to tell him that they really weren't interested in sightseeing right now, but he sensed Thomas had a purpose behind his actions, so he followed without complaint. When they had climbed about halfway, Thomas stopped, and indicated they should sit down.

"I'm sorry about the climb." The words were interspersed with gasps as he sucked in air. "It's steep, but necessary." Finally composing himself, he drew in a few slow, measured breaths. "Anyway, this is the one place we can talk without anyone listening. Not everyone here speaks fluent English, only the Punics, but the natives all speak at least a little bit, and understand a lot. This way, we can have a bit of privacy, and can also watch to see if ScanoGen shows up. The way in is that way." He pointed to the ridge on the far end of the valley.

"Tell us the story," Dane said. "The whole story. We risked our lives to save you, and we deserve answers."

"That's why we're up here." Thomas would not meet his eye. "Where should I begin?"

"How much have you learned much about this place?"

Bones asked.

"Quite a bit, actually. Fawcett is very talkative, and the others are fairly free with information since they know I'm no threat to escape. Kephises was founded by refugees from Carthage who escaped at the end of the third Punic War, just before the fall of Carthage itself. Those who survived the voyage made landfall far to the north, most likely near the southernmost regions of the Mayan empire. The first natives they encountered worshiped them as gods, and followed them into the jungle. Their leader was Hasdrubal, Hannibal Barca's grandson."

"That's one of the things that confused me," Dane said. "I didn't think Hannibal had any children."

"History has been hazy on that topic," Thomas replied. "I suppose that's because his only living descendant headed off to the Americas." His thin smile only made him look more nervous. "Anyway, Hasdrubal was on a mission, given to him by the priesthood, to protect Carthage's greatest treasure. When they arrived in the New World, he told the others that the gods would let him know when and where it was time to stop. They journeyed deeper and deeper into the jungle, picking up some native followers as they went, but losing their fair share of people along the way. When they finally found this place, he deemed it safe and remote enough to settle.

The tunnel, the Path of Five Steps, and the pyramid all were built over the generations using combined labor of the Punics and natives. That's why the pyramid is a bit odd-looking. The Barcids wanted something like the pyramids of Egypt, but the pyramid has distinctly Mayan features, which is why I believe their first landfall was in or near Mayan territory."

"So, the people who live here are a mix of Punics and Mayans?" It bothered Dane to feel like the ignorant half of a conversation with Kaylin's boyfriend, but he wanted to hear the story nonetheless.

"Mostly. Also local natives, some of whom they collected as they went in search of this place, others they collected over the years. There seems to be something of a hierarchy here, depending on how much Punic blood one has, with the Barcids being the most pure. That's actually how Fawcett came to find this place. I assume you found Wainwright?" They nodded. "The young man whom Percy Fawcett encountered was a Barcid who wanted to marry one of the low blood girls. That isn't acceptable in that family. In fact, the only reason Jack Fawcett was permitted to marry into their line was because the husband of one of the women of the line had died. She was of late middle age and thought to be past childbearing years. Anyway, the young man and his lover escaped, and he took with him the secret to the five steps, and he also carved a rough map in stone. I suppose he thought they'd come back some day once they'd had a few children and it was too late for his family to do anything about it. If it hadn't been for him, this place might still be a secret." He lapsed into silence, gazing out across the valley.

"You said you weren't a threat to escape," Bones said, "are they keeping you here?"

"I'm sure if they let you go, they'll let me go, too." Thomas sighed. "Once they understand their secret is out, there's not much reason for them to keep us here."

"I'd like to see them try." Bones grimaced, and his gaze turned flinty as he looked down on the settlement.

"The truth is, unless Salvatore Scano has told the world, which I can almost guarantee you he hasn't, the only people from the outside world who know about this place are sitting right here." Tam frowned. "And what's left of the ScanoGen men, if they survived those zombie people."

"The Mot'jabbur, they call them." Thomas looked up at the sky. "The Dead Warriors."

"Who are they? *What* are they?" Dane asked.

"I suppose you could call them experiments that went wrong, but that wouldn't be entirely accurate."

"What *I* want to know is how you came to have any dealings with ScanoGen in the first place." Kaylin's voice was white hot rage. "You never told me a single thing. Then you disappear, with nothing but a picture as a clue, and leave killers after us. What happened?"

Thomas hung his head for a moment, as if gathering his thoughts, and then stood. "For you to understand that, you'll have to see the tree."

He led them around to the back side of the pyramid and pointed down to a clearing, in the center of which stood the strangest tree Dane had ever seen. It resembled a baobab tree in miniature, with a thick trunk and a few root-like branches spreading out at the very top. But the similarities ended there. The bark was silver and gleamed in the orange sunset. The round leaves were concave and glossy like those of a magnolia, but they were dark on one side, nearly black in color, and a creamy white on the other. A single piece of fruit was visible through a gap in the bizarre foliage. It was the size of a cantaloupe, and it, like the leaves, was dark on one side and light on the other.

"Percy Fawcett was on to something even crazier than anyone ever suspected. Much of what he professed to believe was a smokescreen designed to throw people off the trail of what he knew would be an earth-shattering discovery. It took half a lifetime, but I pieced together, and kept for myself, enough evidence to realize what he was truly after."

Down below, a woman was watering the tree. She glanced up at them, but paid them no particular mind, and went back to her work.

"This tree is the secret the Punics traveled her to protect. It has passed through many hands: Athenian Greeks, Spartans, Persians, all the way back to ancient Israel and beyond."

Dane turned a quizzical glance at Thomas, but did not interrupt.

"The leaves, when divided, have powerful properties if made into a tea and drunk regularly."

"What sorts of properties?" Dane asked.

Thomas gazed into the setting sun, as if uncertain how to explain. "The human propensity for violence exists on a spectrum. Some people have such a tremendous aversion to violence that they cannot abide the thought of it, and will only raise a hand to another human being in the final, most desperate defense of their life, or that of a loved one, if then. On the other end of the spectrum are those who will pull a trigger with no compunction whatsoever. Most of us lie somewhere in between."

"That's one of the things military training does." Dane thought about his own experiences. "From the beginning, you are never told to kill the 'other man;' everything is referred to as a target, even human targets. There are a lot of other techniques they use as well to try to get you past thinking of the other side as human, because most of us have at least some aversion to killing others."

"When I was doing some research about an ancestor who fought in the Civil War," Bones said, "I read that a good many soldiers couldn't even bring themselves to fire their gun. As soon as the shooting started, they'd hunker down and wait it out."

"Very true." The professor in Thomas was emerging. "Those who can kill without thought make our deadliest soldiers, because they don't flinch in the face of danger, and they never hesitate when it's time to pull the trigger."

"They also make for serial killers," Dane added, "because they have no empathy."

"Precisely. Imagine a fighting force in which every man is completely without fear, yet preserves his intellect, and is thus able to follow orders and make appropriate decisions without fear getting in the way. It would make a difference today on the battlefield, but think of the effect it had in the ancient world, where all the fighting was hand-to-hand, face-to-face, hacking apart another human being. It was vicious and very, very personal."

"But an army, even one that was outnumbered, that drank this tea would make for a better fighting force than a larger force filled with frightened men." The pieces were falling into place for Dane. "Hannibal gave this tea to his troops during the Punic Wars, didn't he?" Thomas nodded.

"And the Spartans must have drunk it before the battle of Thermopylae."

"Spies stole it right out from under the noses of Xerxes and his so-called Immortals. Took all the leaves and the sole remaining seed. Xerxes apparently intended to plant a new tree in the western half of his new empire. It didn't work out for him." Thomas grinned. "It passed from Sparta to Athens, which had the most success in cultivating it. They managed to build up a stockpile of seeds, which eventually fell into Punic hands."

"So how did Carthage not win the war if they had the greatest general of his day, plus this tea?" Bones asked.

"The supply is always limited. The tree is slow-growing and produces a limited number of leaves every year. The priesthood that tended to the trees could not produce enough to keep up with the army's demands. Only certain, special units were given the tea in any case."

"So, when Carthage fell, they took what remained of the seeds and escaped?" Dane tried to imagine the courage or desperation required to cross the Atlantic Ocean in an ancient sailing vessel.

"Their Phoenician ancestors had visited what is now the Americas and the priesthood held on to that knowledge. When it became clear that Carthage was going to fall, they sent a remnant to the New World. Hasdrubal and his followers found this place, settled down, and planted a new tree."

"What does the white side of the leaf do? Mellow people out?" Bones grinned.

"Yes. White tea will pacify the drinker for a short period of time. They will temporarily forsake all thoughts of violence. In a way, it's more deadly than the black tea. Slip your enemy some white tea and you can slaughter them. I imagine you could do just about anything you want to someone who drinks enough of it."

A cloud of suspicion passed through Dane's mind. "Do you think that's how they pacified the natives? Maybe it wasn't that they thought the Punics were gods."

"If that's not how they initially gained their allegiance, they definitely have used it since then as a way of developing a servant class that won't be quick to fight back. They even give it to the animals to make them more docile."

"So ScanoGen hired you to bring them, what, seeds, fruit, leaves from this tree?" Dane asked.

Thomas nodded. "They want to develop this into a weapon. Modify people at the genetic level to make them perfect soldiers."

"And turn enemies into pacifists," Bones finished.

"So, what about those zombie guys?" Dane felt something was not adding up. "Did they get too much black tea or something?"

Thomas took a deep breath. "You aren't supposed to eat the fruit, or at least that's what legend said. But the people here didn't heed that warning. There were natives living in the next valley, and once the five steps were in place, the Punics saw in them a potential extra line of defense. Problem was, the effects of the tea were only short-term, and the supply of leaves limited. They took a chance, and used the fruit. At first it seemed like it had worked, but slowly, the people changed. They not only became killers, a threat to anyone who was different than them, but they lost the ability to feel altogether. They don't feel physical pain, and they don't seem to have any emotions, either. They live in caves, hunt, eat, reproduce, and try to kill anyone who enters their realm. It's a miracle I made it through."

"What does the white half of the fruit do?" Dane tried to imagine the polar opposite of the condition in which those natives now lived.

"It puts them in a state of utter contentment, to such an extreme that the person no longer feels the need to do anything. They forsake all human interaction, and just sit and smile. They don't want anything. They stop eating and drinking, and eventually they stop breathing."

"That's even more horrible than the Mot'jabbur." Bitterness singed Kaylin's every word.

"I can see why the Dominion wants this." Tam pursed

her lips, deep in thought. "Shoot, I can see why anyone would want this. Governments, terrorist organizations, the potential is unthinkable." Her eyes grew wide.

"Wait a minute! Project Pan. The Greek pottery..." She gasped. "It can't be."

"Pandora's Box." Thomas nodded. "The Greek urn in which the seeds of the tree were kept."

"You're telling us that *the* Pandora's Box is here?" Why this was surprising to Dane, after everything else they'd seen, he could not say.

"It goes deeper than that." A mysterious smile played across Thomas's lips. "Think for a moment. Have you ever heard of a tree that bore forbidden fruit?" Dane's mouth went dry as Thomas went on. "A fruit that, when eaten, could cause you to be cursed. Could give you the ability to know evil and do evil things."

"No freakin' way." Bones was on his feet. "That is the tree from the Garden of Eden?"

"Hardly." Thomas chuckled. "But I suspect it is a descendant of the tree or trees that inspired the Garden of Eden story."

Dane stared down at the silver tree with its black-and-white fruit, and wondered if his life could get any stranger. How was it that these things kept happening to him? The others were equally silent, gazing at the wondrous sight in awed, reverent silence. As he looked at the tree, though, something else occurred to him.

"You know what that tree reminds me of? Look at the leaves and the fruit. A circle, half black, half white."

"The Yin and the Yang," Tam whispered. "Maybe it's all tied together somewhere back in very ancient history."

"All I know," Dane stood and looked at Thomas, "is you've uncovered a deadly secret, and because of you, we just might have led men here who would like nothing more than to unleash this on the world."

"Thomas, how could you do this?" Kaylin looked angrier than Dane had ever seen her. "You're helping them do Lord knows what? I never dreamed you were this kind of person."

"You don't understand," Thomas pleaded, dropping to his knees in front of her. He reached out to take her hand, but she slapped it away. "For me, it was always about Fawcett. ScanoGen funded my expeditions, and, yes, they paid me well. The money was going to be for us, for our future together. I swear. Once I solved the Fawcett mystery for myself, I was going to tell them I had failed. That I didn't find anything."

"And you thought they'd just let it go like that? I can't believe you." Kaylin buried her face in her hands.

"Kaylin, I…"

"Just forget it. We'll talk about it later." She waved him away. "Talk to them."

Thomas stood, clearly exasperated. "You have to believe me. I didn't intend to give the information over to ScanoGen. I was just using them to finance my work on Fawcett. I've been fascinated with his story all my life. The mystery grabbed hold of me and wouldn't let go. You," he said to Dane, "of all people, understand that, don't you?"

Dane rose to his feet and looked Thomas in the eye. "Do I know that feeling? Yes. Do I think that makes it okay to do something rash and reckless out of utter selfishness? No way."

Thomas looked like he was about to argue, but words must have failed him. He lapsed into a sullen silence and turned away from Dane.

"What do we do now, Maddock?" Bones asked. "I could throw this dude down the pyramid if you like."

Tam suppressed a chuckle as Thomas's face reddened.

"It wouldn't help us any. We need to get our weapons back and be ready in case ScanoGen shows up. I say we give them a couple of days, and if they don't show, that means they're either lost or the Mot'jabbur got them. If Willis is up to it by then, we'll make our way back home."

He turned to Tam. "Do you think there's any chance of keeping this," he pointed at the tree, "under wraps? You said only one person at ScanoGen knows about it."

"As far as I know, he's the only one. I suppose there's a chance he shared the information, but I doubt it. Other than the Fawcett map, Salvatore Scano only knew in a very general way what it was Professor Thornton here thought he would find—an Amazon plant that would allow them to manipulate human aggression. No one dreamed of this."

"If you're really F.B.I., what do you plan on telling your superiors when you get back to the States?" He searched her big brown eyes, seeking whatever truth might wait there.

"I don't know." She didn't look away as she answered him. "I have a duty to my country, and I take that to heart, but I'm almost as afraid of it falling into our government's hands as I am of ScanoGen and the Dominion, whoever they are, getting hold of it."

"I'd say we chop the thing down and get the hell out of Dodge." Bones stood and stretched. "But I suppose they'd plant another one.'

"There's only one seed left." Thomas said in a soft, almost inaudible voice. "Fawcett told me. Some of what they brought with them from Carthage never took root, nor have many of the seeds the trees here have produced. The trees also don't live as long in this place as they did in the old world. They don't say so, but the people here are worried."

"It would be a blessing for them if the tree had already died," Dane said. Of course, it was too late now. "Let's head back down before it gets dark. I have a bad feeling about tonight."

CHAPTER 28

Brian Fawcett was waiting for them when they reached the bottom of the pyramid, a nervous look painting his face. Armed guards stood nearby, eyeing Dane and the others. He had the feeling they were not there by coincidence.

"Quarters have been prepared for you." Brian cleared his throat. "I shall show you to them. We have food and drink waiting there for you as well. Also, your friends are already there."

"These quarters wouldn't happen to be guarded, would they?" Dane was not certain how long he would tolerate being caged, and he knew Bones to be doubly impatient with such things.

"For your safety, only. Some people are suspicious of new arrivals, you know." The words sounded artificial, and Fawcett reinforced Dane's instinct with a quick shake of the head. He mouthed the word "later," and led them away from the pyramid.

To Dane's disappointment, they were given a room, not in one of the huts, which would have been easy to escape from, but in one of the ancient stone buildings. A contingent of guards escorted Kaylin and Tam away to separate quarters. "Don't drink any tea," Dane warned them as they parted ways. Kaylin looked at him with fear-filled eyes, while Tam merely looked calculating, like she was already planning their escape.

At the room that was to be their quarters, Fawcett entered with Dane and Bones, and a guard closed the door behind them. They heard the lock turn, followed by the sound of a bar sliding into place.

Willis, looking weary, sat on a mat of woven reeds, his bandaged leg stretched out in front of him, and his back against the wall. They all stared at Fawcett, who began pacing the room.

"I understand," he said, "how you must feel."

"I doubt that," Bones said. "And I doubt you have any idea who you're messing with."

"Please, give me time," Fawcett pleaded. "You only just arrived. We need to convince Hamilcar that you only came in search of Thornton. Then, he will believe you mean no harm."

"So Hamilcar is in charge?" Dane asked.

"Technically, no, but everyone on the council defers to him and follows his lead."

"If ScanoGen shows up, he's going to regret locking us up and confiscating our weapons. I doubt there's a person here, besides us, who can use them." Dane kept his voice calm. "We came to rescue Thomas. That's all. We're not here to steal anything from their tree."

"Thornton told you about it, did he?" Fawcett chuckled. "I should not have told him, but I fear holding my tongue is not a talent I possess. Besides, I felt that I owed it to him after he told me all about my grandparents and their homeland. The man is quite the expert on Percy Fawcett, you know."

"We know; believe me." Dane grimaced. "If he'd been a little less interested, we wouldn't be here right now, and neither would ScanoGen."

"Maybe the ScanoGen guys were killed by the Mot'jabbur." Matt's flat voice was devoid of optimism. "Then we'll just have to worry about getting ourselves out of here."

"You are welcome to come with us," Dane said to Fawcett. "I know this is your home, and I won't pretend it's not going to be a dangerous trip back, but if you wanted to see the outside world, you can come along. Like I said before, you'd be a famous man."

Fawcett shook his head. "No. I fear it is not so simple in my case. At any rate, I don't want to see anything happen to Kephises, which is why I am trying to convince you to remain patient. If you try to fight, you will be killed, but I don't doubt you are capable of doing your share of harm, even without your weapons. I don't want to see anyone hurt, especially my brothers and sisters here." He ceased his pacing. "This is a magical place. We live peacefully, work together, care for one another, all without the interference of the outside world."

"I hate to tell you, but that's probably over for you." Dane truly did hate the fact that the secret of Kephises was out of the bag. Hopes of keeping it hidden from the world hinged on the silence of a few ScanoGen members, not to mention that of Thomas, once they got out of here. Dane trusted the rest of his group to keep their silence, including Tam. For some reason, he had already developed confidence in her. He hoped she would be an asset, and not prove to be a mole, cleverly placed by ScanoGen. He had been there before. "Forget the Grecian urn you guys have hidden away somewhere," Dane said. "Thomas opened a Pandora's Box when he got in bed with ScanoGen."

Fawcett flinched at the mention of Pandora's Box. "I really should not have been so free with what I told Thornton. But, I suppose it does not matter now. Promise me you won't try anything reckless."

"That's not a problem." Dane ignored the frowns Bones, Willis, and Matt directed at him. "Just make sure Hamilcar understands that, if ScanoGen attacks, the four of us, with our weapons, will give your people their best chance at survival."

"I shall try." Fawcett made an awkward bow and backed to the door. At the sound of his voice, the door was unbarred and opened slowly, several gleaming spearheads filling the empty space. When the guards were satisfied that their prisoners were not making a rush for escape, they drew back and permitted Fawcett to exit.

No sooner had the door closed than Bones was on his case.

"Are you kidding me?" Bones stared at him like he was from Mars. "What do you mean, telling him we wouldn't try anything?"

"What I said was, we won't try anything *reckless*." Dane grinned. "That word, my friends, is subject to interpretation. And what other people think of as reckless is just another day at the office for us."

"That's what I'm talking about." Willis nodded. "You just say the word and I'm ready to move. I can deal with the leg."

"Wouldn't expect anything less." Dane took a careful look at the room in which they were imprisoned. It was a wonderful example of ancient architecture, made of solid stone, each block precisely fitted together. The floor consisted of smooth, square tiles, so precise they looked as if they were manufactured by modern machinery. Truly, they had stepped back in time.

Which was what he was counting on.

Moving to the far wall behind Willis, he put his hand against it, and found it was cool to the touch. He put his ear to the smooth stone, listened intently, and smiled at the soft sound of running water.

"Okay, everybody look around for a hole, or maybe something in the floor or at the base of the wall that looks like a vent."

"Care to let us in on your little secret?" Bones, to his credit, was already searching the floor even as he asked the question.

"This building has Roman-style air conditioning," he explained. "Well, not actual air conditioning, but water is piped through the walls, which cools the room. It might also have an ancient heating system, which consisted of vents that carried warm air from a fire in a central location throughout the building. Also, when archaeologists excavated the ruins of Carthage, they found that the houses had waste holes that ran down into a communal drain. If they went to the trouble of installing the cooling system, I'll bet you they put in waste disposal."

It required only a few minutes to give the room a thorough search, which turned up nothing. Dane gritted his teeth, thinking hard. There had to be a way out.

"Any more ideas?" Matt asked.

"I've got one," Bones chimed in. "Maybe Willis could move his fat butt so we can see if there's anything underneath him."

"Oh, sorry." Willis winced as Dane and Matt hauled him to his feet.

Dane pushed aside the mat with his toe. Up against the wall, where Willis had sat, lay a square floor tile four times the size of all the others. Grinning, he dropped to his knees and ran his fingers along the edge of the tile. Centuries, or more, of dust and dirt had accumulated in the cracks. As he began scraping and brushing it loose, Matt and Bones lent a hand. Finally, the edges were clear. Dane slipped his fingers down into the open space, and felt a groove running all the way around.

"All right," Dane said. "Everybody grab hold and let's do it."

The ancient stone must not have been moved in a long, long while, for it held tight. Veins stood out on Bones's neck as he tugged. Sweat beaded on Matt's forehead, and his face was screwed up in intense concentration. Dane shifted his weight, gave the tile a jiggle, and was rewarded by a bit of movement.

"Come on, you mother." Bones hauled on the stone with renewed vigor, and, a millimeter at a time, the stone tile came free. They laid the heavy tile to the side and Dane looked down into the hole. Cool air drifted up into the room, carrying with at a faint scent of something unpleasant.

"Okay, Andy Dufresne. You going to crawl through the sewage to freedom?" Bones clapped him on the shoulder.

"Matt and I are the only ones who'll fit," Dane said, looking down into the darkness. The drain was just wide enough that he could work his way through, provided it did not grow narrower at any point further up.

"At least it's a small population," Matt observed. "In a bigger settlement, this thing would be stanky." He sighed deeply. "All right. You first, or me?"

"I'll take the lead. You can pull me out if I get stuck." He turned to Bones. "We'll get back as quick as we can to let you out."

"No problem, bro. If they find you're gone, I'll just bash them in the head with this tile." He grinned at the thought.

"Don't get yourself killed, Bones. I'm serious. Worst case, they come looking for us. I doubt they'll hurt you, unless you give them reason."

"You take the fun out of everything." Bones frowned.

"You heard me. I need you to stay alive in case I have to sacrifice you to the Mot'jabbur on the way back." He ignored Bones's insult and, crinkling his nose, slid headfirst into the tunnel.

Four inches of cold water flowed along the bottom of the drain. He headed upstream, in the direction from which the drain would be fed. Matt was right—the smell was not as bad as it could have been, and soon his olfactory senses tuned it out entirely.

"I hope nobody decides to take a leak right now." Matt couldn't hide the disgust in his voice.

"At least we could see something," Dane whispered. They were moving forward blindly, feeling their way through the dark, smelly drain. Dane's shoulder's scraped the walls, and he felt that familiar warning flash of alarm that divers feel when they find themselves in a precariously tight position. He wasn't diving right now, of course, and if he were to feel like he was getting stuck, he and Matt could simply back up.

They continued on, time seeming to grind nearly to a standstill in the darkness. It was difficult to tell what kind of progress they were making, which made it feel even more frustratingly like they weren't moving at all.

"What do you think?" Matt finally whispered. "Did we

make the wrong move?"

Just then, Dane caught a glimpse of gray in the distance. "I see light. I think we're almost there." Now, with a visible goal in front of him, Dane moved as fast as he dared, devouring the space between himself and what he could now see was the night sky shining into the drain.

When they reached the end of the drain, he took a breath of fresh air and peeked his head out. Here, a stream, probably the one that fed the waterfall back in the valley, wrapped around the edge of the village. The drain angled in from the side, so the current and gravity would naturally carry water through it. The calm rush of water was the only sound in the quiet night.

Staying low in the water, Dane crawled out of the drain, and Matt followed. The faint moonlight cast the village in a silvery haze. Firelight flickered in a few nearby windows, but no one was out. He was about to lead the way out when a figure appeared from the darkness, strolling their way.

Fawcett!

Dane froze. He didn't need to warn Matt to be quiet. The man knew his business. He waited until Fawcett passed them, then rose up quickly and quietly, grabbed Fawcett in a chokehold with one arm, and clamped a hand over the man's nose and mouth. Fawcett grabbed Dane's forearm, but could not dislodge his powerful hold.

"Don't make a sound," he hissed into Fawcett's ear. "It's Maddock. He felt the man relax. I don't want to hurt you, but if you call out, I will. Blink twice if you understand."

Fawcett deliberately closed and opened his eyes two times.

"Do you know where our weapons are?" Fawcett blinked twice. "Good. I'm going to uncover your mouth, and you're going to tell me where they are. Try to give us away and I knock you out and hold you face-down in the water until you stop kicking. Understand?" Two more blinks.

Fawcett sucked in a rasping breath, and coughed. "For

God's sake, man," he gasped, his eyes and nose running, "I'll not betray you. I'm trying to help you, remember?"

"Where are our weapons and supplies?"

"They are in Mago's quarters. Right there." He indicated the first door of the building from underneath which they had just crawled. "He is with his father right now, but his door it is locked up tight. You won't get in, at least not without bashing in the door and drawing attention."

Matt smiled at Dane. "I got this" He took a long look at the space between the stream and the stone building, gauging the distance. "You just be ready when I open the door."

Fawcett frowned as Matt slipped back down into the water. "I'll assume he knows what he is doing." He rounded on Dane like an angry schoolteacher. "You promised me you would not do anything reckless."

"I didn't. If I'd wanted to be reckless, I would have sent my friend Bones through the tunnel. He'd have scalped you and set half this place on fire. And that would just be for starters."

"I actually believe you." Fawcett grinned. "Let's move closer to Mago's door and wait for your friend."

They slipped into the shadows of a nearby palm tree and waited for Matt.

"Did you talk to Hamilcar about us?" Dane whispered.

"Yes. He said to treat you well until he decided what to do about you." Fawcett's eyes narrowed and his lips pursed. "I am worried about these ScanoGen people. I fear he does not take the threat seriously enough. He believes our guards will suffice."

Just then, Dane caught a glimpse of movement in the shadows of a nearby hut. He ducked down behind the pitiful screen of the tree trunk, pulling Fawcett down with him. The figure moved closer, the moonlight outlining its frame. Dane could not believe his eyes.

"Tam," he whispered, just loud enough for her to hear. At the sound of her name, she jerked like a hooked fish. Her eyes searched the darkness and finally fell upon Dane. Dane held up a hand, signaling her to wait, and she nodded.

Less than a minute later, they heard a rattling sound, and the door to Mago's quarters opened. Dane waved for Tam to come on, and they all hurried into the room and closed the door behind them.

"How did you get out?" Dane asked Tam.

"They underestimated me, like always. They only put one guard on us. I acted all girly and helpless, and yelled to him that I was hurt. When he opened the door, I took him down and tied him up. You know the drill."

Fawcett looked dumbstruck, but Dane just grinned as he and Matt gathered their weapons. He handed Tam her Makarov and her flash gun.

"How about you?" she asked. "I was trying to figure out how I was going to disarm four guards and spring you guys."

"Came through the drains," Matt proclaimed proudly proclaimed. "That's how I got in here, too."

"So that's what that smell is." Tam grimaced. "Okay, what's the plan?"

"We leave the tents and the camping gear. Just take ammunition and what food we can carry in a day pack. We'll get the others, and get out of here."

They grabbed packs for everyone, and Dane remembered his sat phone, which he hastily pocketed, just in case. Now ready to move, he turned to Fawcett. "Do you know where Thomas is?"

"I saw him only a short while ago. He was on his way to talk to your friend, Kaylin."

Tam frowned. "I guess we're going to have to fight our way back through the Mot'jabbur."

"Can you think of another way?"

Fawcett cleared his throat. "I should not tell you this, but there is another way out. An ancient escape route put in place early in Kephises's history. But I warn you, it might be even more dangerous than the way you came. There is a legend about a monster…"

"We'll take it. It can't be any worse than the Mot'jabbur. Where is it?"

"It is inside the pyramid," Fawcett said. "There is a sanctuary at its center, and a passageway behind the altar. You will not be permitted to just walk in, though. You have to get past the guards and the priests. Perhaps I can help you with that, and show you the way. Understand, I don't want anyone hurt."

Distant cries of alarm rang out in the night. For a brief instant, Dane feared their escape had been discovered, but then he realized the voices were much farther away than their quarters. And then he heard gunshots, followed by an explosion.

"Too late for that." He turned and looked at Tam. "ScanoGen is here."

CHAPTER 29

The world glowed like an alien landscape through Kennedy's night vision goggles. He gripped his F88 AuSteyr combat rifle with M203 grenade launcher attachment, the same weapon with which the three agents had also been outfitted. He'd managed to get by without using it so far, slipping past the guards outside the tunnel while Wesley created a diversion, blowing up a few of the locals. He now crept forward, keeping to the jungle well away from the path that led toward the pyramid.

They all knew their roles. Kennedy and Smithson would take opposite sides and work their way silently through the jungle, moving toward the pyramid, where he was convinced the secret of this place lay. Wesley was to stick close to the path, keeping behind cover and making enough noise to draw defenders his way. If Kennedy had read Wesley correctly, it would not be long before he lost patience and barreled his way down the pathway like a bull in a china shop. For that reason, Brown was to back Wesley up and wait for orders.

"Wesley, don't overdo it," he whispered, his throat mic picking up his barely-audible voice.

"Roger," came the disappointed voice in his earphone.

"Save your ammo. You're going to need it." The promise of carnage in the near future should satisfy the man.

"I've got targets coming my way," Smithson whispered. *"I think they're moving toward the explosion."*

"Let them pass. Your job is to get to the pyramid as

quickly as possible."

Smithson acknowledged the order and went silent.

"Here they come." It was Brown's voice. *"Wesley, you got a line on them?"*

Wesley's reply was a barrage of gunfire.

Kennedy grinned. If that didn't draw the defenders down the path, nothing would. He set off at a quick pace, careful not to make too much noise, and to keep his eyes peeled for movement. Something burst through the brush in front of him and he raised his rifle.

A deer.

He smirked and kept moving. It would take more than that to get him to lose his cool and fire off a shot that would warn the enemy of his approach. Another sound, this of measured footfalls headed his way, and he ducked behind a tree. Through his night vision goggles, he spotted a figure moving toward him. The man was armed with a spear, and his head was turned in the direction of the road. He moved closer, still looking away, and Kennedy attacked.

Dropping his rifle, he struck the man hard in the temple. He staggered backward, his legs tangling in the underbrush. Kennedy kicked the spear from the man's limp hand and leapt atop him, sliding his KA-BAR from its sheath and holding it to the fallen man's throat.

His eyes went wide at the feel of the cold metal against his throat.

"Do you speak English?" Kennedy whispered.

"A little." The accent was weird, but the words were easy to understand.

"What is the secret of this place? What's your special power?"

"Do not know." The man gasped as Kennedy pressed down, cutting into his flesh. "The tree, I think. The tree!"

"What tree? What's so special about it?" Was the fellow trying to toy with him?

"Priests guard it. Is good tree." His words were faint, punctuated by soft gasps. Kennedy hadn't cut his windpipe, so the breathlessness came from fright. Good.

her a backpack.

"All right." Willis scowled, clearly unhappy with his assignment, but he wasn't one to let ego get in the way of doing the right thing. He knew he wasn't anywhere near one hundred percent. "Let's get going."

"What do you want *me* to do?" Thomas's face was white as a sheet.

"Help Willis," Dane said. "Kaylin likes to take risks. Don't let her do anything stupid."

"Right, because she always listens to advice." Thomas managed a faint smile, clearly relieved that he hadn't been asked to take part in the fighting. "Good luck." He offered his hand, and Dane shook it. "And thank you." With that, he was off.

Dane found it odd that, in the midst of an attack, he was contemplating how he felt about shaking hands with Kaylin's boyfriend. Shrugging off the distracting thought, he turned back to the others.

"I think these explosions are a diversion. They've been far away, and always in the same place. Whoever is firing grenades, or whatever they are, isn't coming any closer. I believe they're trying to draw the defenders down the path, and maneuver around them." He turned to Tam. "I killed one of their men during the fighting down in the canyon. How many do you think they have left?"

"Five at the very most, and that's if that idiot Cy is still alive. Last I saw of him, though, he was running like a debutante toward a surgeon's convention." She saw Dane's confused look. "You know, husbands on the half-shell."

Bones chuckled. "I like you."

"Everybody likes me." Tam gave a coquettish smile. "What's the plan?"

"They're going to have to come out of the jungle sometime. The four of us should spread out and take up defensive positions where we can get a good line of sight and maybe pick them off."

"They have night vision goggles," Tam said. "So stay out of sight. They'll see you before you see them."

"All right," Dane said. "We'll rendezvous at the pyramid if they get behind us."

Tam looked at Bones. "Want to be killin' buddies?"

"Don't mind if I do. We'll take the left flank." The two of them disappeared into the darkness.

After a quick look around, Dane positioned Matt on top of one of the nearby stone buildings, and then headed off to guard the edge of the settlement opposite where Bones and Tam had set up.

A group of defenders, led by Hamilcar, rounded a building and froze when they caught sight of Dane. Hamilcar pointed at him and shouted something in his native tongue. His men looked at him in confusion.

"There's no time to argue!" Dane shouted. "The men out there can see in the dark. They have special glasses." With one finger, he drew circles around his eyes, wondering if he was making any sense at all. "If you run into the jungle, they'll just shoot you."

Hamilcar, to his credit, didn't waste time on indecision. "What should my men do?"

"Bows and arrows are your best bet. We have to assume they are coming after the sacred tree. Hide your men all along the way, and shoot them if they come near. You have to stay hidden, though, because their rifles can shoot a lot farther than your bows."

As if the emphasize the point, one of the Carthaginian men crumpled to the ground, his head ruined, just as the report of a rifle reached them. Dane hit the ground and rolled behind the relative safety of the closest hut. Another man fell and his companions scattered. Another report came from behind them as Matt returned fire.

"Get back to the tree!" Dane shouted, peering around the edge of the hut for a muzzle flash that would give away the attacker's position.

Hamilcar barked an order and the men followed him back through the dwellings, toward the pyramid and their sacred tree.

The next shot buzzed high overhead, obviously aimed at

Matt, and Dane saw only the faintest flash of muzzle fire. They must be using flash suppressors. He didn't waste time, but immediately aimed a shot at the place where he'd seen the shot. Matt's answering shot came a split-second later, and from a different spot on the roof. Dane rolled to his right before their attacker could return fire. No shot came, though. Obviously, the man was on the move. He would be a tough nut to crack.

"Next shot, you fire left, I'll fire right!" Dane called out, hoping Matt was close enough to hear him.

"Gotcha!"

The night grew eerily silent as they waited for their unseen attacker to make his next move.

Smithson was running out of forest cover, and he had two shooters to dislodge. Maddock and his crew must have beaten them to Kephises. "Locals are retreating to the pyramid," he whispered into his throat mic. "I've got two shooters in the village."

"Can you slip around them?" Kennedy sounded unperturbed, as always.

"I'm going to try."

"I want you to stay put for a minute," Kennedy ordered. *"Brown, do you copy?"*

"Roger that." Brown sounded equally calm.

"Change of plans," Kennedy instructed. *"I want you to swing around the right and come in hard. Blow the bastards to hell if you have to."*

"Roger that. Over."

"Smithson," Kennedy continued, *"you wait for Brown's attack, and then make your move."*

"Roger." Smithson hoped Brown would be quick about it.

"What about me?" Wesley sounded like an eager kid on Christmas morning who was afraid he hadn't gotten any presents.

"Keep doing what you're doing."

Wesley didn't acknowledge. It was a good thing Kennedy didn't insist on strict military decorum, or he'd have the man's ass. Kennedy wasn't one you messed around with. Smithson grinned. Maddock and his crew didn't know what they were in for.

CHAPTER 30

Bones heard the shots exchanged, but stayed put, despite his inclination to help out. Maddock wouldn't want him to abandon his post. Besides, it had been a while since he'd heard the last shot. He wondered what was going on. Perhaps this meant the battle would soon be shifting in his direction.

No sooner had the thought passed through his mind than he heard the sounds of lots of feet running through the jungle. He raised his M-16 and waited.

A group of men broke through into the clearing, all of them natives of Kephises. From within the depths of the jungle, someone fired off three shots in rapid succession, and two men went down. This was it! His eyes probed the darkness, seeking out a target.

He saw a burst of muzzle flash, and the ground erupted beneath the running men. Bones squeezed off two quick shots and hit the dirt, rolling behind a giant fern. Bullets sizzled through the spot he'd just occupied. Nearby, men cried out in pain. A few struggled to regain their feet, but others did not move at all. Bones had seen too many of those glassy eyed stares in his lifetime.

He wondered if the attacker could see him hunkered down here. The fern wouldn't offer much protection, but it would hopefully hide him from the night vision-enhanced eyes of the ScanoGen men. Another muzzle flash and, before he could return fire, another explosion, this one too close. He squeezed his eyes shut and turned his head as rocks and debris scoured him. Over the ringing in his ears, he heard an explosion from somewhere in Maddock's direction, and then footsteps pounded close by—the guy was coming right at him. In fact, he was almost on top of him!

"Hey!" Tam shouted. Bones looked up to see the man turn his head in her direction just as she pulled the trigger of her dazzle gun.

The man's scream was one of sheer agony. Reeling, he dropped his rifle and ripped off his goggles. A dazzle gun temporarily blinded a man, but what would it do to someone wearing night vision goggles? Bones had no sympathy for this scumbag who had so callously cut down the men of Kephises, who were only defending their homes and families. As the man turned, Bones drew his Glock, took careful aim, and shot him in the groin.

If the man's screams had seemed agonized before, he now reached a whole new level. He collapsed, one hand pressed to his eyes, the other clutching his ruined groin. Blood seeped between his fingers. His screams quickly gave way to pitiful wails, echoing those of the hurt and dying Kephises men. Bones stood and approached him slowly, ready to finish him off, but Tam beat him to it.

She drew a knife and pressed the tip to the man's heart. "All right Brown, who else is with you?"

"Broderick, you traitor!" The man spat. "I'm not telling you anything."

"I'm not a traitor. I'm a Fed. Now tell me, and I'll make the pain go away. Don't tell me, and I'll leave you here to die. I'll even stab you in the gut to make *sure* you don't make it. Of course, you might enjoy being a blind man. Then again, you're not really a man any more, are you?"

"The hell with you!"

"Last chance." She moved her knife to his abdomen and pressed down. "Who is here?"

"Kennedy, Wesley, and Smithson. Everybody else is dead." He groaned again and shuddered as a spasm of pain racked his body.

"What's your plan?"

"They're going for the tree behind the pyramid. Smithson's swinging around the left, Kennedy's going to sneak through wherever he can, and Wesley's holding back until he's called." He convulsed. "That's all I've got. Now finish it like you promised."

Tam nodded and rose to her feet. She drew her Makarov, took aim, and fired a single shot to Brown's head.

"It sounds like Maddock has engaged with Smithson," Bones said. "If this guy, Wesley, is hanging back, that just leaves this Kennedy guy trying to get to the tree. I say we fall back there and wait for him."

"I agree." Slinging her dazzle gun over her shoulder, Tam took up the fallen man's rifle, checked to see if it was loaded, then took off toward the pyramid.

The defenders who had not been killed or seriously injured were dragging the wounded men to safety. "They're going after the tree!" Bones called to one of them. The man nodded, and then barked orders to his men. Two of them put down the injured men they were carrying, picked up their bows and arrows, and followed Bones.

Great! My army is me, a crazy chick, and some dudes with bows and arrows. Bones grinned in spite of himself. *I kind of like my chances.*

As soon as Smithson heard the explosion, he fired off a grenade of his own and took off running. A sharp, stinging pain sliced across his shoulder as bullets buzzed through the air like angry hornets. Whoever was shooting at him hadn't aimed for his muzzle flash, but to the side. A lucky shot, but he'd had worse. It would take more than that to stop him.

Forty yards and he was out from behind cover. Another bullet clipped the ground at his heel, and then he was behind the cover of an old stone building.

He paused and leaned against the wall, catching his breath, when a hissing sound filled his ears and something cracked against the wall just above his head. He ducked down just as another projectile whizzed past. Arrows! He fired off two shots in the direction from which he thought the arrows had come, and kept moving. This was, without a doubt, the craziest operation he'd ever taken part in.

At the first glimpse of muzzle flash, Dane pulled the trigger on his M-16, aiming to the right, just as he and Matt had planned. He assumed Matt fired to the left, but the world was suddenly engulfed in flame as an explosion rocked the hut behind which he was hiding. Burning debris showered him, and he rolled away as quickly as he could. Up above, he heard Matt fire off a single shot.

"Missed him!" Matt called down. "Are you all right?"

"Yeah." Dane climbed to his feet. "I'm going after him."

Kennedy could not believe his eyes. Brown's limp body lay splayed on the ground, blood pooling around his head and between his legs. Rage boiled up inside of him.

"Wesley, do you copy?" He didn't bother to keep his voice down. Nearby, one of the local men who knelt tending one of the wounded cocked his head, as if he'd heard something strange.

"I'm here," came the eager reply.

"Your objective is the tree behind the pyramid. Come at them will everything you've got. I want to kill every last one of them."

"Roger! Over."

Kennedy didn't bother to hide; he didn't bother to creep. He strode forward, cutting down the men one at a time. One actually charged toward him, brandishing a spear. Kennedy's shot took him in the throat. Another managed to fire off a single arrow, which went wide, before Kennedy shot him down, too.

He strode through the village, putting a bullet in every man who didn't look dead. He killed everyone he saw: those who fought, those who ran, those who dropped their weapons and tried to surrender. The pyramid rose up in front of him, and he smiled. His objective lay just on the other side, and anyone who tried to stand in his way would regret it.

Wesley barreled down the winding path, his rifle at the ready, but no one rose up to challenge him. Not a single arrow flew. He didn't even see anyone running away from him. Damn! Kennedy had held him back so long that all the defenders had retreated, probably to the pyramid. It wasn't fair. He had made the same trek everyone else had, and survived the zombie Indians down in the canyon. He deserved his chance to see this operation to the end. He quickened his pace, determined *not* to miss any more of the fighting.

He burst forth into a residential area. Dirt paths worn smooth over the ages ran between stone houses and wood and thatch huts. He saw the glow of fire to the left and to the right. Some of the huts must be burning. He kept an eye out for anyone who might take a shot at him, but still saw nothing. The sound of gunfire told him that fighting was going on up ahead where the pyramid lay.

He rounded the giant stone structure at full-tilt and came out on a well-tended greenspace. Up ahead, a ring of defenders knelt at the base of a tree. One of them spotted him, shouted a warning, and a cloud of arrows flew in his direction. He dropped and rolled, letting the projectiles pass over him. Shoot at him, would they? He'd show them. Springing to his feet, he unloaded with his grenade launcher.

Gunshots rang out up ahead as Dane dashed forward, careful to remain behind cover as much as possible. He heard more shots, and cries of pain as men fell to ScanoGen's assault.

The pyramid loomed up in front of him, and he clambered up to the first level to get a better vantage point.

He reached the far side and stopped short as gouts of flame burst all around the sacred tree. Every man who stood in its defense was blown off his feet by the fiery blast. The shooter kept coming, firing two more grenades, and then switching to rifle fire.

Dane took aim, but before he could squeeze the trigger, something invisible thwacked the ScanoGen man in the gut, and he tumbled backward, rifle falling from lifeless hands. Dane recognized Bones's whoop of delight. Good man.

That was when the shooter Dane had been stalking made his presence known. He fired off a grenade that exploded somewhere near Bones's hiding place. Dane didn't have time to look for his friend. He had finally spotted the attacker, who wasn't watching the pyramid, but was looking to see if he'd gotten Bones.

Cold determination fixed Dane's resolve. He lined up his shot, took careful aim, and squeezed the trigger. He didn't need to look to know he'd hit his target, but he took a grim satisfaction in watching the man fall from a perfect shot to the head.

He dashed around the pyramid, the faint light of the burning tree flickering across its eroded surface. Reaching the far corner, he sprang down and called Bones's name, and was relieved to hear his friend answer, though his voice was weak.

His relief was short-lived, because just then, a dark figure smashed into him, and he tumbled to the ground, his M-16 clattering to the ground. As he grappled with his attacker, he struck out blindly and his fist met bone in a glancing blow that didn't do much damage. The man struck back, but Dane ignored the punch, focusing on trapping the man's arm.

He was a big man with a buzz cut and a scar on his right cheek. This was Kennedy, whom Tam had described as the most dangerous of the ScanoGen force. Dane barely had time to register the thought when Kennedy raised a knife and brought it plunging down.

Dane put up an arm to block the strike, but before the knife could find its target, a snarling black shadow flew out of the night. Kennedy shouted in surprise as he was bowled over. He rolled to the side beneath the dark shape that continued to snarl.

Unburdened by Kennedy's weight atop him, Dane clambered to his feet and saw the man fleeing from Hamilcar, who was brandishing an ancient sword, and three men armed with spears. Isa the jaguar stood protectively in front of Dane, her teeth bared at the retreating figure. She had come to his aid at just the right time.

Dane knelt and scratched her between the shoulder blades. She nuzzled his arm and purred contentedly. "I should take you home with me, girl. Do you think you'd like it on the beach?"

He heard Bones call his name, followed the sound of his friend's voice, and found him lying on the ground, shaking his head. Tam lay in a heap nearby, bleeding from a scalp wound.

"She's not dead," Bones grunted. "But she's out cold. How many did we get?"

"I got the guy who shot the grenade at you."

"Nice one, bro." Bones rubbed his temple. "He gave me one hell of a headache. Tam got one and I got that guy over there. That just leaves one more."

"Kennedy. He just bolted." Dane hauled Bones to his feet.

"Looks like we failed." Bones shook his head sadly as he stared at the ruined tree. Despite his devil-may-care exterior, Bones retained some of his people's values, and his regard for nature was one of them. He would not relish the destruction of any ancient tree, but this one was particularly tragic.

Dane looked at the charred remains of what, just minutes before, had been a one-of-a kind, miracle of nature. Its silver bark was now a scorched, black hull. The limbs had been blown apart, the leaves incinerated, and now the single fruit was a shriveled ruin in the midst of the burning remnants. No one would ever make use of its power again, but perhaps that was for the best.

"Do we go after Kennedy?" Bones asked.

“I don’t think you’re up to it. Besides, he’s alone and unarmed. I think they can handle him. Let’s get help for Tam.”

“I’m all right.” Tam was sitting with her head between her knees. “Just a little cut.”

Dane knelt and inspected the wound. It wasn’t deep. Still, the girl was tough. “Let’s get this patched up, and then we’ll get out of here.”

CHAPTER 31

Matt met them at the entrance to the pyramid. Willis stood guard just inside.

"Is it over?" Willis asked, a touch of disappointment in his tired voice.

"We think so." Dane helped Tam inside, where Matt hastily cleaned and bandaged her wound. Thomas and Kaylin joined them, and Dane and Bones recounted the details of the fight.

"At least it's finished," Kaylin sighed. "Please tell me we can go home now."

"Kaylin, can we talk?" Thomas shifted his weight from one foot to the other, his eyes flitting from side-to-side.

"What is it?" There was a wariness in her voice, as if she feared the subject he was about to broach.

"Let's go somewhere private, all right?" Thomas took her hand and turned to lead her away, but froze at the sound of someone running down the corridor.

Fawcett burst into the room. "You've got to get out of here right now!" he gasped, sweat pouring down his pallid face. "They're coming for you!"

Dane couldn't believe what he was hearing. "Who is coming? More ScanoGen agents?"

"No. The locals. They blame you all for leading the ScanoGen men here, and they plan on punishing you for it. They're still arguing amongst themselves, but it won't take them long to work up the courage."

"We saved their butts." Bones looked like he was ready

to take them all on. "And this is how they thank us? Bring 'em on!"

"Forget it, Bones," Dane said. "We'll go. No point in fighting to save their lives only to kill them ourselves. Let's get the hell out of here."

Hand on his Walther, he pushed past Fawcett and headed down the corridor, headed toward the exit. He didn't want to fight these people, but he and his friends *would* walk free, whether they liked it or not. No going quietly; no being locked up again.

"Not that way!" Fawcett snapped. "You'll walk right into the middle of them. You'll have to take the other way out. The escape route I told you about." He indicated the dark, downward-sloping passageway that led deep in the heart of the pyramid.

"You heard him," Dane said to his friends. "Let's go. Anyone need a hand?" He looked at Willis and Tam, both of whom shook their heads. They, along with Bones and Matt, followed Fawcett down into the darkness while Dane hung back to cover the rear. Kaylin tried to follow the others, but Thomas pulled her back.

"Kaylin, wait a moment. I wish I could do this another way and," he glanced at Dane, "in another place. I want you to stay here with me." Kaylin gaped. "Hear me out. It's wonderful here. The people have lived in peace for over two thousand years. Even the animals are tame. You didn't see the real Kephises. It's a paradise! We could have the perfect life here. There's a lifetime of study here. You can learn about their history, culture, language, architecture, even their art and music. There is a whole Kephises you haven't seen yet, and we can discover it together in a place of peace and beauty."

Dane thought this was the most absurd thing he'd ever heard. These people would likely hold Thomas, and certainly Kaylin, just as responsible for the carnage ScanoGen had inflicted on their home as they did Dane and the others. He expected Kaylin to laugh, or at least tell him he was insane, but instead she looked… uncertain. Her eyes flitted from

Thomas to Dane, and back to Thomas again.

"I don't know..." she began.

"Stay with me." Thomas dropped to his knees. "Be my wife. They accepted me here. They'll accept you, too. We can help them rebuild their city. Just think, we can be a part of an ancient race that has lasted for two millennia. No one gets that chance. Not ever!"

Kaylin appeared frozen in place. How could she even consider this? She looked at Dane, and a question seemed to hang in the air. What did she want him to do? Talk her out of it? The hell with that! If she was crazy enough to stay here, let her.

And then it struck him. What was it that really bothered him? The fact that she might choose, in his estimation, the dangerous course of staying here and risking the wrath of the people of Kephises, or that she couldn't seem to decide whether she wanted him or Thomas? In any case, there was no time to ponder it further.

"I think you're both crazy if you stay here," he said. "Mobs aren't known to be judicious, and if they're half as angry as Fawcett seems to believe, it's not a risk you should take. Whatever you decide, though, you need to make up your mind now. They could be here any second, and we're bugging out."

Kaylin took Thomas's face in her hands. "Come with us," she whispered. "It's not safe for you here."

"I see." Thomas's tone was as flat as the expression on his face. He pulled her hands away and stepped back. "You made your choice." His eyes flitted in Dane's direction for the briefest of moments. "Now go."

"Thomas, please."

"No!" Thomas turned his back on Kaylin, crossed his arms, and stared at the wall. "Hurry, before they catch up with you all. I'll tell them I think you went into the forest. That should buy you some time."

Tears running in rivulets down her cheeks, Kaylin bolted the room, and Dane followed. He didn't know what to say to Kaylin, and frankly, he wasn't inclined to talk to her right now. Maybe, if they both got out of this mess in one piece, they would talk about it then.

The passageway led down into an antechamber, the walls of which were carved with scenes from Carthage's history, mostly great military victories. Dane felt a pang of regret that he could not stop to examine them more closely. *I find Fawcett's lost city and I don't get to stay but for a few hours,* he thought.

The antechamber opened into a room about forty feet square, its walls angled inward, approximating the shape of the pyramid outside, meeting at a tiny shaft far overhead. Two flickering oil lamps flanked an ancient Grecian urn atop a stone altar, which was supported by a four foot-high block of stone, in the room's center. Dane did a double-take, realizing this urn was very likely the legendary Pandora's Box.

"About time," Bones greeted them. "Thought you'd decided to stay here and play hero a little longer."

Dane shook his head and inclined his head toward Kaylin. Bones took one look at her face, still wet from tears, and understanding filled his eyes. "Gotcha. Sorry, Kaylin."

"This is the temple," Fawcett explained unnecessarily. "The way out is back here." He waved for them to come around to the back side of the altar.

"I'm surprised no one is in here," Dane observed. "No priests?'

"The guards have all left to fight. The priestess who was to have been here tending the flame is, um, a close friend of mine. She chose to tend to the wounded for a little while. Long enough for you to make your escape."

Dane rounded the altar and watched Fawcett place his hand over a symbol carved in the stone block on which the altar rested, and press down. A trap door sprang open, revealing a low, dark tunnel.

"In here," Fawcett said, motioning toward the opening. Bones took the lead, and the others followed, until only Dane remained. Fawcett grabbed his arm. "Listen carefully. You will come out at an underground river. Follow it down to where it ends in a box canyon. At the far end of the canyon, you will find the black water.'

"What is the black water?"

"You followed my great-grandfather's map, did you not?" Dane nodded, and Fawcett continued. "All I know is that you should have left the river and passed into the black water."

"Okay. I know the place you're talking about." He meant the lagoon where they had left their boats. Perfect.

"Take this." Fawcett shoved a small pouch of woven grass into his hand. "It is the last seed from the tree. Take it somewhere safe. Its power is great, as is its potential for harm, and for that reason, we cannot risk those men coming back for it." He paused. "But something so wondrous should not pass from this world."

"But, this rightfully belongs to Kephises!" Dane protested. "It's their secret to guard, not ours."

Fawcett laughed. "It is a secret that once belonged to Carthage. Before that, it was Athens's secret, Sparta's before that, and so on. The tree does not belong to any one people. Not forever, at any rate."

"What happens when they find it gone?"

"I rubbed ash on an avocado seed and switched them out. It looks quite similar. I don't doubt the priesthood will discover the switch when it comes time for planting. By that time, you will be long gone, and hopefully they will blame one of you. No offense."

"None taken." The bag had a long drawstring of vine, so Dane hung it around his neck and tucked the pouch inside his shirt. "Thank you." He shook Fawcett's hand and turned to make his escape.

"One last thing," Fawcett said. "The legends say the box canyon is the domain of the mapinguari. Be careful."

Dane was halfway into the passageway, but he stopped and looked back. "What is a mapinguari?"

"A monster, I suppose. That's all I know." Fawcett looked around. "I had better go. They can't know that I helped you. It is not my life I care about, but my friend's.

Good luck!" He hastily pushed the trapdoor closed, leaving Dane in darkness.

It had been far too easy to elude his pursuers, Kennedy thought. They certainly lacked the tracking skills of the natives of this region. If this place truly was a remnant from the ancient world, isolation had caused them to go soft. He had outdistanced them, doubled back, and slipped past their line. It might have appeared that he'd fled in panic, but it had been a strategic retreat. He was out of allies and weapons, save his KA-BAR.

How had he let himself lose it like that? When he saw Brown lying dead, something inside him had snapped, just like in Kandahar. He couldn't let it happen again. This mission was a hair's breadth from failure, and it would take all his skills and a bigger dose of luck to get him through.

The minutes crept by, and gradually the people retired to their quarters, leaving only a few out on patrol. He needed to catch one of them alone so he could get some answers.

As if on cue, a man came strolling down the path toward Kennedy's hiding place. Incredibly, he appeared to be unarmed and unconcerned about his own safety. When the man passed by, Kennedy raised up, grabbed him from behind, and dragged him into the undergrowth.

"You speak English?" Kennedy growled his hand pressing down on the man's nose and mouth. The man nodded, though his eyes were on Kennedy's KA-BAR, which hovered a few inches from his face. The man held Kennedy's wrist in a firm grip, keeping the knife at bay, but Kennedy was stronger; even as the man held on, the knife moved incrementally closer.

"I want to know what Thomas Thornton was after."

The man gave his head a little shake, as if he did not know what Kennedy was talking about, but there had been a momentary flash of understanding in his eyes that Kennedy did not miss. He knew something! Kennedy leaned a little harder, and the knife moved closer. The man was turning purple from lack of air, and the blade of the knife was dangerously close to his eye. Finally, the fight went out of his eyes and he nodded.

"Tell me everything, tell me quiet and fast, and you might live." He removed his hand and the man sucked in a breath. In short order he had spun an incredible tale of a tree with the power to make a man a killer or a pacifist—at least that was how Kennedy understood it. Apparently, it was also what had spawned those zombie men they had encountered previously. The warrior he had questioned earlier had also claimed the tree was special. A sudden, disturbing thought turned his insides cold.

"Tree? You mean the tree Wesley blew up?" He had seen it happen from a distance. The reckless soldier had gone barreling in to the fray, not even thinking, and started blowing up everything in sight.

"Yes." The fellow was either too smart or too frightened to look triumphant. "It's gone."

Kennedy thought hard. Had he lost all his men for nothing? There had to be an answer. "Can they plant a new one?" Once again, the truth was in the man's eyes, and he didn't try to deny it. "What do they have? Cuttings? A seed?"

"The seed is in the temple, in an urn on the altar."

"Show me." Kennedy yanked his knife hand free from the man's tiring grip, stood, and hauled him to his feet. "Don't make a sound. If we see someone, we hide. Don't you do anything, *anything* to rat me out. I can spill your guts and be gone in an instant, and you'll die slowly and painfully for nothing. Got me?"

The man nodded, turned, and guided them back down the path, Kennedy holding on to his shirt tail. They reached the pyramid without incident, and the man led him up a sloping tunnel, then down a steeper one. He wondered if he was being led into a trap, but how could one have been set?

He spotted the urn the moment they stepped into the gloomy temple.

A brown-haired woman with olive skin knelt before the altar. At the sound of their entry, she turned and her eyes went wide with shock. "Brian," she gasped. "What has happened?"

"Miri, I…"

"Don't say another word, or you both die!" Kennedy might just kill them anyway. He'd had more than his fill tonight. "Is this the urn?" The man, Brian, nodded, and Kennedy gave him a shove that sent him sprawling on the ground at the woman's feet. She knelt beside him, scowling at Kennedy and taking Brian in her encircling arms like a mother bear protecting her cub.

Kennedy mounted the steps to the altar, reversed his KA-BAR, and brought it down hard. Miri cried out as the urn shattered. Fishing through the shards, he pulled out a large, grayish seed. He held it up in the lamplight to get a closer look.

"That is not…" the woman began. Too late, Brian clapped a hand over her mouth.

"What do you mean?" Kennedy formed each word like a death sentence, because that's exactly what it was—Brian's death sentence.

The woman shoved Brian's hand away, and they both clambered to their feet and backed away. "That is not the seed," she whimpered. "That man must have taken it. The one from outside."

"Dane Maddock?" The name was a curse on Kennedy's lips. He leapt down and stalked the pair as they backed around the altar.

"I suppose so. He and his friends took the seed and left through the door. Look back here!"

"Miri! No!" Brian's words fell on deaf ears as Miri ran to the altar, pressed something, and a hidden door swung open.

"This is the way out," she said. "It will take you under the land of the Mot'jabbur. The dead warriors. You will not have to pass through their lands this way."

Kennedy's eyes narrowed. What if this was a trick? Maybe she had just opened the door to a pit like the one that had taken the life of one his guides just two days before. Then again, why would you build a death trap into the back of an altar?

Kennedy leaped forward, grabbed the woman by the wrist, and yanked her to him. "Tell you what, lady. You go first and show me the way." She screamed and clawed at his arm, trying to get loose.

"No!" Brian yelled. "Take me! I'll show you the way." He started babbling, explaining how he had stolen the seed, replaced it with a fake, and given the real one to Maddock. He even described the woven grass pouch in which he'd placed the seed.

Kennedy was seriously considering killing him just to shut him up when a roar filled the temple, and he whirled to see a burly man with brown hair and a short beard bearing down on him, holding an ancient sword aloft. This was Hamilcar, the one who had chased him earlier. Kennedy owed him. He turned and charged.

Hamilcar's sword sliced through empty air as Kennedy dodged to his left and delivered a swift kick to the man's foreleg. The man was sturdily built, though, and the kick didn't faze him. Hamilcar was also faster than Kennedy expected, and his backhanded swipe nearly opened Kennedy's throat, but the miss left him vulnerable. Seeing the opening, Kennedy struck, and his KA-BAR opened a gash in Hamilcar's side.

Hamilcar didn't even wince, but took a step back and resumed his attack. The Bronze Age sword was no more than two feet long, but that still gave Hamilcar a decided reach advantage over Kennedy with his knife. Kennedy parried a thrust and danced to the side, looking for an opening.

Something flew through the air, just missing his head. Brian was atop the altar, hurling pieces of the broken urn at Kennedy's head as fast as he could.

The distraction was almost the death of him. Hamilcar aimed a vicious thrust for his heart, but Kennedy spun at the last second. The sword whistled past him. Hamilcar had overextended his attack, and before he could draw back,

Kennedy lashed out with his KA-BAR, going for the throat. Hamilcar ducked, and the blade caught him on the crown of his head, nearly taking his scalp. He roared in pain and swung his sword at Kennedy's legs. Kennedy sprang back and crouched, ready to finish it, when a half-dozen armed men burst out of the passageway and through the antechamber.

Out of options, Kennedy turned and ran for the trapdoor.

Chapter 32

The passage spiraled downward as if a giant had twisted a corkscrew into the ground. Dane walked hunched over, one hand on the wall, the other on the cold stone above, until the ceiling was finally high enough that he could stand. Deeper into the darkness he went, with every step seeming to heap a greater weight upon him. Two thousand year-old passageways didn't inspire confidence, but he reminded himself this place had stood for this long. Why shouldn't it last a bit longer? He soon caught up with the others, and was pleased to see Matt had held on to his flashlight.

"You didn't think to snag a few of those for the rest of us?" Dane joked.

"Nope. You were all guns and munchies, so that's what I got for the rest of you. Besides, we were sort of in a hurry." Matt let the light play around the sloping passage. The stonework was solid, with every block fitted together with precision.

Breathing easier now, Dane checked on Willis and Tam, both of whom insisted they were fine, though Willis was keeping one hand on the wall and moving slowly.

"What's supposed to be down here?" Bones asked. "Jimmy Hoffa?"

"A subterranean river. We follow it, and it will take us to a canyon close to the lagoon where we left the boats. This way, we won't have to fight our way through the Mot'jabbur."

"Sweet!" Bones clapped him on the shoulder. "Looks like things are finally going our way. In fact," he cocked his head to the side, "I think I hear the river up ahead."

Dane listened intently, and could just make out the whisper of water running over rocks. "Great. Now, let's take stock. What do we have in the way of weapons and provisions?"

"I have my flashlight!" Matt replied. "But you already knew that."

Willis still had his Mossberg, but was running low on ammunition, and everyone except Tam still carried a side arm. If they did manage to avoid the Mot'jabbur, they should be okay. Food was in short supply. Everyone carried a pack with a few freeze dried meals and a canteen. They would try to supplement along the way back, but there was no reason they couldn't make it back to what passed for civilization in these parts on what they had, though they'd all probably be a few pounds lighter when they arrived. The worst part would be listening to Bones complain, but it would hardly be the first time.

The passageway came to an abrupt end at a rock ledge that jutted out into the swift-moving water. Matt directed his light downstream. Stalactites dangled from the ceiling like sinister chandeliers, waiting to fall on unsuspecting travelers.

"So, do we swim it?" Tam pursed her lips, looking doubtfully at the dark water.

"We can take off our pants and make flotation devices out of them." Bones sounded eager. "Ladies first!"

"You couldn't handle it, sweetie," Tam said. "Not in a million years."

Something in the corner of his eye caught Dane's attention. "Matt, turn your light this way." Leaning against the wall, just a few feet upstream from where they stood, was a raft.

"A two thousand year-old raft from Carthage? No thank you," Bones scoffed. "I say we put my 'no pants' idea to a vote. Who's with me?"

Dane and Matt took a closer look and were surprised by

what they found.

"This thing is new." Matt rapped on the logs and tested the vines which bound it together. "I wonder who put it here and why?"

Dane knew in an instant. "It was Fawcett. He was the one who told me about this place."

"How do you think he got it down here without them noticing?" This was the first thing Kaylin had said since leaving the temple.

"I got the impression he has someone, maybe a girlfriend, in the temple priesthood. I suppose she could have let him slip a few things down here at a time. It wouldn't have taken much."

"Look here, Maddock!" Matt knelt and looked behind the raft. "There's a basket of food here: nuts, dried fruit and meat. There's even a gourd for water. You don't think…" He looked up at Dane.

"He was planning on leaving." The full impact of what Fawcett had done for them hit him hard. Fawcett had been preparing for his escape, was possibly even planning on taking his priestess girlfriend with him, but he had given it up so they could get away.

"We'd better not let his sacrifice go for nothing, then." Kaylin's voice was husky with emotion, but her resolve was clear. "Let's get out of this place."

The raft could not bear everyone's weight, so Dane and Bones handed their guns over to the others for safe-keeping, and swam behind, holding on to the back. The water was frigid and Dane immediately missed his diving suit.

"Dude, I am never going to be able to have kids after this," Bones said. "Matt, we're trading places in a few!"

"Can't. Somebody has to hold this flashlight."

Dane laughed. "Bones, you don't want to have kids anyway."

"I don't know. Heck, I might already have kids scattered all over the world. Who can say? Lots of little Bones running around."

"Stirrups," Tam said absently.

"Say what?" Bones looked at her like she was crazy.

"The stirrup is the smallest bone in the human body. You know, 'lots of little Bones…'"

Bones grimaced. "Science hurts my head. Of course, I'm not feeling any other pain thanks to this ice water. I might not feel anything ever again."

"Do us all a favor," Dane said, "and stick your mouth in the water until it's numb."

Everyone, including Kaylin, laughed, and they relaxed as the current swept them along. They shared some of the food Matt had found, and as the distance between them and Kephises increased, their spirits rose in turn. Soon, they were laughing as they ducked low-hanging stalactites and the miles swept away behind them.

It was difficult to track the passage of time, but Dane knew they were making much better time floating down this river than they had hiking through the jungle. He assumed they had to be getting close to their destination.

"Um, Maddock," Matt called. "Do you see what I see?"

Dane peered up over the raft and saw a faint glow in the distance.

"We must be getting close to the end. Cool!" It would be a relief to get out of this cold water and onto dry ground."

"That's not what I'm talking about!" Matt's voice rose as he called out. "Look in front of us!"

At first, Dane saw nothing but low-hanging stalactites shrouded in gray mist. Then he realized that the sound of the river had been growing progressively louder for some time now. He raised up a little higher to get a better look.

"Aw, hell!" Willis exclaimed. "Waterfall!"

Thirty feet ahead and closing fast, the river poured out over a rock shelf and tumbled into a void. There was no way they could all leap from the raft to the rock shelf—the water was moving too fast.

Dane and Bones grabbed hold of the vines that knotted the raft together and began kicking furiously, trying in vain to swim against the current and arrest the raft's momentum.

Tam and Willis both began paddling backward on the same side, almost upending the craft.

"It's not going to work!" Dane looked all around, but the walls were worn smooth by the passage of water and time. There was nowhere to get a handhold. And then he looked up. "Grab a stalactite!"

Everyone looked at him as if he was crazy, but then understanding dawned on Willis's face. He reached up and grabbed hold of the closest one.

It broke off in his hand.

"Damn!" Willis tossed the stalactite aside and reached for another, but by this time, Matt had stood and wrapped his arms around the biggest stalactite he could reach. The raft pivoted under his feet and Dane and Bones were spun about so that they were now downstream of the craft, their feet precariously close to the edge of the fall.

"It's going out from under me!" Matt shouted, still hanging on. By this time, Willis had gained his feet and found two handholds. He stood, arms spread apart, holding on for dear life.

"You look like Samson!" Bones shouted. How he could still make his wisecracks at a time like this was beyond Dane.

"Let's hope for a better outcome than that story." Tam grunted, struggling to find a handhold of her own without tipping the raft.

"Bones, can you at least be serious when we're feet from going over a waterfall?" Dane was working his way to the corner of the raft, which would put him close to the rock shelf, but still not close enough to reach. "Okay," he called to the others on the raft. "We need to start working the raft over to one side. Willis, can you reach a little to your left and grab that next one?" Willis nodded and shifted his grip. The raft wobbled as he reached out, but didn't tip. One at a time, each person on the raft took hold of a new stalactite and, on Dane's command, pulled. The raft inched closer to the side.

"Again!" Dane shouted. He was holding on, still kicking for all he was worth, but he could feel the water inching him closer to the edge. The moments seemed to melt into hours as they hauled the raft ever closer to the edge.

Finally, the raft struck the side and Dane scrambled out onto the ledge. He hauled Bones up, and the two of them helped Kaylin and Tam to safety. Now only Matt and Willis remained.

"You first!" Matt shouted.

"Naw, man. I'm closest to the edge. You'd never make it over."

"But you've got the hurt leg."

"Just go, and make it fast. And when you get off this thing, get the hell out of my way." Willis took a deep breath and tightened his grip. Veins bulged in his neck and cords of muscle on his powerful arms rippled in the half-light under a sheen of sweat and mist as he held the raft in place against the powerful current.

Matt took two steps, leaped, and rolled as he landed, clearing the way for Willis, from under whom the raft was already moving.

Willis let go, bent his legs, getting his balance, and, as the raft came even with the rock shelf, jumped. The wobbly foundation of the moving raft, plus his injured leg, betrayed him, and his leap fell short. He hit the water inches short of the ledge and was swept downstream.

Dane leaped and caught Willis's wrist. His wet skin was hard to hold on to, but Dane maintained his grip as the heavier man pulled him down toward the edge of the waterfall. Dane tried to dig in with his feet in order to arrest his slide, but he found no purchase on the smooth stone.

Then he felt strong hands grasp him by the legs, holding him fast. Matt stepped over him and hauled Willis up out of the water.

"You don't have to do everything by yourself, Maddock." Bones stood and helped Dane up.

"Like I'd be anywhere without you guys." He took a moment to assess their situation. No one was hurt. They had lost his and Bones's backpacks, the basket of food, and Willis's Mossberg.

"There goes our raft." Kaylin pointed down to where

the river flowed across the subterranean chamber in which they stood, dropping out of sight at the other end, continuing its descent to places unknown. Pieces of the shattered raft bobbed in the churning water, carried away by the current.

"That's okay. We don't need it anymore." Dane pointed to a spot on the far side of the chamber, where a shaft of light shone through the mist. "We've found the way out."

The climb down was an easy one, save for Willis, but he managed. They picked their way across the stone, buoyed by the promise of daylight and warmth.

Bones crinkled his nose. "You smell that?" He sniffed and frowned. "It's like a pole cat or something."

He was right. There was an unpleasant odor in the air, faint, but definitely that of an animal. "Could be anything. All sorts of creatures in the Amazon."

"Can't be any worse than what we've already bumped into." Bones grinned. "It's not a zombie native smell, so I'm game for whatever we find."

The morning sun was a blessed relief to Dane's waterlogged body, and he soaked in its warmth with a smile on his face. As Fawcett had described, they were in a high-walled box canyon. Kapok trees towered above a forest of palm, Brazil nut, and other trees he couldn't identify. All around, he heard the calls of bird as they welcomed the break of day.

"Now this is nice." Kaylin managed a weak grin. All they had been through was taking its toll on her, even more so than anyone except Willis, who, despite his brave exterior, looked like he was about to drop. A blue macaw landed in a nearby tree and turned its head to look at them in curiosity.

"How about we find a place to rest for a few hours?" Dane suggested. No one looked at Willis, but they all knew why he made the suggestion.

"Naw, I'm good. We all got some sleep on the raft."

Dane knew it was pointless to argue, so they set off. The going was excruciatingly slow as they hacked their way through the tangled undergrowth. If any non-flying creature lived here, it would have to be one that either slithered on the ground or swung through the trees.

"My kingdom for a machete," Matt grumbled as he hacked away with his knife. "Why didn't I grab them when I broke into Mago's quarters?"

"Hush!" Tam waved a hand at Matt. "What's that sound?"

A high pitched sound, somewhere between a squeak and a chirp, rang out above the sounds of the jungle. "It's over there. Take my pack." She slipped off her pack, shoved it into Willis's arms, dropped to the ground, and crawled into the underbrush.

"Seriously?" Bones shook his head. "Just crawl around down there with the creepy critters. We'll wait for you."

Tam returned a minute later clutching something small, white, and fluffy to her chest. "It's a baby harpy eagle. It was nuzzled up against its dead mother. Must have tried to fly to her and fell."

"I've never heard of it." Bones leaned down for a closer look.

"It's the largest eagle in the world, and they're nearly extinct in some parts of the world. Deforestation is wiping them out." A grim expression fell across her face. "Something else wiped out this one's mother. She was nearly torn in half."

"Wonder what did that to her?" Dane was suddenly wondering if there was something to the mapinguari legend after all. "Say, have any of you ever heard of the mapinguari?"

"Hell yeah!" Bones fist pumped. "It's like Bigfoot meets the giant sloth."

"How do *you* know about it?" Tam asked as she took her pack from Willis and set about making a comfortable place for the baby eagle to rest. Apparently they now had a mascot. "You don't seem the scholarly type."

"Bones only studies things that are, umm…" Kaylin began.

"Controversial," Bones finished.

"Bullcrap is more like it," Willis said.

"Hey, somebody's got to know about Bigfoot and Nessie and all that good stuff. That somebody is me."

Tam finished making a nest for the bird inside her backpack, and put it on backward, like a baby carrier. Bones took the lead as they resumed their trek, happily carrying on about the mapinguari.

"There are all kinds of stories about it. The far-fetched ones say it has caiman skin, backward feet, and a mouth in its belly."

"The 'far-fetched' stories?" Kaylin smirked.

"We just discovered a two thousand year-old Punic city in the middle of the Amazon. Do you really want to take a tone with me?"

"Fair enough," Kaylin said. "Go on. We're all ears.'

"Anyway, it seems most likely that it's a descendant of Mylodon, an ancient, ground-dwelling sloth. It was ten feet tall." Bones slashed at a low-hanging limb and dodged as it sprang back at his face. "Supposedly, the mapinguari is a carnivore, and it can move in total silence through the thickest vegetation. Then again, some people think it's not a ground sloth, and can swing through the trees, as long as the limbs are strong enough to hold it."

"What else?" Dane found himself searching the upper reaches of the kapok trees, keeping an eye out for the legendary beast.

"It's hard to kill because of its thick skull, and sturdy bones. And it's got a tough hide and this coarse, matted fur that arrows bounce off of if you don't hit it just right. It hates the scent of a human, and people get dizzy when they look at it, but that's probably because of its strong odor..." His words trailed away and he stopped and turned to face Dane. "Just out of curiosity, why do you ask?"

"Oh, it's no big deal, really. According to Fawcett, this canyon is where it, or they, supposedly live, and it's supposed to be death to pass through here."

Five seconds of stunned silence hung in the air as everyone stopped and stared at him.

"Why are you just now telling us this?" Matt sounded uncannily like Dane's father, back when Dane was a child and had neglected to mention something important, usually a failing grade or a paper that needed signing.

"What would have been the point? We didn't have any other choices. Besides, it's probably just a legend, anyway."

"And if someone asked you if the chupacabra was real?" Bones arched an eyebrow.

"Fine! I get the point. Let's just get the hell out of this canyon." He brushed past Bones, who, unlike the others who were still staring at him in disbelief, was looking crest-fallen.

"What's wrong with you?" Dane frowned.

"We came all the way to the home of the mapinguari, and I don't have a camera."

Kennedy knelt in the shadow of a kapok tree, chewing on a Brazil nut and letting the humid air bathe his frozen body. It had been child's play to use his clothing as a flotation device as he rode the river, but the frigid water had nearly been the death of him. He'd scarcely been able to pull himself out of the water before what would have been a certain fall to his death over the waterfall. His body temperature had fallen, too, and he found himself feeling sluggish and confused as he made his way out of the underground cavern.

He would be all right, though. He'd been through worse in the service. Already, his senses were sharpening. He'd immediately spotted tracks left by Maddock and his party, and followed them to where they had cut a trail through the undergrowth.

He grinned. Nice of them to clear him a path. It would take him minutes to cover distances that had taken them hours to hack their way through. Best of all, he doubted they had any idea he was on their trail.

CHAPTER 33

"Did you hear that?" It was about the third time Matt had asked the question, but this time, Dane did hear something. It was a rustling somewhere in the distance, and it was coming closer.

"Can't be the mapinguari. It's silent, but deadly." Dane could tell Bones was trying to sound more positive than he felt.

"Smells like a silent but deadly." Willis grimaced.

He was right. Borne on a gentle breeze, the same foul odor that was evident in the underground cavern now assaulted Dane's nostrils. He drew his Walther, regretting the lost backpack with his reloads. He had four bullets left in this clip. "Bones, do you have any more wisdom to share about this thing?" The rustling grew closer and the stench was almost overpowering.

"They're afraid of water. Won't cross it." Bones said, tapping the handle of his Glock. Unlike the others, who were visibly nervous, Bones was as calm as ever. Then again, perhaps he was just crazy. "I'll bet there's a stream or something running across the end of this box canyon. That would explain why they haven't expanded their territory."

"All right, everyone. If we get separated, make for the end of the canyon as fast as you can. We'll meet up at the lagoon."

The rustling sound ceased. They all turned and looked in the direction from which the unseen thing had been approaching. What was it doing? From inside Tam's backpack, the little harpy eagle sounded a shrill cry, and then, all was bedlam.

The attack came from behind. With an unearthly roar, a monstrosity of tangled reddish-orange fur dropped down in the midst of their group. It swiped at Matt with a clawed hand, cutting him across the chest. Dane whirled and fired, catching the moving beast in the head. It roared again and vanished in a flash, scrambling on all fours into the jungle.

It wasn't over.

Another of the creatures, probably the one they'd heard stalking them, burst from the tangled forest, knocking Bones to the ground. Dane aimed for the gut this time, but the mapinguari was fast, and his bullet caught it in the thigh as it sprang toward him.

Dane dropped and rolled as the beast flew past him. It rounded on him. It had a long snout, beady, black eyes, and a mouth full of razor sharp teeth. Its body was covered in red-orange fur, like that of an orangutan, except its belly, which was leathery, dark red flesh. Moving faster than Dane would have thought possible, it attacked, but Matt, Bones, and Willis were ready. They all opened fire. There was no telling how much damage the bullets actually did to the strange beast, but it fled, leaving a trail of blood behind.

"Whew!" Bones said. "That was freakin' crazy."

Just then, the jungle behind them came alive with the cries of angry mapinguari.

Bones looked at Dane. "What now?"

"Now we run!"

"What the hell?" Kennedy stopped short, looking all around. Up ahead he heard the cry of an animal like none he'd ever heard before, followed by gunshots, people shouting, and more roars. The outburst only lasted for a matter of seconds, and then silence…

…followed by bedlam.

They were in the trees and in the jungle all around him. Big, furry, orange things swinging toward the sound of the gunshots. He didn't know what they were and he didn't care. He just wanted to get out of there.

The jungle seemed to grab at him as he ran, as though nature itself was working in concert with the unseen creatures. Gunshots occasionally broke through the din of bestial roars. He didn't know whether to hope Maddock's men were killing these creatures, whatever they were, or if he should root for the beasts. Then again, he had to have the seed. He *had* to have it.

One of the monsters broke through the foliage to his left and came for him. He saw a flash of white teeth and long, razor-sharp claws. He hit the ground and rolled under it, stabbing up into its exposed gut as it flew past him. His KA-BAR dragged across the tough hide, but didn't pierce the flesh.

He came to his feet, knife at the ready. The creature turned, circling him warily. He didn't understand why. He certainly hadn't done it any damage. Snarling, the beast struck at him with its wicked claws.

Kennedy leapt back, breaking through a tangle of brush, and nearly falling into a twenty foot gorge. He teetered on the edge, staring down at the swift-moving stream that tumbled over and around jagged boulders. Righting himself, he turned to face the monster. Its head broke through the foliage and it froze. It sniffed the air, roared, and turned and ran.

What had just happened? Why had it not finished him?

There was no time to contemplate this turn of events, because just then, he looked around and spotted Maddock helping the blonde, Kaylin Maxwell, up onto a fallen tree that spanned the gorge. On the opposite side he saw figures vanishing into the forest. The others had already crossed. He was almost too late.

Maddock stood with his back to Kennedy, watching the girl. Perfect. Kennedy drew his KA-BAR and attacked.

Dane heard the approach of his attacker only an instant before the man was upon him. He whirled around, barely dodging the knife thrust. It was Kennedy. How had he caught up with them? It didn't matter now.

Dane drew his Recon knife just as Kennedy rolled to his feet and came at him again. Dane wished he had even one bullet left in his Walther, but he had expended them all fighting off the mapinguari, which, just as Bones had said, did not seem to want to come anywhere near the water.

Kennedy feinted and Dane stepped to the side, flicking his knife at Kennedy's eyes. The man moved his head just enough to avoid the blow, and slashed at Dane's knee. Dane shifted his feet and made the man pay with a quick slash that missed his throat, but opened a gash in his cheek. Now he'd have another scar to match his first one.

Kennedy, baring his teeth, crouched, looking for an opening. They circled one another in silence. Dane could see Kaylin out of the corner of his eye. She was more than halfway across, and must not have heard the attack over the sound of the rushing water far below her. That was fine with him. She didn't have any bullets left either, and even if she did, he wouldn't want her involved. He wanted her to get to safety with the others.

"Just give me the seed and I won't kill you," Kennedy growled.

"What do you want it for?" Dane kept his voice conversational, though his every nerve was charged.

"I don't want it, but those whom I serve want it very badly."

"Those you *'serve'*? What kind of talk is that for a tough guy? ScanoGen must pay you pretty well if you'll grovel like that for them."

Kennedy barked a laugh. "You're as ignorant as I thought. ScanoGen pays me well, but I only work for them. I serve the Dominion. Perhaps you've heard of them?"

The words caught Dane totally by surprise, and Kennedy used the moment of shock to make a quick thrust at Dane's midsection, one which he barely avoided.

"I don't know what you did in Utah, Maddock, but rest

assured, the Dominion knows your name, and they know Bonebrake. When I make my report, you're both dead men. If you give me the seed, though, I'll ask them to spare the lives of your friends Barnaby, Sanders, Dean, and Maxwell." His confidence was growing as he spoke. "I know your type, Maddock. You don't want their blood on your hands. Not that I think you're noble, I think you just don't like feeling guilty."

"Thanks for the therapy session. My copay's in the mail." Dane made a feint of his own and Kennedy danced back out of reach. So he wasn't so caught up in his little speech that he could be taken unaware. "Sorry to disappoint you, but I don't have the seed."

"Liar! That guy, Brian, gave it to you. He told me himself. He even described the pouch he put it in!"

"True, but I gave it to Tam Broderick. You remember her," Dane taunted. "By the way, she's F.B.I. Did you know that? She's got the seed, and she's already on the other side of the river." He hoped Kennedy could not see that the pouch still hung around Dane's neck. "You can go after her, but you're going to have to get through me first, and then she's got all those friends of mine you mentioned to protect her. Good luck with that."

Kennedy's eyes flitted across the river for a split-second, and then he attacked. He thrust for Dane's midsection, but changed his direction at the last second. Dane felt the blade slice across his thigh. It would hurt later, but the adrenaline coursing through his veins dulled the pain.

Dane lashed out, cracking Kennedy across the forehead with the butt of his knife, and slicing back down at an angle, opening a gash over his collarbone. Kennedy's return stroke was not quick enough to catch Dane's throat, but it sliced open his shirt and left a shallow cut across the breastbone. Dane had been ready for the strike, though, and as Kennedy's knife hand swept past him, he struck him with a vicious backhand swipe that nearly severed Kennedy's wrist.

Kennedy roared in pain and leapt at Dane, his good hand clutching at Dane's throat. Kennedy's shout had finally caught Kaylin's attention, and she screamed Dane's name as he was borne backward by the heavier man. Dane plunged his knife into Kennedy's exposed midsection, but it seemed the man was as far beyond feeling pain as Dane was. They were now only inches from a fifty foot fall to the rocks below.

"Ready to die?" Kennedy growled, his eyes afire with madness as he pushed Dane backward. Then his gaze fell on the grass pouch hanging from Dane's neck, and understanding dawned on his face. "The seed!" He released Dane's throat and ripped the pouch free.

The moment of distraction was all Dane needed. Free from Kennedy's controlling grasp, he pivoted to the side and shoved Kennedy to the edge of the gorge. As Kennedy staggered and caught himself just at the edge, the small pouch holding the sacred seed slipped free from his grasp.

"No!" Kennedy cried as it fluttered down and was swept away by the fast-moving water. Roaring like an angry bear, he turned on Dane, who was ready for him.

Dane drove the heel of his palm up into Kennedy's chin with all of his might. Kennedy's eyes rolled back in his head and he wobbled, out on his feet.

"I think we're done here." Dane placed his index finger on Kennedy's chest and pushed. Like a felled tree, Kennedy tumbled to the rocks below. Dane watched as his lifeless body was swept away. With a deep sigh, he turned away.

Kaylin waited on the other side of the river, her face buried in her hands.

Dane made his way across to her, and she fell into his arms. This time, it felt… different, like the comfort shared with an old friend. Whatever he had felt for her, or thought he had felt, was gone. He searched his heart, like a tongue probing the empty socket of a lost tooth, but he found nothing there.

"Are you all right?" he whispered.

"No," she sobbed. "I just can't take this anymore. I'm not like you, Maddock."

"I know. I think I finally get it. You're a tough girl, and

you can handle yourself, but that doesn't mean it feeds your soul to go traipsing through the jungle risking life and limb. I saw the look on your face when Thomas asked you to stay. I don't even think you wanted to stay with *him* so much as you loved the idea of the life he was describing." He held her at arm's length and looked down into her teary eyes. "You're a beautiful woman, a talented artist, and you love beauty. It's not your fault your father also made you a badass."

She laughed a little. "Not badass, exactly, but I guess I can take care of myself."

Hand in hand, they headed off through the jungle in the direction in which their friends had gone.

"Exactly, but just because you can do something doesn't mean that's what you're meant for."

"Kind of like us? We're not bad together, but maybe we aren't meant for each other."

"Could be," Dane agreed. "Of course, I wouldn't say no to being friends with benefits." He fixed her with a roguish grin and she smacked his chest. "Ow! Did you forget my lovely knife wound?"

"I'm sorry!" she gasped. "I'll tell you what." Now she was the one who looked like she had something up her sleeve. "Get me somewhere where I can get a hot meal and an even hotter shower, and I'll make it up to you."

"You've got a deal." He laughed inwardly as they came in sight of the dark lagoon, where the others were just dragging two boats into the water. Maybe Bones was right. Dane needed to spend less time trying to figure life out, and more time enjoying it.

The return trek, though grueling, was blessedly uneventful. They encountered no more deadly natives, giant anacondas, or legendary beasts, not to mention ScanoGen agents. By the time they had returned to the main branch of the Xingu River, Dane felt like he was waking up from a bad dream.

"You know something, Maddock?" Tam stroked her

baby eagle, which she had clearly adopted. "You guys are wasting your talents finding sunken treasure."

"I don't know about that." Dane closed his eyes and laid his head back, soaking in the warm sun. "We're pretty good at it."

"You know what I mean." She laughed as the little eagle snatched a grub from her hand. "Seriously, though." She fixed him with a grave expression. "The government could use guys like you and Bones. Men like you are rare."

"We've served our country. Now we're doing our own thing, and we're happy."

"It's not only that. Kennedy said the Dominion knows about you. What if they come after you? You and Bones might need us on your side."

"We can handle ourselves." Dane's voice was as cold as his insides. She might be right. If the Dominion was truly the powerful organization Tam said they were, and he and Bones were on their radar, no telling what they might try.

"I know you can," Tam sighed. "That's why I need you. I've already talked with my superiors." She held up her sat phone. "It looks like the Dominion is going to be my white whale." She lowered her voice. "I'm forming a team whose sole job is to find out who and what they are, and put a stop to their schemes. I told them I want you and Bonebrake."

"You're taking me by surprise here." Dane's head was spinning. "I'm flattered, but, I don't know. I like my life the way it is."

"I don't blame you, but if the Dominion comes after you, your life will never be the same." She smiled down at the eagle, which now lay asleep in her lap.

"How are you going to get that thing through customs?"

"Don't have to. I got our ride home all taken care of, and we ain't flying commercial." Tam grinned. "Sometimes it pays to work for Uncle Sam."

"Works for me." He looked out at the lush, green forest as it slid by, trying to imagine going back to work for the government. He couldn't fathom it.

"You don't have to give me an answer right now," Tam

said. "But think about it. I can just about guarantee you'll be paid a visit by my employers sometime soon. Maybe you can decide on your answer by then."

"We'll see." Dane closed his eyes again and lost himself in the gentle rolling of the boat as it cut through the water. He had thought trekking off into the Amazon was a challenge, but he had the feeling his life was about to get a whole lot more complicated.

EPILOGUE

The small grass pouch was no match for the rapid current and sharp stones that tore at it as it rode the water. It snagged on a limb and hung there, buffeted by the current, until it fell apart.

A gray seed, large enough to fill a man's palm, floated free. For days, weeks, the water carried it deeper into the depths of the jungle, into land which no human foot had trod, until it came to rest on a sandbar.

A parrot, its emerald feathers glistening in the sunlight, took the seed in its beak and carried it away. Choosing a suitable perch, it set about trying to crack the seed, but soon gave up trying to penetrate its hard exterior. In a rustle of wings, it took flight, letting the seed fall to the ground.

It came to rest in a sun-kissed clearing, where it lay undisturbed. It baked beneath the warm sun, and, in time, it settled beneath the soft earth, nestled in its nourishing arms.

The rainy season came and went, and, in the fullness of time, the seed sprouted, and brought forth life into its secluded domain.

A tree grew in the jungle.

~The End~

From the Author

I hope everyone enjoyed the latest Dane Maddock adventure. As usual, I have taken some liberties with history and reality for the sake of crafting a fun and entertaining tale. The most obvious departures from reality relate to Percy Fawcett's connection to the ship, *Quest.* Fawcett did not, in fact, travel with Shackleton and party on said ship, nor did *Quest* sink near Ascension Island. I hope readers won't mind these alterations to history. I believe these disparate elements came together to make a great story! As always, thank you for reading.

Until next time,
David Wood

About the Author

David Wood is a fan of all things historical, archaeological, mythological, and cryptozoological, and his writing blends all these passions. When vacation time rolls around, he passes on the exotic locales, preferring ruins, caves, Indian mounds, mountains, and sites of historical interest.

David is the author of the Dane Maddock adventures, the historical adventure Into the Woods, and the young adult thriller The Zombie-Driven Life. A proud member of International Thriller Writers, when not writing, he co-hosts the ThrillerCast podcast.

David and his family live in the Atlanta, Georgia area.

Visit him on the web at www.davidwoodweb.com.